# FOREVER GANGSTA

**Lock Down Publications and Ca$h**
**Presents**

# Forever Gangsta

**A Novel by *Adrian Dulan***

**Lock Down Publications**
P.O. Box 870494
Mesquite, Tx 75187

**Visit our website @**
**www.lockdownpublications.com**


First Edition December 2019
Printed in the United States of America



**Lock Down Publications**
**Like our page on Facebook: Lock Down Publications @**
**www.facebook.com/lockdownpublications.ldp**
Cover design and layout by: **Dynasty Cover Me**
Book interior design by: **Shawn Walker**
Edited by**: Sunny Giovanni**

# Stay Connected with Us!

Text **LOCKDOWN** to 22828 to stay up-to-date with new releases, sneak peaks, contests and more…

Thank you.

## Submission Guideline.

Submit the first three chapters of your completed manuscript to ldpsubmissions@gmail.com, subject line: Your book's title. The manuscript must be in a .doc file and sent as an attachment. Document should be in Times New Roman, double spaced and in size 12 font. Also, provide your synopsis and full contact information. If sending multiple submissions, they must each be in a separate email.

Have a story but no way to send it electronically? You can still submit to LDP/Ca$h Presents. Send in the first three chapters, written or typed, of your completed manuscript to:

LDP: Submissions Dept
Po Box 870494
Mesquite, Tx 75187

*DO NOT send original manuscript. Must be a duplicate.*

Provide your synopsis and a cover letter containing your full contact information.

Thanks for considering LDP and Ca$h Presents.

## Acknowledgments

All Praise and Glory is to Allah. How grateful I am to be your servant. I want to thank CA$H and Shawn Walker, for looking down through there and pulling me out the mud. I truly appreciate this opportunity. Adrianna Dena Dulan, LET'S GET IT! Donovan, good looking out, bruh. Your hard work is very much appreciated. To those of you that have supported me by listening in on "Adrian Dulan Lic Talk," on YouTube, to purchasing my first novel, "Pound Game". Thank you for your support. Know that my work only get's better and better. Stay tuned. Peace

## Prologue

While standing in my father's living room, I stood dazed at the sight of a small black duffel bag. The contents alone were enough to render me frozen in time. Under any other circumstance I'd probably be one of the happiest people alive. But, if you were to consider how I came up with the small treasure that lie before me, you'd surely understand. I was in grave danger. After zipping up the duffel bag, I slung its strap over my shoulder to prepare to leave. I looked carefully around the living room just to be certain that I'd left nothing behind. All it took was one tiny thing overlooked. One tiny thing to say I'd been there, and the consequences would be devastating. I couldn't bear the thought of something bad happening to the people that I loved, all because of something I'd done. To think of something as crazy as that made me sick to my stomach.

A cool evening breeze blew through the window as I snatched up my keys off of the dining room table. The cool air brought in the scent of a stream nearby. I could hear the soothing rustle of leaves touched by the wind around my father's home. It's the little things like this that'll be sorely missed. I could only pray that the day would come that I'd be allowed to return. But for now, I'd best be on my way. An urgent feeling of danger was growing stronger by the second.

"Kevin! Kevin! Come outside for a moment. I need to have a word with you." My father's voice instantly filled me with a dreadful disappointment. I'd avoided contact with him for weeks, hoping beyond hope that we never had to have the conversation that he surely wanted to have now.

After slipping outside onto the back patio, I hurried along, anxious to say what needed to be said so I could leave. My father's dogs barked excitedly at the sight of me. They jumped up and down as if they were trying to leap over the fence that they'd been contained in. I saw my father under the hood of his old black pick-up truck. The clicking sound from his socket wrench tightening down on a bolt was a sure sign that he was consumed in doing what he loved.

"Dad, you wanted to see me?"

My father continued to bear down on the bolt, shaking the entire truck until he was certain that the bolt had been tighten. He sat his socket wrench on the fender, then turned his attention to me. "It's been awhile since the last time I heard from you," he began by saying. "I called your phone, but you didn't answer. I even stopped by your house, but your car wasn't there. It almost makes me feel like you've been avoiding me, or as if you're hiding from someone."

I looked down at the ground, then out into the woods. Fireflies lit up the night while a steady chorus of crickets sang a harmonizing tune. I looked back at my father just as he swat at a swarm of moths fluttering around his droplight. "I haven't been avoiding you. I just felt like it'd be best if I stayed away for a while. I done messed around and got into it with the wrong group of people. The—"

"I've been telling you for years to leave them boys 'round there alone!"

"But these aren't the people that you think they are. I'm talking about your—" How could I look my father in the eye and tell him about the dumb ass shit that I'd got myself involved in? He'd raised me to be a better person than I'd become. He'd done everything he could to try and teach me a better way. "Look, all I can really tell you is I'm in some serious trouble. I don't wanna drag anyone else into this messed up situation and end up putting their life in danger."

My father scoffed and gazed out into the night as if he were gauging my explanation for credibility. His eyes wandered down by the dogs still barking, then back at me. Even in the shadowy darkness I could tell that he was disappointed by what he saw. I was dressed in all-black— black t-shirt, black cap. In his book I'd be labeled as being dressed as a thug. In mine, I'd say I was simply trying to blend in with the night. "Is there anything that I can do to help you?" My father asked. "I can't see someone being hell-bent on killing you, especially when—" The gentle hum of several cars pulling up out front temporarily distracted him. "Were you expecting company?" My father asked, but I was speechless.

Just as my father began to walk toward the house, I reached out and stopped him. "Don't," I pleaded in a trembling whisper. "That might be the people that have been looking for me."

Gunfire suddenly erupted, killing silence with its deaf-defying roar. Bullets ripped through my father's home, destroying everything inside. I heard glass burst, wood blown to smithereens. After what felt like an eternity, the shooting finally stopped.

"We've gotta' get outta' here," I hissed, trying my best not to give away our presence.

"Go where?" My father spat, while peering up at me from his cowering position against the truck. "The only way out was through the front."

I scanned every possible escape route, starting with the alleyway behind our neighbors' home. Surely if we were fortunate to make it through, the shooters would have someone waiting for us on the next street. Finally coming to the conclusion that we had no other option, I took my father by the arm and pulled him to his feet. "Stay close. I think I know a way we can get outta' here."

We made a mad dash toward the stream; bobbing and weaving through old junk cars, past the dogs still barking, running head on into the night. The density of the woods was suffocating. The air was as thick as oil. Gnats assaulted our nostrils with every breath, while mother nature had come alive and tried to stop our escape. Twigs slapped at our faces while thorns clawed at our ebony skin.

I heard a rip. "Oh shit!" I frantically felt over the bag, checking to make sure I hadn't lost any of its contents.

We pushed further into the night, guided only by the sound of the stream. I knew those woods like the back of my hand. All we had to do was follow the sound of the stream until we came to it. Then, follow the stream until it led us to a small make-shift bridge.

"Kevin, wait!" My father cried out. "I-I can't keep up." Fatigue had set in on my father in the worse way. He was far too old to be doing any of this.

"Come on, Dad. I got you. If we can just make it up to the bridge, they'll probably never find us." I grabbed my father by the arm, hoping to pull him along to safety, but our pursuers were upon us. They released a hailstorm of bullets.

*Plllllldddddd! Pllllllddddddd! Pllllddddddddddddd!* Bullets whistled through the night, sending chunks of wood splashing in our faces. Instinctively we cringed, while stumbling blindly into the night. We held on to hope by following the nearby sound of the stream. But we were no longer being guided by the sound of the stream. We were being guided by the will to survive.

I heard a grunt. “Dad!”

“Keep running!” He cried out.

I burst through the brush, up by the stream. I looked back hoping to see my father following closely behind, but something strange happened. Everything became visible, even in the darkness of the night. The moon rained its heavenly glow just as bright as the sun would on a hot summer’s day. Time had even changed. Time was no longer governed by the laws that we as human beings understood; everything was much slower. I saw my father stumble into view just as a bullet ripped into his back. His eyes were as wide as saucers, filled with a tremendous amount of pain. It was a pain that was so great, so heart wrenching, I froze. Maybe this is what it felt like when a man was about to die. Maybe at any moment I should expect to see my entire life flash before my mind’s eye. Maybe now it was time for me to make do for my past and present mistakes. Just maybe. Something hot pierced my shoulder and thigh, spinning me around, and I slipped off of the bank. My arms flew out in every direction, grasping nothing but air. I could hear the water getting closer behind me. I could see the stars of heaven shinning brighter than I’d ever saw in my life. I saw a flash.

## Chapter 1

I grew up in a small town about 30 minutes outside of Oklahoma City called Guthrie. My hometown is what many would consider as old-fashioned or behind the times. We didn't have the luxury of big beautiful skyscrapers to decorate our downtown city streets. Instead, my city was filled with historical sites, even brick roads. You could walk along the street at night, and might not see a streetlamp for several blocks. As country and boring as all that may sound, I loved my city. It might not have had the buzzing night life that other cites had, but it was enough for me. I was raised in a nice house, on a hill, on a street called Drexel. Drexel is on the eastside of my city. There were 3 other houses on my street; all built the same as mine, and all occupied by people doing good for themselves. My house was the last on the block. It sat next to the woods which had a stream that ran through it.

I used to wake up some mornings and look out to see a fox or some other wild creature shoot across our lawn. That shit used to fuck me up, but that was home, though. In my neighborhood there was a mixture of all types of living conditions. There were people that had plenty of money, property, and several rental houses. Then, there were those that didn't have anything. Those were the ones that did whatever they had to do to get by. Some people were blessed to live in a nice house such as mine. While others lived in what we called wooden shacks. I was fortunate to be raised around such a diverse group of people. When I say that I was fortunate, it's because I was able to learn from those people. I was able to see first-hand from the point of view of the haves and the have-nots. My father was a welder that made a decent living for us, while my mother, whom had divorced my father, was still trying to find her way in life. She lived in Dade County, Miami Florida. Them niggas down there wasn't playin', not even a little bit. I saw dudes get their whole head blown off just so certain people could control a certain area. What made all of that even more interesting was that them same cats that were laying niggas down wasn't trippin' about no gang shit.

They were trippin' about that almighty dollar. Although I was just a shorty, watching and learning things from a distance, I still picked up somethings. Things that would later lead to my downfall.

**22 Years Ago**

"Kevin, wake up!"

I was startled; awakened by the sound of my father calling my name. I could tell by the sternness in his voice that he was either upset about something, or he wanted me to do something.

"Are you just going to lay around all day? Or, would you like to come outside and help me work on these cars?"

I sat up on the sofa, stretching as I swiped away the crust from my eyes. I went through that same scenario every weekend. My father liked to fix up old school cars to be sold, whenever he had any free time. He once told me, working under the hood of them old cars is how he found a peace of mind. I kinda find that hard to believe, especially considering all the work it involved.

"Nah, I'm good." I finally replied. "James called earlier and asked if I'd come over. I told him that I would, but I accidently dozed off when I sat down and started watching television."

My father peered down at me as if he'd suspected me of lying to him. He had a funny way of tilting his head, studying me over the rim of his glasses. That's how I knew I was either in trouble, or he wasn't buying what I'd just told him. "Alright, suit yourself! I figured you might wanna make a few extra dollars. Especially since I know that you've already spent up your allowance." I watched as my Pops threw on his straw hat and exited the back door.

Ain't no way I could see myself slaving in that hot ass sun. My father worked all week, just to turn around and work all weekend. Sometimes, I think he was addicted to that shit. Besides the fact that he worked on them old school cars, he cut other people's yards to earn extra cash. Now that was way too much strenuous activity if you were to ask me.

I was a fly, young nigga. In my eyes, my only problem was that I never had any real money. Don't get me wrong, my father spoiled me. He just never put anything over $20 in my hand. While standing in the bathroom mirror, I couldn't help but smile. Some people say I looked like Wood Harris that played Ace in the movie Paid in Full. Besides the fact that I'm tall, dark and handsome, I have no idea of how they came up with such a conclusion. I was 14 years old, and I know that nigga Wood Harris had to be 30 something, pushing 60. After freshening up a little, I touched up my waves and hit the door. The sun had just set so it wasn't as hot outside as I thought it'd be. In fact, the evening was the time of day when everyone was out and about. You might stumble across a handful of people out doing the same thing as you. Or, you may spot a few junkies in route to get their next fix. In my neighborhood, the main spot for a junkie to get their next fix was at a place called The Ghetto. Basically, The Ghetto was an old, rundown apartment building. It didn't even look like any apartment building that I'd ever seen before. The building itself was made with a mixture of wood, siding, and shingles.

Old-fashioned.

My father was adamant about me not hanging around The Ghetto; although the place literally sat around the corner from our home. The only time I really got a chance to see what the place looked like was when I was with my father, and we drove past it. Of course, being that we lived in a small town, everybody knew everybody. So, whenever we'd drive past The Ghetto and I saw people that I knew, I grew curious as to what they were doing there.

*BAM! BAM! BAM!*

30 minutes later, I was at James's front door. Everybody called him O-Dawg because his last name was O'Dell. Not to mention, he was the spitting image of Lorenze Tate. O-Dawg was the type of nigga that always stayed into something. He wouldn't hesitate to up that pistol on a nigga, and he always had a gang of bad bitches. On the low, I really looked up to the homie. Although he was just a year and a half older than me, his Pops was already letting him drive his car. Every night we'd hit up the bootleg and buy a half-pint of Gin. Then, we'd holla at the big homie Po, and get a dime sack of weed. My hometown is small, so people talk. If I wanted to keep my daily ritual of staying faded a secret, then I had to be discrete about how I did things.

*BAM! BAM! BAM!*

The burglar-bars that outfitted the homie's front door rattled as I beat on them.

Just as I lifted my hand to pound on them some more, James's big sister, LaShura, snatched open the door. "Fool, why are you standing out here, beating on our door like you crazy?"

I just looked at her fine ass, at a loss for words. LaShura was the only girl in the whole wide world that I was madly in love with. She wasn't like all them other tramps in my neighborhood; fucking and sucking dick, hoping to come up on a quick buck. LaShura was way too classy for that. The most a nigga might get outta her was a friendly ass smile, or a wave goodbye. "Is O-Dawg here?"

LaShura gave me a disapproving onceover, then unlocked the burglar-bars so I could go inside. I couldn't help but notice how good she looked in her Guthrie Blue Jays track shorts. She even wore a hot pink cut off shirt with matching slippers. Sexy.

"Why you always being so mean to me?" I asked as LaShura closed and locked the door behind me. "You know, when I get a little older, I'ma make you my wife."

LaShura smacked her lips and rolled her eyes as if she was disgusted. "Boy, bye! You know damn well that I'm too old for you. What you need to do is take yo ass back there with my brother before I tell my Momma that you in here messing with me."

I couldn't do nothing but shake my head and keep it pushing. The homie's Mom was off the chain. She stayed faded off that drank, and wouldn't hesitate to cuss a nigga smooth the fuck out. Almost every time I came over, I'd see her posted at the edge of her bed with a cup of drank. And almost every time she saw me, the first thing she'd say was, "Kevin, what in the hell are you doing in my house?"

"Oh, hi, Ms. O'Dell!" I'd reply cheerfully. "I just stopped by to holla' at James."

Ms. O'Dell looked at me skeptically and said, "You and James better not be havin' none of them fast ass girls in here while I'm gone to work."

I looked at her as if she'd just offended me. "I'd never disrespect your house like that. Besides, I'm still a virgin."

Ms. O'Dell's eyes grew wide with curiosity. "Boy, if you still a virgin at fourteen, then you must be gay!"

I left her drunk ass sitting right there where I'd found her. It was one thing to get cussed out by the homie's Mom. But, when she got on that bullshit, it was time to step. "What up, bruh?" I greeted O-Dawg as I walked into his bedroom. "What chu' got going on back here?"

O-Dawg peered up at me with a devilish smirk and said, "Hurry up and shut the door! Moms is already trippin'. Plus, I got something that I wanna show you."

Naturally, I did as the homie had asked. Whatever he had to show me must have been important. He never called, asking for me to slide through early. He didn't have to. We did the same thing every day at the same time. Dark-thirty. After closing and locking the door behind me, I moseyed over to the homie's little brother's bed and plopped down. I sat patiently while he rummaged through the dirty clothes basket searching for something.

"What chu' know about crack?" O-Dawg asked, while peering back over his shoulder.

"Noth-nothing. Why?"

O-Dawg pulled out a small pill bottle and twisted the lid off. He poured five tiny rocks in the palm of his hand, then stood, smiling proudly. "Lookey what I've got." He whispered, while shaking the tiny stones in the palm of his hand. "I'm fixin' to take this shit right here, flip it, then I'ma use some of the money to go shopping."

I looked closer at the five tiny stones, trying to imagine their worth. Each rock appeared to be about the size of a peanut. If each of those bitches were worth one dollar, it'd take that nigga forever to save up some money and go shopping. "Smmth. That's what you called me all the way over here for? That little ass shit gon' have the hood roastin' yo ass!"

O-Dawg smirked and scooped his small fortune back into his pill bottle. "This little ass shit is worth twenty bucks a pop! I bet when I flip this shit right here, we'll see who's the first one to cop them new Jordan's."

I peered down at his orange tinted pill bottle with a newfound respect. Twenty bucks a pop? That nigga was balling. It'd take me five weeks to see that kinda dough. That'd mean no more smoking weed. No kicking it. The only thing I could really see myself doing was slaving outside on them old ass cars. "Where you get those at?" I asked, trying my best to sound intrigued.

"My Uncle Tim," he replied, nonchalantly, while hastily tucking the pill bottle in his front pocket. "He gave me this shit so I could start getting my money straight. He tol' me I ain't have to pay him back, either. He just want me to be able to look out for him, if he ever need me."

Instantly, 1,008 questions flooded my mind. One being, why would a dope-fiend give someone the product that they used? I knew O-Dawg's uncle was strung out on crack because I heard Ms. O'Dell call him a crackhead whenever money would come up missing. "Do you think your Uncle will give me a few stones so I can get my money straight too?"

"Give? I doubt that nigga gon' give you shit. Besides, this all he got anyway. But, seeing as though you my nigga, and I fucks wit' you, when it's time for me to get some more, I may throw you a little."

That nigga had no idea how hot I was. With each passing moment my facial expression was falling miserably to conceal the envy that I had in my heart. Finally, having had enough of feeling like a stone-cold hater, I moved the conversation along. "I think my relative, Justin, be selling that stuff too. Every time me and my Pops ride past The Ghetto, I see fam posted outside. Whenever it's time for me to head back to the crib, I think I'ma stop by and holla' at him."

O-Dawg shrugged and pulled a white t-shirt over his head. "Good luck wit' that shit! I got lucky to get this. If it weren't for my uncle being plugged in, I'd be shit outta' luck just like you."

I just let that last little comment roll right off my back. O-Dawg's uncle wasn't the only muthafucka in America that had the hook up on some crack. I figured, if any dope was being sold at The Ghetto, then my relative could get it. Justin was like the black sheep of our family. He always kept his hands in something illegal. Although, most of my family was divided by some invisible barrier, Justin was the only one that didn't care about that barrier. He wasn't my real blood relative, but we still treated each other as if we were. His mother and mine were best friends while they attended the Guthrie Job Corp back in the day. Although his mother had been killed in a car-wreck when Justin was much younger, we were still raised to treat each other as family.

Shortly after Ms. O'Dell left for work, me and O-Dawg sat outside in his father's 5.0 Mustang. As always, we had a dime sack of weed and a half pint of Gin. Normally, we'd be plottin' on which hoes we planned to fuck with that evening. But that night, O-Dawg was already getting money. His Uncle Tim kept a steady flow of traffic coming in and out the driveway. Although most of the customers wanted dimes and nicks, the homie was still stacking his paper. I couldn't help but feel the slight sting of jealousy, so I decided to call it a night.

"I'ma get up with you tomorrow." I said, as I open the car door to get out.

"Damn, it's like that?" O-Dawg exclaimed. "We still got one mo' blunt left. You ain't trying to smoke the rest of the sack before you leave? Or, is you really sitting over there in your feelings about something?"

Reluctantly, I pulled out the sack of weed and twisted our last blunt. Instead of going back and forth about why I wanted to leave, I simply split the blunt in half and hit the streets. My mind was reeling at the endless possibilities I had if I were able to get plugged in by my relative. I figured the least thing I'd be able to do was stack up my dough. Before anyone had the chance to catch on to what I'd been doing, I'd already have me a nice size stack saved up.

Shortly after I left O-Dawg's, I was mobbin' up Grant Street, headed toward The Ghetto. Not soon as I set foot on the block, it felt like I was stepping into a whole new world. The street was shrouded in darkness, with the exception of a few porch lights sprinkled here and there. On one side of the street sat a small group of houses; 2 of which were abandon, and another was barely visible because of all the trees in the yard. The last house on the block was a spot where several hustlers were known to hang out. If I had any chance of hooking up with my relative, that'd be the first place I'd start looking.

"Is Justin here?" I asked a group of junkies that sat on the hood of an old, broken down car. They all looked at me as if I had *stupid* written across my forehead.

"Who is you ta' be askin' for Justin?" A man quipped.

I mugged him so hard because I already knew he wasn't nothing but a smoker. You could pass by there any time of the day and see him standing out there. "My name is Kevin," I replied. "Justin is my relative. Now, if you don't mind, would you tell him that I'm out here?"

The man that I'd been talking to studied me momentarily. The way he was checking me out had me thinking that he must have known me from somewhere. Just as I started to ask him what his problem was, he reluctantly went to do as I'd asked.

"What up kinfolk!" Justin exclaimed. "What chu' doing out here in front of the spot?" I turned to see Justin standing next door on the porch.

"I'm here to see youf," I replied and walked over to greet him. "I got something really important that I need to holla' at you about."

Justin stepped down off the porch and shook his head. He looked every bit like the zombies that he be out there serving. Seems like every time I saw him, he'd be sporting dusty ass brown dickies with a red t-shirt. That night would be no exception. "Boy, if yo Daddy pass by and see you out here, somebody is gon' be in trouble!"

I shrugged, not really giving a damn about what could happen. I was there to talk about what needed to happen. "Look, fam. I really need to get at you about some important business. I already know how my Pops is going to wig the fuck out if he drive past and see me out here. That's why I need for you to take me somewhere so we can talk."

Justin sighed and waved for me to follow. I'm sure his better judgment told him not to talk to me, but his ever-growing thirst for money had him chasing that dollar. Justin led me across the street and into the drug-infested apartment complex. My mind was in awe at all the crazy things I saw. People were huddled up smoking crack like it was the thing to do. Some people had the decency to try and hide it, while others kept right on doing what they'd been doing. By the time Justin led me inside the club and to a discrete place where we could talk, I was already having second thoughts. It was one thing to be at the homie's house while he sold a few stones. But, being at The Ghetto was totally different. I was amongst real hustlers, now. People that survived off of other people's weaknesses, and wouldn't hesitate to end your life if you ever tried to get in their way.

"So, what was so important that you felt the need to come here and talk?" Justin asked.

I sat down in the booth across from him, trying my best to appear calm. The loud cries of laughter, mixing with the shouting and blaring music had my nerves on tilt. I literally had to force my mouth open just to say something. "I-I know you remember my friend, O-Dawg, right?"

Justin sighed and slowly nodded.

"Well, his uncle gave him some work so that he could start hustling. I was trying to see if you could plug me with a little something. That way I can start making some money too!"

Justin chuckled, and asked, "Do you think you're really ready to start gettin' this money?"

I nodded, feeling my courage growing stronger by the second. "I been ready! If you'll just fuck with me this one time, I promise I'll bring every dime of your money back."

That must have been all Justin need to hear. He quickly dug into his pocket and pulled out a small plastic bag. "Check this out," he said. "I'm going to give you ten stones to start out with. That's five stones for you, and five stones for me. All you gotta' do is bring me back a hundred dollars. Everything you make over that, you can keep!"

My mouth almost hit the table. I was about to have two hundred dollars go through my hands within the next couple of days. That was more money than I'd ever had at one time. True, half of the money belonged to Justin, but the other half belonged to me.

"The fuck is wrong with you, Kev? Do you want this shit or not?"

I was so caught up in the moment that I failed to realize that I'd been sitting there with a stupid look on my face. "Hell yeah, I want it! I was just thinking. Thinking about how I'ma get this money."

But now, Justin sat studying me. He appeared to be having second thoughts, but there was no way I'd let him back down on me now.

"Come on, cuzzo. Don't act like that. You know I ain't ever came to you on no bullshit, and I ain't about to start now."

Justin shook his head again, obviously shaking off his doubt. "Make sure that you put this shit up, where you won't lose it. I'd hate to see you explain to your ol' man about why you owe me money."

I nodded and quickly wrapped the work in a piece of plastic that he'd given me.

"You've got one week to bring me my dough." Justin continued by saying, "That's one week to get out there and prove to me that you're serious about making this money. I'll be here every day from sunup to sundown. If you're really trying to get off that pack, come through and I'll show you how it's done."

## Chapter 2
## The Present

The cold water inside the stream embraced me as if I was a sacrifice being used to quench its dying thirst. I fought desperately to stay afloat, but couldn't. The current was just too strong. Recent showers from days gone past had turned the stream into a deadly force of nature. The water surged forward, whisking my away, driving me deeper into its belly.

My lungs burned with an intensifying furry. My eyes stung as if they were being pelted with millions of tiny needles. Memories of my daughter awaking me washed over me like a tidal wave. She wore her favorite pink dress with shiny black slippers.

"Daddy?"

I felt my body twisting and turning head over heels; spinning, spinning, spinning.

"Will you play with me?"

Spinning. Spinning. Spinning. Head over heels; twisting and turning, deeper into darkness. Just as the idea of being hopelessly lost surfaced in my mind, I was found. My feet drug along the bottom of the stream just as I was suddenly whisked away again. Spinning. Spinning. Spinning. Head over heels; twisting and turning. I went head over heels one final time, and the next thing I knew, my face had slammed into the earth.

*BAM!*

Unconscious.

### 22 Years Ago

"Do you know what it means to self-destruct?" My father asked. "Because that's what you're doing every time you put this stuff in your body. You are *destroying yourself*!" He marched across my bedroom with one hand clinched, wearing a mask of frustration.

I quickly sat up in bed, trying to make sense of what was going on.

"What could possibly be so wrong with your life that you feel the need to use drugs? Don't I provide a roof over your head and nice clothes on your back?"

I hesitantly glanced up at the ceiling, then at my closet, finally back at my Dad.

"Boy, answer me!"

"Yes, sir. I mean, no. I mean, I guess so."

"Then why are you using drugs?"

I hesitantly looked around my room once again. I hoped he wasn't talking about the pack that I'd just got fronted. *Lord, please tell me he wasn't talking about the pack that I'd just got fronted!* "I-I-I u—"

"Kevin, don't lie to me."

"But, I'm not!"

My father thrust out his hand, revealing what he'd had all along. It was half of a blunt.

"Psst." I sighed, remembering now that I'd left the work in my sock. "It's just weed, Dad."

"*Just weed*!" My father sat down at the foot of my bed, clearly disturbed by what I'd just said. "Son, once you start messing around with drugs, you'll eventually wanna try another and another. Before you know it, you'll been done got ahold of something that you can't so easily put back down."

I nodded, knowing in my heart that he said what he said out of love.

"I can't allow you to stay here if this is the kind of stuff you're gonna be bringing in here."

"But, Dad—"

"No buts! This is against the law. I go to work every day just to keep food on the table, and nice clothes on your back. Do you think I'm fixing to just sit back and let you turn my house into a place where you store drugs at?"

"No, sir."

My father glared at me momentarily before looking away. I know he was fighting with everything inside of him not to send me to live with my mother. "You don't go to school anymore because you're too busy trying to run the streets. You don't do the simple things that I ask you to, because you think you're grown. I've tried everything that I can think of to get you back on the right track, but you refuse to listen!" My father ran his hand over his smoothly shaven bald head. He sat silent, hands folded, elbows resting on his knees. "Th-Thi-This is the last time that we'll ever have this conversation, Kevin. Just because I love you, don't mean I'm fixing to let you keep running over me." My father stood up, tugging at his gray suit jacket as he prepared to leave. Every Sunday morning he'd get up, get dressed and be at the Kingdom Hall by 9. "Why don't you come with me," my father offered, now peering down at his watch to check for the time. "If you hurry and get a move on it, we probably won't miss too much of the meeting."

I peered up at my father as if I were actually giving his invitation some thought. To let the truth be told, I'd never set foot in a place like that again. I'd went through hell just to be a part of something that I didn't even understand. My father was on this crazy religious kick and always tried to force-feed me things about his religion that I wasn't quite ready to accept. I gave up everything that I wanted to do with my life for something that he believed in. If I wanted to live in a nice house on a hill and not have to worry about looking over my shoulder, then I had to abide by my father's rules. Now, true, all of that was fine and dandy when I was much younger. But the older I got, the more I was starting to understand how the world really worked.

"Nah, I'm cool," I finally replied. "I was supposed to go shoot some hoops with the fella's later on. I think I'ma just kick back and wait on them to call."

A hint of sadness flickered across my father's face. "Whatever you say," he replied. "You may think that you're fooling me, but you ain't fooling nobody but yourself."

Deep down something was telling me that I should go. Although I'd distanced myself from going to church, I never stopped believing in God.

Later that day, I hit the streets on a mission. Instead of sitting under my relative Justin all day, I'd devised a plan to make my money before he made his. Lucky for me, I had a friend that lived right down the street from The Ghetto. As far as I knew, his mother and father were never at home.

Every time I went by Stutter's house, he'd always be there and he'd always be alone. He didn't go to school, any after-school functions, or anything else that consisted of being around lots of people. My nigga was a loner just like me. Some people thought he was a little weird because he had a speech impediment. But, not me. The homie was funny as shit. As long as you didn't get him too excited, or wasn't talking about some pussy, then you could easily understand everything he was saying.

Stutter was 5'10", brown skin with a baby nappy ass afro. He lived in a 2-story house on the corner. His house was one of those spots that was borderline from being called a wooden shack. Instead of curtains or blinds to cover up the windows, fam had yellow sheets to cover them bitches up. Judging by the looks of things, it'd be easy to assume that his Moms and Pops were strung out on drugs.

"What it do?" I greeted Stutter as I mobbed up on his front porch. "Is you ready to get this money like we talked about over the phone?"

Stutter sat smiling from ear to ear. "He-He-Hell-Hell yeah!" He exclaimed. "Is-is-is you still gon' give me some money?"

I laughed out loud and replied, "You know I got chu, bro. All you gotta do is help me get rid of this work, and it's on."

I saw a flame ignite in the homie's eyes. I'm sure he must have figured that this was his chance to come up. Stutter was the type of nigga that ain't ever had shit. His clothes were always dirty; his shoes were busted. And his hair always looked like it hadn't seen a comb in weeks. Being that no one from the hood really fucked with bro, fam was just out there. I always knew he was good peoples, that's why I stayed fucking with him.

Over the next couple of hours, we sat outside flagging down every car in sight. Anyone that even looked like they were headed in the direction of The Ghetto, we was pulling their ass over. Some kept on going while looking at us like we were crazy while others pulled over and spent that bread with us. We were so caught up in the excitement of making money we were flagging down people that didn't even smoke crack. One old lady threatened to call the police, while another simply drove away laughing at us.

By five o'clock that evening, we'd sold everything I had, and what made that accomplishment that much sweeter, I'd made $50 more than I was supposed to make. When we noticed how excited customers were to buy my shit, when I pulled out my sack, Stutter made the suggestion to start cutting them bitches in half. Shortly after finishing up for the evening, I hit up the big homie, Po and bought a dime sack of weed. I ended up giving Stutter 40 bucks for helping me get rid of the pack, then I sat Justin's money to the side.

"Nigga, we rich!" I shouted. I'd never had that much money in my possession. Sure, I'd saw way more money than I had, but seeing and having is two different things.

After we finished smoking a blunt, Stutter and I mobbed up the hill to The Ghetto. I couldn't help but notice the new air of confidence in the homie's stride. He'd usually be acting shy; afraid to be himself because of what other people might think. But now that he had a little paper, bro was acting like a totally different person.

"What up? Where's my relative, Justin, at?" I asked the same two men that I'd saw posted up out front the night before.

One of the men immediately hopped up and scanned the block. The other simply sat watching us. "You back already to see Justin, huh?"

I sized the man up. "Yeah, what business is it of yours?"

The man jumped to his feet, openly challenging me. We stared each other down before he reluctantly went to get Justin.

"Damn, my nigga. Did you see that shit?" I looked back to see if Stutter saw what had just happen. But, instead of looking up at me, he stared shamefully down at the ground. "What's wrong, fam? You aiight?" He nodded like he was, but I could tell that he wasn't. "What is it? Do you know that fool or something?"

Stutter nodded again, all the while his lips trembled as he struggled to speak. "Tha-That-That's my DDDDDDDad."

I looked back just in time to see his ol' man stroll back up. Something about that fool didn't sit right with me. Forget the fact that he was a stone-cold junky, it was something else. I could feel it. "Do you think your Pops is gonna wig out on you, 'cause you over here?"

Stutter nodded again, except this time he wore a long, sad expression as if he wished he wouldn't have ever came.

"Don't even trip, my nigga. When my relative come out here, I'ma tell him ta' holla at cha' Pops."

"Damn, Kev!" Justin quipped, as he stepped outside on the porch. "I thought you was serious about puttin' in some work. If you would've slid through earlier like I told you to, you'd already be done!"

I spared a reassuring glance back at Stutter and winked. "I told you that I'd bring you all your dough. In fact, here's every penny that I owe you, right here." I pulled out a wad of cash and peeled off five crispy twenties.

Justin's eyes slightly bulged as I walked up and handed it to him.

"Now, I'm trying to see if we can do that same thang again?"

Justin chuckled as he folded up the money and shoved it in his pocket. He walked past me and gave Stutter a curious onceover before waving for me to follow.

"I'll ca-ca-caaaatch up with you tomorrow!" Stutter yelled out from behind us.

I stopped and spun around. "Why you leaving?"

Stutter cut his eyes over to his Pops, then back at me. "I-I-I got t-t-t-t-t-t-to get home and clean up," he said. "Just hit me up whenever you got some free time."

I watched as Stutter struck out walking back down the hill. To see my nigga so shook had me feeling some kind of way. I wanted to find out what the deal was, right then and there. But, seeing as though Justin was ready to talk business, I figured I just stop by before I went home.

"Nigga, you killin' me with these spaced out episodes you be having." Justin said.

I frowned and dismissed his assumption. "Ain't nobody having no spaced out moment. I was just thinking about something."

Justin stepped into my line of sight, and said, "Distractions will get you killed out here. When you out here on the block, there shouldn't be but one thing and one thing only on your mind."

"And what's that?"

"Gettin' this muthafuckin' money! Bitches are gonna come and go, even your closest homies are gonna come and go. But, if you ever get distracted and allow yourself to get caught slipping, it's a wrap! Ain't no coming back from the dead. When you play this game out here, it's for keeps."

I nodded as Justin spun around and strolled off. On the low, I still felt some kind of way about the shit I'd just saw. It was because of Stutter that I had a spot to get rid of my packs at. I'd be a fool not to make sure he was straight.

Justin led me back through the apartment complex, and toward The Ghetto. Just like before, shit was going down all around me. I saw two junkies arguing over some dope. One of the men looked like he was ready to fight, while the other appeared to be trying to cop deuces. I started to ask Justin to hold up so we could watch and see what would happened next, but then I saw some even crazier shit. Some ol' head was posted in the cut, straight getting his dick sucked. He had his back against the wall while some woman was on her knees in front of him. I couldn't help but burst into laughter while I strained to get a better look.

But, when the ol' head noticed me watching, he shoved the woman off of him and said, "The fuck is you lookin' at, lil nigga?"

I tripped and almost broke my neck. That nigga scared the shit outta me.

Justin turned and saw what I was looking at, and snapped, "That's why you need to mind your own business!" He snatched open the door to the club, and quickly led me inside. "If you don't wanna find yourself in a fucked up situation, then I suggest that you take heed to what I'm telling you."

I couldn't help but look at Justin like he'd lost his mind. "Why you ain't check that nigga when he started talkin' shit? We family, right? I thought all these niggas worked for you."

Justin smirked and continued to lead me over to the same booth we were in the night before. "I got a few workers," he begun by saying. "But, this ain't my spot. It's plenty of niggas up in here gettin' money. That ol' head you saw gettin' his dick sucked— this is his spot. He own every house on the block. I don't get in other people's business, no matter who it is. How you think I've managed to be out here gettin' money for so long?"

"I thought if somebody tried you, you were supposed to get at they ass."

Justin chuckled. "This ain't TV, kinfolk. This is the real world. You have to think before you react. If you go around bustin' caps at every Tom, Dick, and Hank, ya' ass will be in jail so fast it'll make your head spin." Justin laid some real heat on my dome that night. Although we were family, he helped me to understand that it was a cold game out there. "How much money did you make off that work that I gave you last night?" Justin asked, as he pulled out a small Ziploc bag and sat it on the table.

I softly chuckled and said, "I learn quick, my nigga. You just gave me this long ass spill about minding my own business. Now here you are, trying to see how much money I made."

Justin laughed hardily. "I'm just saying, kinfolk! I'm trying to see what you trying to spend. Sooner or later you gon' have to pay for your merch. That front shit is punk shit. I'm willing to help you get on your feet. But after that, you on your own." Justin dug into his sack and pulled out an individually wrapped chunk of crack and said, "This weighs seven grams. They call it a quarter piece. I'll sell it to you for two hundred once you get your money right." He dug into his bag once again and pulled out an even smaller chunk. "And this?" He held the small chunk out, inspecting it as if it were a shining diamond. "This is an eight ball. I'll front it to you this time for—"

"Wait, wait. That quarter piece cost two hunnit?"

Justin nodded.

"Well, how about I give you a hunnit for that right now, and I'll bring you the rest when I finish servin' it?"

Justin slid the work across the table and asked," Do you know how to chop up dope?"

I looked at him crazy. "You know I just started selling this stuff. You gon' have to show me everything I need to know about this shit."

Justin chuckled and went on to school me. He showed me how to work a scale, how to cut up work. He even showed me the different quantities that I could buy once I stacked my money a little higher. When Justin finally finished lacing me up with game, he led me back outside into the parking lot. We briefly spoke about our plans for the following day before we were rudely interrupted.

"I gotta' leave a little early tonight," Stutter's father said, as he walked right between us as if my presence meant nothing. "It's some shit going down at the house that I need to get down there and take care of."

Justin simply nodded and continued to walk along, talking as if we'd never been interrupted.

When I was certain that Stutter's Pops was safely out of listening range, I asked, "What's the deal with that nigga?"

Justin looked at me quizzically. "Who?"

"Dude that just walked off," I replied, while still staring in the same direction that he'd just walked away from us. "Bruh was acting like he wanted to get on some bullshit earlier, when we first walked up."

Justin dismissed my assumption with the flick of his wrist. "That nigga ain't talking about shit. He out here workin' to get high just like his bitch do."

I peered over at Justin skeptically. "His girl get high too?"

"*Do she*? That bitch be suckin' every nigga's dick that'll give her a hit of dope. And the killer part about it is, that's that fool's wife! That was her that you saw earlier sucking Nate's dick. I'm surprised that her husband, Leonard, ain't figured out what that bitch be up to."

I instantly felt bad that my nigga Stutter was having to deal with some crazy shit like that. I don't know what I'd do if I was in that kind of situation. On the real, I kinda felt sorry for his Pops too. The whole hood was running up in his wife and wasn't a damn thang he could do to stop it. "That's deep, cuzzo," I said and quickly gave Justin some dap. "I'ma get up with you some time tomorrow, fam. I really need to stop by Stutter's crib and make sure he's alright."

Justin looked at me skeptically before turning to leave. "Do whatever you feel you need to do," he said over his shoulder. "But, just remember what I told you."

"Which part?"

"*All of it*!"

I laughed and strolled away into the night. Everything I'd saw throughout that day began to replay in my mind. There wasn't nothing that a dope-fiend wouldn't do for some dope. To think that my nigga, Stutter, had been dealing with this all along had me sick to my stomach.

By the time I made it down to Stutter's house, I was anxious to show him the new pack that we'd be working off. Really, I just wanted to know that he knew everything was going to be alright. But, the closer that I drew near to Stutter's home, the more I wasn't so sure that I was going to be able to give him that kind of reassurance.

"*Where the hell have you been*?" Leonard's voice boomed from inside their home.

"I've been here!" A woman cried out. "I swear! I *sweeeeeeear*!"

I stopped dead in my tracks, peering up at Stutter's house from the street. My relative's last words echoed in my head like a bad song stuck on repeat. Had I not seen Stutter sitting on the top step, I'd have surely turned around and went home. "Stutter!" I shouted, before trotting up to him. "What's wrong? Are you alright?"

Stutter peered up at me with a face streaked with tears and said, "He-HeHeeeeee won't stop."

I kneeled beside him and placed my hand on his shoulder. His shirt had been nearly ripped off of him, leaving his left side exposed. "What's going on in there? Is your Pops trippin' about us showing up at the spot earlier?"

Stutter shrugged while wiping at his tears in vain. "I don't know. All-all-all he wanna do is-is-is fight!"

I peered inside their home, hoping to catch but a glimpse of what was going on. The front door stood ajar, revealing the inside of the house, which was completely dark. A few candles glowing could be see, here and there. But no sign of his mother, or father. "Where are they?" I asked.

Stutter opened his moth to reply, but then we heard a loud *BANG*, ending with a *CRASH*.

"*Help*!" His mother screamed.

We were up and through the front door in a flash. The whole house was rank with the smell of rotting food. While Stutter bobbed and weaved through the darkness with the skill of a trained acrobat, I stumbled and almost fell over everything in my path.

"Get off her!" Stutter yelled, no sooner than we ran into the bedroom. The sight of his mother fighting for her life caused me to stop dead in my tracks. "I said *get off her*!" Stutter's fingers worked feverishly to pry his father's hands from around his mother's throat.

She kicked, squirmed, and clawed at his massive forearms. I saw her fight to live slowly getting weaker. I had to do something. *Now*.

"*Let her go*!"

I guess the sound of someone else being in the room must have caught Leonard's attention. He peered up at me with a sinister look, giving Stutter just enough time to break his grip. "The fuck are you doing in my house, nigga?" He spat and slowly rose to his feet. His bare chest heaved as if he could hardly breath. "Do you think you wanna piece of this?" He slammed his fist into his chest and yelled, "Bring it!"

"Dad, no!" Stutter cried out.

Leonard spun around and flinched as if he were going to strike. "*Shut the fuck up*, crying like a bitch!" He scolded him. "You brought this pussy ass nigga in my house, not me."

"Look, I didn't come in here to start any problems with you," I said in a weak attempt to defuse the situation. "I saw Stutter crying outside and that's how I ended up coming inside. I know I have no right to be all up in your business. But, how can I just walk away while you're about to kill my best friend's mother?"

Leonard glared down at his wife in disdain. Her dress had been ripped straight down the middle, exposing her plump, sweaty bosom. "Bitch, get up!" Leonard spat through clinched teeth. "Get cho' trifling ass the fuck outta my face."

His wife rolled to the edge of the bed where Stutter helped her to her feet.

Leonard turned his menacing gaze back to me and said, "You don't know me. You don't know shit about me. What I do in this house is my muthafuckin' business. You got that?"

I glanced over at Stutter who looked like he was practically begging me to say yes. "I got it," I replied.

Leonard turned his gaze upon Stutter and gritted. When he was certain that his point was understood, he strolled past me but intentionally nudged me with his shoulder. I acted like I hadn't felt a muthafuckin' thang. Fuck him. I'll be damned if he had me stretched out choking the life outta' me. When he nudged me with his shoulder, I'm sure that was an open invitation for whatever.

Shortly after all the confusion, Stutter and I walked back outside into the cool night air. I saw his father gazing up into the starry sky. He appeared to be much more relaxed now. He stood with his hands resting in his pockets, legs crossed, leaning against the wall.

"Do you smoke weed?" I asked.

Leonard looked at me like I was crazy and forced a weak laugh. "Why? You got some?"

I pulled out our last blunt from earlier and sat down next to Stutter. I really just wanted to make sure everything was gonna be cool before I left. The way that nigga was snappin' earlier had me thinking he was nuts for real. I couldn't just walk away and leave my nigga to face his Pops all by himself. If he'd been beating his mother's ass like that for several years, I figured she was probably just as crazy as he was.

For the next couple of hours we sat outside, chopping up game. Stutter's ol' man turned out to be more levelheaded than I'd thought. He told me all types of things that helped me to understand why Justin had him on his team. He even told me a few stories about when he was my age and hustling. Some of the things he told me was hard to believe, but some of the things he said, I couldn't help but believe. The look he had in his eyes while he spoke made a believer out of me.

When it was all said and done, Leonard agreed to get on board and help help us make some money. He gave me some lame ass spill about how he saw something in me that reminded him a lot of himself. I can't say whether or not he was just running drag to get what he wanted. The only think I knew for certain was that I had someone on my team that knew what they were doing.

**STUTTER**

"So, you and Kevin been hustlin' here at the house?" Leonard asked.

I groaned softly and replied, "Yes, sir."

"How much money did y'all make?"

I gazed out into the night, in the same direction that Kevin had just walked away. I wished like hell he didn't have to go. "Tw-Tw-Twenty dollars," I finally replied.

Leonard turned and looked at me. The cherry at the tip of his cigarette lit up as he inhaled a thick cloud of smoke. "Don't lie to me, boy," he warned. Smoke trickled up alongside his face where it disappeared into the night. "If I have to, I'll come over there and shake ya' down. Now, come clean with me. I know you don't wanna piss me off, do ya?"

I slowly got up and pulled out the forty bucks Kevin had given me. "Thi-This-This all I got." I held the money out and looked down at the ground.

Leonard walked across the porch and stopped right in front of me. He

snatched the money out of my hand, and said, "Look at me."

I couldn't look at him. My eyes felt like they were glued to the ground. I already knew what was about to happen next.

"I said *look at me*!" *WHAP!* The sharp sting of his hand across my face sent me airborne into the wall behind me, where I slid to the ground. "Get cho' lying ass up and face me like a man!" No matter how fast the world was spinning around me, I knew better than to hesitate for one second. When Leonard said move, you moved. “Why did you lie to me?” He asked, while resting his hand on the back of my neck.

“I-I-I-I ain’t ate-ate nothing all day!”

“So, because you ain’t ate nothing, you think that gives you the right to lie to me?”

I said yes, he’d probably choke-slam me on the porch. If I said no, there was no telling what’d happen next. “I-I was just hun-hungry, Daddy.”

Leonard flinched. “Call me that one mo’ time,” he spat.

“I’m sor-sorry. I swear, it won’t hap-hap happen again.”

Leonard smiled triumphantly and smacked the back of my neck. “You better not,” he said. “Because if you do.” He snatched me closer, forcing me to look him in the eye. “I’ll break yo’ got-damn jaw! You got that?”

I nodded as he shoved me into the wall and disappeared back inside the house. I wanted to sit down on the top step and cry my eyes out, but what good would that fucking do? At fifteen years old, I’d endured things that the average adult couldn’t stand under. Day in and day out, my life consisted of the same chaotic bullshit. My parents constantly fussed and fought about who stole what from whom. And don’t let the realization settle in that neither of them had eaten for the day, then they’d be looking at me to go out and steal something. I hated life and everything about it. I hated that everyone seemed so fucking happy, while I was stuck over here in this hell hole.

When Kevin showed up with a plan to make some money today, I saw a way I could possibly fix this shit. I saw a way to put some food on our table, and maybe some new clothes on our backs. I don’t know how serious Kevin was about what we’re about to get involved in, but regardless of how he felt, I was about to get mine.

## Chapter 3
## The Present

The continued squawk from a bird stirred me awake. The hot, scorching sun hovering high above took me by a bit of surprise. It was a whole new day and I had no idea of where I was or how I'd gotten there. I groaned softly as I tolled onto my back. I heard the flutter of wings as the bird took flight back to the safety of the heavens. In the trees around me, I saw hundreds of tiny birds. All of them fluttering about, squawking, watching, waiting for something. I strained trying to lift myself from the bank, but the pain was excruciating. I'd been shot in the shoulder and thigh, and lost a ton of blood. My head felt like it'd been split in half and cluttered with millions of confusing images.

I envisioned my mother when she told me not to come back to Oklahoma; my daughter pleading with me to stay home, my father. I cringed. Vomit spewed out of my mouth and splashed on my chest; where it oozed down my shoulders, dripping to the bank.

Images of last night's bloody nightmare flashed vividly through my mind. Twigs slapped at our sweaty faces. Thorns clawed at our ebony skin. I heard a rip.

*SQUAWK!*

*The bag!* I bolted up into a sitting position. Fuck the pain. Fuck feeling weak. I frantically looked around the bank. To my left; nothing. To my right; still nothing. I looked further down the stream, and there it was. At the edge of the water lay a deflated bag of nothingness.

"*Fuck*!" My voice echoed through the wilderness like a raging demon. Half a million dollars gone. Half a million dollars lost, somewhere in the stream. Sprinkles of muddy blue notes could be seen scattered about the bank. I even saw stacks of soggy, muddy, ruined money seemingly tossed along the brush.

I rolled onto my stomach, clawing at the bank, straining to pull myself along. The wind blew, releasing a howl. I heard the rustle of something moving along in the tree line. The rustle of weeds and dead leaves crackling drew closer. I scanned the tree line following the sound until I saw something peeking through the brush. I slowly inched closer toward it, only trying to identify what it was that I was looking at. But then I noticed that wasn't the only creature watching me.

One by one seven coyotes filed onto the bank. The first, inching dangerously closer. Its eyes were strangely human, calculating pools of madness. Its fur, black as a raven's feathers, bristled and trembling with rage. It bobbed its head as if trying to catch the scent of something. *Maybe they're attracted to the smell of blood*, I thought. Maybe they've been watching me the entire time, thinking my body was nothing more than a corpse.

I eased back to the stream, although I had no intention of going in. I couldn't swim, but hopefully they couldn't either.

*Grrrrrrrr!* The terrifying sound of the pack growling caused me to stop. My heart felt like it was about to burst out of my chest. The leader of the pack lowered its nose. A long, thick trail of saliva dangled from its lips. He bared his teeth, snapping, never once barking. Snapping. I edged closer to the water, so close that my hand was now touching it. My actions caused a reaction. The pack charged.

"*Aaaaaaahhhhhhh*!" I threw my arm over my face, bracing for the assault.

Just as the pack charged, hundreds of black birds blanketed the sky. A wave of birds swooped down, squawking and must have startled the pack. The coyotes cowered away whining, before reluctantly retreating back into the brush.

I sighed, ready to collapse at any given moment. There had been too many near death experiences in such a short period of time. I needed rest. I needed to get home. I needed my family.

I peered up into the light blue sky, watching as hundreds of black birds disappeared into the distance. I was trembling weak, almost to the point that I didn't think I'd make it. The sun still shown high above. I had plenty of time before nightfall. That was plenty of time to gather my strength and get ready for a journey that I'd damn well be ready to make.

## KEVIN

Seven years had flown by since the day I started selling dope. It had been seven years of living life on the edge. Seven years of having no drive, no determination to do anything better with my life other than what I was doing now. Grinding.

I was on the block 24/7 pushing my luck far beyond its limits. I'd grind all day just to turn around and blow my money the same night. I didn't have any worries about if I'd be able to make my money back, I had a spot that was rolling. Fiends would line up down the block, just to buy up everything that I had. If the spot got too hot because the rollers started creepin', I'd just switch positions like I was fuckin' a bitch, and make the money start cumming from another way.

When Leonard laced me up on how I could really shut the game down, I took that shit and ran with it. I made it hard for the average nigga to eat. I knew all the heavy hitters in my city. I knew where they sold dope at. I knew what time they opened up shop. I even knew what time they went back home to their little wifey. Whoever had the spot that was rolling the hardest, I'd simply post up down the street from their crib, shortstop their customers and have them coming by Stutter's house the next time they wanted to re-up.

Stutters house had turned into a rolling ass spot. It was also my home away from home. I still lived around the corner at my Pops' house, but I spent most of my time with Stutter. My father didn't do too much trippin' about anything anymore. He once told me that it felt like he was losing me to the streets. He didn't want to say something or do anything that may push me further down the path that I was on.

I can't say that I knew what to think after he'd told me that. In my mind, I was doing what I was supposed to do. I'm sure I'd counted more money in my 21 years of existence than he'd seen in his entire life. I know if I were him, I would've wanted a piece of the action. I figured, if I was considered as being lost because I was counting up all that money, then let me just be lost. I'll leave it to them broke ass niggas to be found.

## 15 Years Ago

"Seven!" I yelled as I bent over and scooped up my money off the concrete. "I been breaking you niggas all night. Anyone wanna bet that I don't hit again?"

Everyone in the garage fell deathly silent as I glared at all of them. Some dudes still stared down at the dice as if them bitches would magically roll off of seven, while others wouldn't so much as make eye contact with me.

"They-They-They don't want these problems," Stutter said while standing next to me. "The stars must be in alignment for you. You ca-ca-can't lose!"

As I stood, stuffing handfuls of money in my pocket, I couldn't help but think, *maybe he's right!* Today was my 21st birthday, and everything I'd planned for the day had turned out exactly as I'd planed. I threw a 90's themed birthday bash for myself, and the whole hood showed up. I bought plenty of drank, weed, and food for everyone. And what really set everything off, everyone came in costume.

Stutter showed up dressed like Tupac, when he played in the movie Above the Rim. He wore an oversized black hoodie with a black bandana tied tightly around his head. O-Dawg came out dressed as only he would. I guess because he already dressed like O-Dog in the movie Menace II Society, he felt like he didn't have to wear anything different. But, LaShura, she killed it. She was the Lady of Rage— the rapper from Death Row Records. LaShura wore a pair of tight leather black shorts with a matching top. She even had her hair done up in two neatly picked out afro puffs. I didn't think she could've done anything that would fuck up her grand entrance, until I noticed who she brought with her.

"I'll take that fade!" Her guest exclaimed. The crowd parted as Stanley shouldered his way through with LaShura in tow.

"Well, if it isn't the damn dummy that I've been waiting to break." I said.

Stanley chuckled and replied, "Your money ain't long enough to be talking about breaking me. You need to be glad that somebody is givin' yo broke ass action at gettin' some real money."

The crowd erupted in laughter, adding more fuel to a fire that was already ablaze. Everyone knew how I felt about Stanley. He was the one person on the face of this planet that I wished would just die. Besides the fact that he thought he was God's gift to the world, he also stole LaShura from me. Although we were technically never together, still—just die.

"Shoot a hunnit!" I challenged him and tossed five crispy twenty dollar bills on the ground.

Stanley looked as if he was ready to spit on my money and said, "Shoot five hundred!"

Everyone in the room that had the long face just moments ago, was looking at me like I'd been looking at them. But there was one big difference between me and them. I ain't ever backed down from a challenge. If that pretty ass nigga was there to break me, then that's what he was gon' have to do.

"Bet!"

The crowd gathered around as I scooped up the dice and started shaking them. Them hating ass niggas wanted to see me lose so bad, they didn't wanna give me enough room to shoot.

"Lil' Joe!" I exclaimed. One of the dice rolled and stopped on four. "Bet a hunnit that I roll ten or four."

Stanley forced a weak laugh. "Nigga, you gon' stop comin' at me with that broke nigga shit. Bet five hundred on your point. And bet another five hundred that you don't roll ten or four!"

I just mugged his dumb ass. He knew damn well I didn't have money to be calling bets like that. I'm sure all he wanted to do was stunt in front of LaShura. But, if I missed my point, it ain't like he was walking outta there with my money, anyway. "Bet the rest of this." I said, and pulled everything out of my pockets, and tossed it to the ground. "It ain't nothing but three hunnit and some change."

Stanley peered over at LaShura, smiling as if he'd just exposed some deep, dark secret. Everyone knew he had way more money than me. He was the only one there that drove an all-black Benz sitting on rims. I drove a 1986 Cutlass. It was all white, sitting on hubcaps. I didn't know anything about the lavish lifestyle that he was living. The people in my city were country as fuck. We didn't wear all the latest fashions with big jewelry laced with diamonds. We wore Levi Jeans with Glocks at our waistlines. Although I ain't never shot a nigga in my life, if I missed my point, I was gon' put one in his ass.

"Bet!" Stanley replied, accepting my wager. "I can't wait to break yo young ass and send you running back home to your Daddy."

I picked up the dice and started shaking them bitches as if my life depended on it. I knew I could've been making a major mistake by shooting dice that night. The money I used to gamble with, was the money that I needed to re-up. I'd already spent more than I was supposed to when I threw my party. I figured, if I win, at least I'd have most of my money back. But if not, I was certain that Justin would throw me a line to get back on my feet.

"Nine!" Someone shouted, after I rolled the dice and stopped on nine.

"You lucky you ain't got any more money," Stanley quipped. "Niggas where I'm from like to bet more money every time the dice roll."

Lord knows I wanted to tell him how I felt about niggas where he was from. Had I not already had so much on the line, I'd have surely started some shit.

"Seven!" Stanley yelled when the dice rolled and landed on seven. "Nigga, you was talkin' all that shit, and now you broke?"

Everyone ooooooh'd and ahhhhh'd, surprised that I'd missed my point. I glanced from left to right, taking note of the astonished looks staring back at me. When I looked over and saw how LaShura was looking at me, I couldn't bare the shame. I went with my move.

"You need ta' fall back with all that touching my money!" I said. "All that loot in your hands is *my* muthafuckin' bread." I pulled out a chrome P89 just to let him know I wasn't bullshittin'.

Stanley ice-grilled me, unphased by the gun that I held in my hand. "You ain't 'bout that action." He snarled.

I racked a bullet in the chamber and said, "Try me."

"Kevin, what the hell are you doing?" LaShura jumped in front of me. "I'm not about to let you shoot him because you lost a bet."

I gave her a menacing onceover, unable to believe what the fuck she was doing. “LaShura, move!”

“No, you move!” She fired back.

I saw one of Stanley’s homies make a move for his strap, so I aimed my gun at him. “I wish the fuck you would,” I spat through clinched teeth. “I’ll melt cho’ face off with everything I got in this clip.”

LaShura snatched the gun away from his face and said, “You ain’t killing anyone!”

Stanley snickered as he kneeled and continued to scoop up the rest of his money. By now, the people he’d came with had their straps out as well. I was outnumbered, out gunned, and my ego was bruised.

“This the type of shit you on?” I asked LaShura.

She glared at me and replied, “Is this the type of shit you on, Kevin? You bringing guns into my Momma’s house and threatening to shoot people, now?”

“Who the fuck told them niggas they could come to my party in the first place?”

“I did! This is my mother’s house, remember? If you and all your little friends don’t like it, then all y’all can get the hell out!”

I started to hack up a wad of phlegm and spit that shit dead in her fucking face. I practically worshipped the ground that bitch walked on, and this was the thanks I got? “Fine! If you want these bitch ass niggas to be up in here instead of me, then I’m out!”

**LASHURA**

As I stood, watching Kevin make his way through the crowd, it kind of made me feel bad about what I’d just said. But it sadden me to see him try so hard to be something that I knew he wasn’t. The Kevin I knew wasn’t some gun-toting, pants sagging gangster that everyone feared. The Kevin I knew was humble, quiet, more of the churchgoing type. He’d always had an unrestrained crush on me, but I’d never entertain it. Being that I was three years older than Kevin was— quite frankly— not my type.

I was attracted to men with a little more swag and finesse about themself. Men that knew how to treat a woman and without a doubt, have the finances to be able to do it. My idea of that special kind of a person was none other than Stanley. To me, he possessed all of those qualities and some. Stanley stood at 6'4" with a flawless bronze complexion. He had naturally curly hair curtesy of his Native American and Black heritage. His deep-set eyes, coupled with sharp facial features was enough to drive any woman insane. Had I not been well versed to see beyond a man's physical appearance, maybe I too would be head over heels madly in love with him.

"LaShura, you and I need to talk."

I didn't have to turn around to know that was Stanley breathing down my neck. The little incident between him and Kevin most definitely had him ready to flip out on somebody. "Talk about what?" I asked snidely as I spun around, peering up at him with an attitude. "You got your money. He's gone home. So, what else is there to talk about?"

"Oh, you got jokes? That nigga just pulled a gun out and threatened to shoot me. Do you think I'm fixing to overlook that shit simply because you know that nigga?"

I crossed my arms over my chest and rolled my eyes. Everyone that had been watching filed through the garage door back inside where the party was still going on strong. Some people timidly glanced in our direction, while others moved with haste to join the party.

"So, you just gon' stand there and act like I ain't said nothing?"

"If that's what it takes to keep this from escalating into something else!"

Stanley chuckled. His eyes panned the room until they locked on someone else. "Now, see, that's another muthafucka' that I'ma fuck around and have to check."

I turned to see my brother, James, glaring at us. He greedily guzzled down the last of his 40 Ounce then hit us up. "Westside muthafucka!" he shouted.

"See what I'm talking about?" Stanley quipped while pressing against me in an effort to push past me.

"Stanley, no!" I stood firm in my position to stop him. "That's my brother. Are you serious?"

"I don't give a fuck who it is. He over there throwing up gang signs like that shit means something to me. If that fool really got a problem with me, I'm trying to see about dat!"

I grabbed Stanley by the arms and forced him to look at me. "James isn't even in a gang. He probably just drunk, trying to start some shit."

Stanley eased up as if my line of reasoning made sense. "I'm warning you, LaShura, you better put a muzzle on that clown ass nigga before he fuck around and get murked. I ain't fixing to keep sparing these young ass niggas just on the strength of you knowin' 'em. The next time they get outta' line, I'ma just handle the shit myself." Stanley snatched away from me and gave his crew the head nod to roll out. Although James and Kevin had been spared, I knew this beef was far from over.

**STUTTER**

That night after Kevin dropped me off, I sat outside trying to figure out what in the hell we were going to do now. I would've never thought Kevin would be dumb enough to fuck off all the re-up money. I figured him to be way smarter person than that. With what little cash I had stashed away, I had to help out with the bills. My family depended on me, just like I depended on them to raise me. I couldn't blow money like there was no tomorrow. I had to use a little more discretion. The moves I made not only affected me, they affected the people around me.

Being raised in a household where both of my parents were strung out on dope made me learn how to manage my money. If I didn't manage my money, shit was all bad. The lights might get cut off. Next, we wouldn't have any food to eat. Although all the added pressure did was make my life a living hell, it also made me stronger. Without the struggle, I would've never learned to fight.

"What chu' doing sitting out here looking all depressed for?" I looked back to see Leonard step out on the porch behind me. He wore a long sleeve, blue checkered flannel and a pair of jeans. A Milwaukee's Best beer dangled from his hand.

"Ke-Ke-Kevin done did some stupid stuff."

Leonard chuckled as he sat down on the top step beside me. "I don't know if this is the first time you've noticed this or not, but Kevin has been doing stupid shit since the first day I met him. He takes life for granted and doesn't appreciate the lifestyle his father provides for him. If he isn't careful, he'll look up one day and find himself in a bit of a situation."

I sighed, peering out into my neighborhood, thinking, *if only he knew*.

"So, what Kevin done did now? I'm sure it's got to be something serious. I rarely ever see you lookin' so depressed."

Just because Leonard was on some laid back, sociable type shit, that don't mean the nigga wouldn't flip like a light switch. I had to be careful how I told him things. Sometimes he could be very understanding, but often times he wasn't. "Kevin, los-los-lost all the re-up money."

"*He did what*?"

I took a deep breath and prepared myself for what I knew would come next. The look of anger and frustration etched on my father's face was a clear sign that trouble was brewing.

"How did he lose the money, Stutter?"

I turned and looked him straight in the eye. My elbows rested on my knee, and my legs were shaking like a leaf. "He spe-spent some on-on-on his birthday party, and the rest he lost in a dice game."

"You let him lose it gambling? Why you ain't stop him?"

"I-I did! But-But-But-But..." I couldn't get shit to come out right. As bad as I wanted to tell him that I'd tried, I decided to let well enough alone.

Leonard forced a weak laugh while bobbing his head and said, "Oh, I get it. Neither one of you niggas know how to play your position. You his right hand man, Stutter. It's your job to make sure he don't do no stupid shit like that. All you niggas had to do was stick to the script. That's it. Just stick to the fucking script!" Leonard gulped down the remainder of his beer, crushed the can and hurled it far out into the streets. “Go in the house and put everything up,” he went on to say. “Don’t bring nothing with you except thirty bucks to pay the neighbor.” Suddenly he paused and glared at me and said, “You do still have that money put up, don’t chu?”

I nodded, and turned to peer back out into the neighborhood.

“Good. Make sure and take that damn bandana off your head too. We don’t wanna tip anyone off to the shit that I’ve got planned to do.”

**LEONARD**
**1 Hour Later**

There’s an art to being a leader. Some people are built for it, some people ain’t. Some people are born into a situation that made them learn how to lead. Stutter is the leader.

Folks might say that it’s a crime for me to expose him to the raw essence of the game. I say that it’s a crime to raise a child unprepared to face the truth. The world can be a cruel, miserable place if you let it be. But, if you nurture it with all the right things, you’ll look up one day and be living in paradise.

“Wh-Wh-Where we going?” Stutter asked as I drove down a dark country road. I suppose being out in the middle of nowhere must have had him spooked.

“I’m fixin’ ta’ show you how to play your position.” I said. “The problem with you and Kevin is, neither one of y’all understand the importance of playing a role. Kevin don’t have the slightest clue what it take to be a leader. And you have no idea what it means to be a right-hand man.”

I turned onto a long, winding gravel driveway that led up to a mobile home. The man that lived there was an associate of mine. I credited his 30-year run of never being arrested, robbed, or taking so much as one loss, to strict discipline. “When we go inside, I want you to keep your mouth shut! I don’t need these Hill Billy Peckerwoods thinking anything other than what I want them to think.”

Stutter peered outside his door. “We-We-We ‘bout to go-go in there? What about them ddddogs?

I reached under my seat and pulled out a chrome snub-nose .38. I'd had that gun for years. When times got hard, I could always count on That Bitch to bring us through. "Do you see this?" I lifted my gun just high enough for him to see it. "Them dogs don't stand a chance against this. The only thing you need to be concerned about is watching my back! Nothing else even matters."

The porch light popped on just as someone opened the front door. I instantly recognized Tom by his long, scraggly white hair and fluffy beard. "Who's out there?" Tom shouted. He obviously didn't recognize my neighbor's beat up Lincoln we were in. It was burgundy with a bad tint job. If it weren't for the small spare tire on the front driver's side, the car could have easily been mistaken for a getaway car.

"It's me, Leonard!"

Tom whistled for his dogs to stand down as he slowly descended the steps one at a time. He cautiously walked around to the driver's side and peered down inside the car. "What brings you out 'dis time uh night?" He asked.

I chuckled but played it cool. Tom may have been a country bumpkin, but he was far from stupid. "You know any time I drive way out here, it's to score some good smoke. My friend here got about eighty bucks he wanna spend with you."

Tom bent down some more, straining to get a better look. He kept both hands wrapped tightly around a double barrel sawed off shotgun. "Who's he?"

I looked at Stutter, then back at Tom. "Just call him, The Money," I replied. "The Money don't like folks knowin' his real name unless they have to."

Tom seemed to ponder my line of reason if only for a second. I could tell that he didn't like the idea that I'd brought someone new to his home. "I'll do business with you and Mr. Money this one time. But the next time, your friend wanna score some smoke, you'll have to come alone." Tom shooed his dogs away while Stutter and I got out.

When Tom led us inside, I couldn't help but notice the look of disdain etched on his wife's face. She was in the kitchen drying dishes. But when she saw Stutter and I walk in behind Tom, she threw her dish rag on the counter. "Damn it, Tom!" She shouted. "I thought you promised me there wouldn't be no more company after dark."

Tom chuckled and plopped down at the table, where a half-eaten sandwich awaited him. "I know what I promised ya'," Tome replied. "It's just, Leonard and his friend Mr. Money wanna score an ounce this time. If you could, would ya' grab one of them there bundles out the back. I'll sit right here and keep Mr. Money and Leonard company while you're gone."

Tom's wife glared at us momentarily before storming off to the back room.

There was one obvious thing about Tom and his wife that had been the same since we first started doing business. They never hid the fact that they didn't like black folks. And I never hid the fact that I didn't like crackas either.

"That'll be 80 dollars!" Tom's wife snapped as she waddled back into the living room and dropped an ounce on the coffee table.

I glanced down at the bag, then peered over at Tom. "You ain't gon' weigh it up for us?"

Tom dropped his sandwich on the plate as if I'd just offended him. "Do it look like I need to cheat yooooou?" He snarled.

I smirked, but kept it cool and said, "Naw, but this is business. It's only right if you come straight with me, like I've always came straight with you."

Tom scuffed and peered over at his wife sternly. "Momma Bear, run back yonder and grab that scale from underneath the bed."

His wife spun around and shot him an evil look. "Do I look like a dog ta' you?" She spat. "If you want 'dem damn scales, then you run along and get 'em yourself!"

While Tom and his wife started bickering, I slowly pulled my gun from under my flannel. Just as Tom's wife started to walk back into the kitchen, I reached out and grabbed her by the hair. "Ahhhhhh!" She screamed.

Tom scooped up his shotgun from beside his chair and pointed it at us. "Da' hell do you think you're doing, L?"

I snatched his wife in front of me so that her fat ass could be used as a human shield. “Now, Tom, we can either do this the easy way, or things can get ugly.” I pressed my gun against the side of his wife’s head so hard she winced.

“Kill ‘em, Tom!” His wife yelled. “I tol’ ya’ not to be foolin’ around with his kind, no how.”

Tom shifted his gaze from me to Stutter; from Stutter back to us. He then slowly lifted his shotgun as if he were trying to get a better aim. “I’m warning you, Leonard. If you hurt my—”

I yanked his wife’s head so hard I felt some of her hair break loose from the scalp. “You’re in no position to be makin’ any threats, Tom. I’ll give you to the count of three to put that there gun down. You can play a game with this bitch’s life if you want to. I really don’t give a fuck. It’s all up to you.” I knew Tom was a thinking man. He hadn’t made it all these years without taking so much as one loss, without using his head.

“Alright. Alright!” Tom exclaimed. “I’ll put down my gun, but you’ve got ta’ promise me you’ll let her go.”

I simply nodded just to see what Tom would do. Low and behold, Tom slowly took his finger off the trigger, and sat his gun on the table.

“Stutter, go over there and get that gun.” The look he had on his face was priceless. I could tell he was having second thoughts. I knew he hadn’t ever done anything like this before. But when it was all said and done, he’d know exactly what it took to be a leader.

**STUTTER**

I picked up the gun and just held it. I didn’t know what to do with it. Tom sat there looking at me as if he hated my guts, and my Pops looked like he was loving every moment of it. Whatever money Leonard was about to take from these people couldn’t have amounted to much. They looked like ordinary trailer trash if you were to ask me. The type of people that still hung their clothes up on a clothesline, and sat around all day drinking beer.

“If that muthafucka even blink, blow his got damn head off!” Leonard snarled, then guided Tom’s wife across the room and slammed her face-first into the table. "You know what this is about," Leonard went on to say. "I want everything in this bitch worth value."

Tom glared at Leonard for what seemed like an eternity. I'm sure the way Leonard had his wife pinned facedown on top of the table had something to do with it. "I ain't done nothin' but right by you!" Tom spat. "You come to my home and I treat you with respect. I give you whateva' it is that you askin' for. I 'on't cheat you outta' nothin'." Leonard lifted Tom's wife's dress and positioned himself against her ass.

"Don't make me fuck this bitch right in front of you," he said. "I'll run something so long and fat up in this bitch, she'll be beggin' for me to stay."

Tom leaned forward as if he were trying to stand, so I smacked him with the butt of his shotgun. *Whap!*

"Umpf!" He grunted and covered his nose. "Damn you, Leonard! Damn you ta' hell! You want the fuckin' money, it's over there under the sofa. Just take whateva' you want and get the hell outta' my house!"

Leonard glanced back over by the sofa, then looked back down at Tom's wife. It was obvious that his attention was consumed with her. "It's a got-damn shame that you got a problem with niggas," Leonard said as he pulled her head back, forcing her to stand up. "If you weren't such a racist ass peckerwood, I might've let you live." *BOOM!* Leonard shot her in the back of the head.

"Noooooooooo!" Tom cried out and jumped to his feet.

His wife's dead body slid to the floor just as Leonard turned his menacing gaze upon me. "What does it take to be a leader?" Leonard asked, but I was so shook I didn't know what to say or think.

"I-I-I ddddon't kn—"

Leonard raised his gun and pointed it at me. "If you tell me that you don't know, I'll kill you."

I looked down at Tom who was now kneeling next to his wife. He gently kissed the back of her hand, while repeatedly telling her that he loved her. "Heart," I finally replied. "It ta-ta-takes hea-hea-heart to be a leader."

Leonard chuckled softly as he slowly lowered his gun. He looked over at Tom, then back at me. “Well, kill him.”

The whole world felt like it stopped, but I knew that it hadn’t. Although my father peered over at me with a smile on his face, I knew he was dead serious. I know that I didn’t wanna end up like Tom’s wife, and I sure as hell didn’t wanna get beaten. So, instead of prolonging the inevitable, I closed my eyes and just squeezed. *BOOM!*

# Chapter 4
# The Present
# KEVIN

"Hey, mister. Are you sleeping?"

I could hear someone talking, I could even feel their touch. But strangely enough it felt like I couldn't move.

"I guess you're too sleepy to wake up. I'm going to have to tell my father that you didn't wanna wake up!"

I did want to wake up. Lord knows I wasn't asleep. I couldn't allow whomever was talking to me to think I didn't wanna be bothered. I just felt weak, tired; so tired that all I wanted to do was sleep. "I'm not asleep. I need help. Run and tell someone that I'm down here and bring a bottle of water."

A beautiful song sang by hundreds of tiny birds chirping, mixed with the thunderous roar of rushing waters, heighten my sense of awareness. I was still by the stream. I must've collapsed.

"If you're thirsty, I can give you something to drink. But first, you've gotta' open your eyes."

My eyelids fluttered like a moth's wings would after it had been smitten to the ground and lay helplessly on its back. I felt someone's fingers prying at my eyelids. They wanted my eyes open. They wanted me to see something. And then came the light.

"There you are!" A little boy exclaimed. "I've been waiting for you to wake up all day." He paused, seemingly distracted as if he were looking for something. "But you wanted to play sleep. I can't believe you wanted to play sleep on me!"

The little boy couldn't have been no more than five or six. He was barefoot and covered in filth. His clothing resembled a long scarlet t-shirt, except the sleeves had been torn off.

"I need help. I've been shot several times and lost a ton of blood. It feels like I can barely move, and I'm dying of thirst."

The little boy suddenly perked up as if that was something he could help me with. "If you want water, I can give you water." He said.

I was damn near in tears. "Yes, please. Give me water."

The little boy sat down next to me and crossed his legs Indian style. He ran the back of his hand over his lips, then began. "Once upon a time lived a man named David. David had allllll the money he could ever want, plus a big ol' pretty house. He had two dogs and uhmmmmm." He paused, thought about it, held up two fingers and said, "And five chickens. One day, David's friend, who was a warrior, decided they should take a trip. Do you wanna know where they went?"

I could care less where they went to. I wanted to punch lil' nigga dead in his chest and tell him to quit tryin' to play me. "Please," I said trying to control my temper. "I'm dying, my nigga. If you don't wanna go get help, then at least get a nigga some water."

The little boy sighed as if he'd suddenly grown impatient. "Alright already! You didn't give me a chance to get to that part." He drummed his fingertips across his chin and peered up into the sky. "Oh yeah!" he exclaimed, remembering now where he'd left off. "They went to the jungle."

*Christ, save me.*

"In the jungle, there's all types of mean ol' ugly monsters. Some of them will try to get you while you're awoke, and others will only get you while you're asleep. The first day David and his friend were in the jungle, they spent the whole day hunting. But, while they were hunting, they kept coming across mean ol' ugly green monsters. David's friend told him to kill them whenever he saw them. But, David didn't. He didn't believe he could do it. The whole time David and his friend were out hunting, David depended on his friend to protect him. One night, after they'd spent the whole day hunting, they both fell into a deep sleep. While David and his friend were sound asleep, a big ugly green monster came into their camp. At first, he looked at David's friend, then at David. David looked to be about the right size meal for him to eat. But right before he had the chance to take David, David's friend woke up and saw him.

"'Hey, what are you doing?'" He growled. "The monster said, 'I'm about to eat your friend!' David's friend hopped up and said, 'You ain't eating nothing,' and chased the monster far, far away. While David's friend was gone, David was still asleep. He never knew about the monster that came into the camp. By the time he woke up and his friend wasn't back, he instantly grew afraid. He hadn't ever been alone and around so many ugly monsters. He had a bunch of money, though. He had a big pretty house, two dogs and..." He paused, obviously in deep thought; held up four fingers and said, "I think three kittens. But you wanna know what David didn't have?"

*That's it!* I couldn't take it anymore. I hadn't ever put my hands on a child before, but I was about to fuck his little ass up. "Just give me the got-damn water!"

The little boy glared at me momentarily, then peered down by the stream. He looked back at me skeptically before scurrying down by the stream. I saw him kneel and scoop up two handfuls of water. Then he turned back to me and yelled, "I got it! Give me one second, and I'll be right there." I watched as he took his left foot and carefully placed it over his right foot; careful not to spill a drop. By the time he'd finally made it back to me, he was smiling proudly. "Here! You wanted water, so I brought you water."

I groaned as tears welled up in my eyes. I wasn't going to make it. He didn't understand. "I can't drink that kind of water; it'll make me sick if I do."

The little boy slowly lowered his hands allowing a few droplets of water to drip to the ground. "I already tried to give you the water that you needed," he said. "But you wouldn't drink it."

Darkness.

If you were to say I was heartbroken after what happened last night, I'd surely tell you that you weren't even close to understanding the way I felt. What could possibly be the reason that LaShura chose Stanley over me? I'd asked myself that question more than 1,008 times. Was it because his money was longer than mine? I had to consider that possibility, but then again, LaShura wasn't a gold digger. Maybe it was because Stanley was a well known factor and I wasn't. Now, when I considered things from that perspective, that could've been it.

Stanley had major clout in the streets. No matter where he went, or how he showed up, people respected him. At 21 years old, I hadn't matured enough to understand why that was. While I ran the streets thinking it was all fun and games, Stanley showed me that there was another lever to this shit. The game was more than just smoking weed and chasing girls. I'd never had a reason to think about things like that, until last night. But after Stanley took my money and embarrassed me I had every reason to.

My relative, Justin, had always been my only source to re-up. I didn't understand the importance of having a real connect. Or, better yet, what a real connect even looked like. If you were to line up Justin and Stanley side by side, and ask me to tell you who was the plug, I'd say Justin. Stanley wasn't nothing but a pretty boy in my book. I'd yet to identify him for the factor he was.

Justin, on the other hand, well, he'd stepped his game up since I first started hustling. He was no longer just a fat, shaggy beard-wearing, same pair of Dickies sporting muthafucka' that sold dope at The Ghetto. He'd cleaned himself up, and now done all his business strictly by delivery. The Ghetto was now ran by a group of individuals that I didn't know much about. Rumor had it, they were shutting spots down and taking over the streets. If you weren't buying or selling dope for them, then you weren't getting money.

Now, I don't know if Justin had had a run-in with these new niggas, or if it was just coincidental that he was suddenly out of pocket. All I knew for certain was that I was dead broke, with no other means to re-up. Whatever I didn't know about putting in work, I was definitely about to learn.

***

"Here-Here-Here's what I think we should do." Stutter said as we sat in my car, parked outside of his home. "We should pull up, like-like-like we trying to buy something. When they walk up asking what we need, *BAM!* Break yo'self fool!"

I damn near died laughing, listening to his plan for us to come up. The homie didn't know the first thing about how to rob a nigga. He barely knew how to sell dope. "I don't think it's going to be that easy, bruh. For one, they ain't fixin' to let us just roll up, draw down on 'em, and not do nothing. They probably got dudes posted in the cut waiting for some shit like that to pop off. And secondly, don't forget them niggas been shuttin' cats down out here. Not only do they have a team of straight savages behind them, but they strapped the fuck up!"

Stutter sighed and turned to peer out into the night. I could tell that he wasn't going to be too quick to abandon his plan as I had. "So-So, what do you suggest that we do?"

I shrugged. "I don't know. We fuck around and have ta' wait until Justin get some more work."

Stutter smirked, just as a set of headlights appeared at the top of the hill. The first set of headlights was followed by two other cars; creeping, seemingly inspecting each house as they passed by. The way they crept down the street instantly drew our attention. We both crouched in our seats so low that we could barely see over the dash-board. Generally, when we saw several cars trailing one another, it was the police. But as the three cars drew closer, I noticed the first set of headlights didn't belong to a police cruiser. The first set of headlights belonged to a black Benz.

"I wonder what the fuck that nigga Stanley doin' over—"

Stanley swerved and stopped in front of us. The second car whipped in behind us. The last car parked right outside of my door. We were trapped.

"Get out the car!"

I slid my hand down trying to get my strap. Somehow, it'd slid further under my seat and I couldn't reach it.

"I said, *get out the muthafuckin' car*!" Suddenly, they snatched open our doors and pulled us both out by our shirts.

Stutter was thrown to the ground, while I was slammed against the hood with a gun jammed in my face.

"This the type of action you was lookin' fo', lil nigga?" Stanley snarled. "You was poppin' that gangsta' shit last night, right?"

I couldn't answer that mark ass nigga even if I wanted to. One of his homies had the barrel of his gun lodged in my cheek so hard he'd caused my lip to bleed.

"How much money you niggas done made me today?" Stanley snatched at my front pocket and ripped it. He forcefully dug inside only to find my cell phone." Where's the muthafuckin' money at? You broke ass niggas was poppin' all that shit. Where it at?" He slapped my other pocket, only to find that it was empty as well.

"This nigga ain't got shit either!" Another man quipped while holding his foot on the back of Stutter's neck. "I'm willin' ta' bet they got a stash spot somewhere around."

Stanley scanned the front yard as if he'd somehow be able to find something that I didn't have. He glanced back at me, then went to check my car. "Looky what I found." He said mockingly, as he held my gun out for all to see. "Ain't this the same piece of shit that you pointed at me last night?" I never said a word. I just stood there and mugged his punk ass. The way they was handling me and my nigga, all I wanted to do was murk something. "Let him go!" Stanley barked, assuming the reason that I hadn't spoke was because of the gun that was practically jammed in my mouth. "Now, I'ma ask you one more time," Stanley said, now standing in my face. "Is this the same piece of shit that you pointed at me last night?"

I sized that fool up from head to toe and spat next to his feet. "Fuck you think it is?"

*Whap!* Stanley smacked me with the butt of my gun which split me above my eye. Blood trickled down my face as I tried to brace myself on the fender. I heard laughter erupt all around me, then someone shoved me to the ground. Just as I steadied myself and lifted back up on my knees, somebody kicked me dead in the fuckin' face. *BAM!*

Unconsciousness.

**STUTTER**

Like the old saying is told, what goes around, comes around. How true that statement proved to be after what happen to us that night. The same element of surprise that we'd used on Tom and his wife, was the same tactic that Stanley used on us. If it weren't for my mother coming outside when she did, I'm sure Kevin would be dead. The look Stanley had in his eyes, as he stood over him with that gun pointed at him, I thought surely it was a wrap. At any moment I expected to hear the blast of a gun echoing in the night.

But instead, my mother screamed, "KEVIN!" She bolted outside, running full speed at Stanley. Had it not been for his two goons that stepped in and stopped her, she'd have surely plowed straight into him. "Get outta' my way!" My mother pushed and shoved at the men that stood in her path.

The sound of her in distress only sent me into a frenzy. I squirmed, straining to lift up, only to have my neck almost snapped in half.

"Be still befo' I crush yo shit!" A man snarled as he pressed down harder on the back of my neck.

That's when Momma saw me. She peered in our direction as if she couldn't believe what she saw. "Get off my son!" She then bolted across the yard and attacked the man holding me down.

"Somebody better get this bitch before I dome her stupid ass!" He shoved my mother to the ground and turned and pointed his gun at her.

In the split second his attention was drawn away from me, I scrambled in between the gun and my mother. "Momma, be cool." My statement fell on deaf ears.

Momma was already back on her feet with an old box cutter in her hand.

"You a bitch!" She fired back at the man. "That goes for you and that stankin' ass bitch you came out of."

I frantically tried to calm Momma down, all the while ushering her back to safety. In my haste to make sure she was safe, I accidentally cut my hand on her box cutter. "F-F-Fuck!"

Instantly, my mother's fight to push past me eased. She knew I was hurt. She boldly stood taunting Stanley as he reluctantly walked back to his car. With a crowd of spectators growing larger by the moment, it'd only be a matter of time before the cops showed up.

"Don't chu' ever try and stop me from handling mine, after a nigga done put their hands on me!" Momma scolded me. She gave me a thorough once over and spotted blood dripping from my hand. "Take that damn shirt off and wrap your hand up. After you've got it good and tight, go call your Daddy. Tell him ta' bring me, That Bitch!"

## LASHURA

It'd been a long, restless night. I lie awoke tossing and turning, wondering if or when Stanley was coming home. I'd called his cell phone several times, only to get forwarded to his voicemail. The lack of communication between us as of late was killing me. It felt like he was trying to hide something from me. I couldn't help but wonder where he was, who he was with, or who he's sleeping with.

Regardless of how perfect Stanley fit into my idea of a man that I'm attracted to, he still had many flaws. Sometimes, I found myself wondering if I could really put up with all this for the rest of my life. The late nights out running the streets was one thing. But, to sit around and wonder had something terrible happened to him was driving me insane. And that's not to mention the threat of losing everything we own in the blink of an eye. The sprawling three bedroom condo that we lived in was purchased with drug money. The cars, the clothes, everything was purchased with drug money.

No matter how many times I tried to reason with Stanley that one of us needed a job, at least to help make things look legit, he'd never listen. He'd simply say, "Bae, I got this! Stop trying to speak negative bullshit into our lives."

Lord knows I wish it could be that easy. Who wouldn't wanna wake up in a beautiful condo that overlooked downtown Oklahoma City? I could sit in the comfort of our very own living room, and peer out to see all the beautiful lights come to life at night.

As much as I wanted to believe what Stanley had told me would work, in the back of my mind I knew it wouldn't. For the past several months, I'd been having these strange feelings. Like something bad was about to happen. Between my ever growing suspicions of where Stanley was, or who he was with, I couldn't get a good read on why those feelings had come about. After awhile, those nagging gut feelings became so intense I told Stanley about them. I thought surely my sudden paranoia would be met with some sort of empathy. Instead, he told me that it was all in my head, and I needed to relax.

The sound of keys rattling against the doorknob prompted me to sit up. I'd been lying in the living room on the sofa. I didn't have on any lights, the TV, or nothing. I figured the stove light and the flickering lights of Downtown gave me just enough light for what I needed to do.

Think.

"I already told you," Stanley said, speaking into his cell phone as he closed the door behind himself. "Let me get back at chu' in the A.M. I'm home now, and you already know how my girl be trippin'."

I watched as Stanley walked into the kitchen and over to the microwave, checking to make sure that I'd left dinner waiting for him. I started to sit there and listen to his little conversation, but I'd allowed curiosity to get the best of me. "Who's that?" I asked.

Stanley paused and looked back at me surprised. I could tell by how low his eyes were, and his slurred speech, that he'd been drinking. "Yo, chill!" He exclaimed with a slight chuckle. "I'ma hit you back first thing in the morning, shorty. Aiight? Peace."

The first thing that popped up in my mind, was who the hell was Shorty? I wondered why he didn't wanna talk now, but what in the hell did he mean by I be trippin'?

"Damn, bae. You eavesdroppin' on ya mans now?"

I paid his feeble attempt to try and turn things around on me no mind. I wanted to know who he was on the phone talking to. "I wasn't eavesdropping on you," I stated calmly, as I sauntered across the living room and went to stand next to an island that divided the living room from the kitchen. "I just heard you talking to someone on the phone, and if I'm not mistaken, you mentioned something about me."

Stanley bobbed his head as if that was the answer I'd been looking for. He quickly busied himself, getting ready to eat, then set the timer on the microwave for 2 minutes.

"Why haven't you been returning any of my phone calls? I've been calling you all day. I text you at least a hundred times. You could have at least text me back and let me know that you were alright."

Stanley turned around and leaned against the counter. "I was busy, bae. Don't you think I would've called back if I had the chance?"

"Whoever you were on the phone with obviously had their chance. I thought communication between me and you was a must."

The timer on the microwave went off, filling an uncomfortable moment of silence.

"Look at chu," he said mockingly. "It must be nice to sit around all day, dolled up, without a care in the world. You get to sit back and twiddle ya' thumbs while I'm out there huggin' the block."

"Why are you talking to me like that?"

"What chu' mean, why am I talking to you like that? You wanna question me about *my* phone, like I'm your child or something. And, I still haven't forgot about that stunt you pulled last night. The way you protecting that bitch ass nigga, Kevin, is starting to make me thank you fuckin' him."

"Wowwwwwww, seriously?" I walked around the island while tying the strap on my olive-green robe tightly around me. "What was I supposed to do, let you and Kevin kill each other over a dice game?"

"That fake ass—" Stanley's cell phone rang, which temporarily distracted him.

"Answer it." I said, then folded my arms across my chest just to keep from answering it myself.

Stanley peered down at me with a devilish smirk. "LaShura, you trippin'! This is my muthafuckin' phone. I ain't gotta' answer shit if I don't want too."

The phone had stopped ringing. I stood there glaring up at him, then back down at his phone. I could remember part of the number, 405-651-3... *Shit!* As I stood there trying to remember what the last three numbers were, his cell phone rang again. "*Answer it*!" But when he just stood there with a stupid look on his fucking face, I went for it.

"Nah, hold the fuck on!" Stanley quipped, while holding a firm grip on my wrist; forcing me to drop the phone. "What is you doing? Ain't nobody tell you, you can answer my phone."

"Let me go."

"Not until you chill the fuck out! Don't be touchin' my fuckin' phone, aiight?"

This negro must've had me confused with one of them scary ass bitches he used to fuck with. I'll be damned if I cowered away, just because a man raised his voice at me. My parents had 3 kids, 2 of which were boys. I used to kick James's ass so much he started telling, and my youngest brother knew better than to ever test me. "Don't tell me what I can do!" I spat. "I can answer your phone if I want to."

"No, you can't."

"Yes, I can."

"LaShura, you trippin'."

"I'm tripping? Nah, I'm about ta' show you tripping. Let me go."

"I ain't letting you go until you chill."

"I said—" *WHOOSH!* I swung with an overhead left, but he caught it. "Damn."

"Oh, you tried to hit me?" He had a death-defying hold on both wrists now. He squeezed so hard that he made my knees buckle.

"Stanley, you're hurting me."

"You should've thought about that before you tried to hit me."

"I'm sorry."

"No, you ain't. You just saying that shit so I'll let you go. Then, you gon' try and hit me again." We wrestled briefly. Him tugging and pushing. Me twisting and turning, trying to bite a hole in his chest. Before I knew it, he'd pinned me against the island. "LaShura, you need to chill. All this ain't necessary."

"How you gon' tell me what's necessary? I want to know who's calling your phone at three o'clock in the got-damn morning!"

Stanley forced a weak laugh and said, "You really wanna know?"

"Yes! Who the hell were you talking to, Stanley?"

He released me and turned to go back over by his phone. "Her name is, Toyia."

"T-Toy-who? Toyia?" I was having a hard time trying to wrap my mind around what just came out of his mouth. "So, are you fuckin' this bitch, Toyia?"

"Mannnnn, miss me with the fuck shit! You knew what it was gon' be when we first got together. I give you everything you want. You ain't wanting for nothing. I shower you in nothing but the finest and you don't think that shit come at a cost?"

I wished I could slap the hell out of his ass. I couldn't believe he'd think I was willing to share the person I loved for a price. "I didn't ask for any of this, Stanley."

"Yeah, but you sho' in hell ain't turned shit down either. You knew damn well how I was getting money when we first hooked up."

"Wait, wait, wait," I said, waving both hands in the air to silence him. "So, I should've known you were going to cheat on me, because I knew you sold drugs?"

Stanley looked at me like I was crazy. "The fuck you think? Do you remember when we first got together and I told you that someone broke into my storage unit and stole everything?"

I shrugged and looked confused. "And? What's that have to do with anything?"

"Everything! When I told you someone broke into my shit, I also told you I'd have to change some things around. I tried to explain what some of those things would be, but you didn't wanna listen. You kept talking about, you didn't wanna know because you don't wanna be involved. Remember that?"

"Oh, so now you're trying to turn this thing around and make it my fault?"

"I ain't said shit about makin' nothing your fault! I'm trying to help you understand why things are the way they are. I can't just rent a house somewhere and put drugs and money in there. If the police run up in that bitch, it's over! They gon' say everything in that bitch belongs to me, because the place is in my name." Stanley snatched up his cell phone off of the counter and marched across the kitchen to me. "DO you see this?" He said, then unlocked his phone and scrolled through several pictures until he found the one he'd been searching for. "This is Toyia. She ain't shit, but a fat, nasty hood rat that don't nobody give a fuck about. I lost everything when them people broke into my shit. Do you understand me? Everything! I had to switch things around and be smarter about how I do shit. Either I could make some gullible ass bitch fall in love, so I can hide everything at her spot. Or, take a chance on getting caught with a bunch of dope and money. Now tell me, LaShura, which would you prefer?"

I couldn't believe what he'd just asked me. And to think that I thought he was my perfect idea of a man for me. "Do you wanna know what I think? I think you should be with that bitch! If she's willing to hide all your shit, and put up with being second place to me, then she deserves you. I cannot and will not ever be able to do what she does. You can have her!"

# Chapter 5
# KEVIN

The next morning came barring warm sunlight raining down on my battered face. I squinted, simultaneously wincing because of my aching jaw. My face felt numb, puffy, even monstrous. Slowly I sat up on the sofa, careful not to cause myself anymore pain than I was already in. O-Dawg slept peacefully in a recliner across from me. He cradled an empty 40-ounce bottle and a black 9-millimeter in his lap. Leonard sat at the dining room table, obviously in deep thought. He continuously tapped a red Bic lighter on the table.

"Where's Stutter?" I asked.

Leonard sparked his lighter and lit a cigarette. "He's upstairs still asleep," he replied as smoke poured from his nostrils, splashing over the table. "The pain killers that I gave him should have him down for a while."

I nodded in understanding just as Kathy sashayed into the living room. Her once plump bosom was now nothing more than two leather straps dangling in a dingy white wife beater. "How you feelin' this mornin', suga?" She asked, and sat a plate of scrambled eggs and toast in front of me.

"Fine, thank you."

"I made you and your friend something to eat. Hopefully, this will give you two boys enough energy to get out there and do what you have ta' do!"

I looked down at my plate just as a roach shot across the table. I looked back up to see if Kathy had just saw it, but she'd already spun around to wake up O-Dawg. The cut off shorts that she wore sagged miserably revealing ashy butt cheeks covered in stretch marks.

I cringed.

"So, what's the plan to get back on your feet?" Leonard asked, while watching me intently from the dining room table. "I know you're not gonna allow that one little setback to put a stop to your hustle. When you're in this game, you're gonna take a loss. It's what you do after you take that loss that matters."

I leaned back on the sofa, wondering what my next best move was. There wasn't a doubt in my mind whether or not I was going to bounce back, but how? "You know what I thought about after that shit happen last night?"

Leonard spun his lighter around on the table, appearing to be uninterested in what I was about to say. "What did you think about?" He said.

"I thought about your old connect. What ever happen to them niggas you used to deal with back in the day? I remember everything you told me about how they made sure that you wanted for nothing. If you had a problem with someone, then they made sure that that problem went away. If you wanted more work, they made sure you got more work than you could handle. After what happen to us last night, I'd say we need someone like that on our team."

Leonard smirked, and took a long hard pull from his cigarette. "They're still around," he said. "They ain't stop doing what they'd been doing because I fell off. They just found someone that could do what I did, and kept it moving."

I sat up to the edge of the sofa. "Well, why don't you hook me up with them? The way you say you were balling back in the day, I think if we put our heads together— we'll go way harder."

Leonard peered out the dining room window as if he were on a long trip back down Memory Lane. From what he'd told me, he was a monster back in his day. He was the very nightmare that made federal agents wake up having cold sweats. "I don't think that'll be such a good idea," Leonard said, softly. "The people I used to be in business with, ain't like dealing with any of these other knuckle heads that you're used to dealing with. These people will kill your whole family, then turn around and bury you alive just for coming up short with their money."

"What if I brought my own money? That way I can eliminate the chance of messin' up their money. Do you think they'll sell us some work?"

Leonard ran one hand over the bald spot at the top of his head and ruffled the hair around the sides. "I don't know," he replied. "Those people are dangerous, Kevin. Ain't no telling what they'll do. And besides... how much money you got to be spending anyhow?"

I thought about it for a second, then looked over at O-Dawg. He quickly stabbed at his eggs with a fork then greedily crammed a fork full into his mouth. "What if I sell my car? I'm sure I can get four or five gee's for it. Do you think that'll be enough?"

Leonard chuckled and snipped out the rest of his cigarette in the ashtray. "Number one, four or five thousand for something that ain't worth half of that, is a feat in itself. But, to take that kind of money to a group of people that only deals in kilos, is almost begging for trouble."

I looked down at my plate where a family of roaches had gathered together to say grace before they ate. The thought of what they're about to do didn't bother me. The thing that bothered me was I wasn't eating. I wasn't getting money. Every dope-boy I'd ever heard of always had a connect. Even the songs I heard on the radio talked about niggas pushing kilos because they had a good connect. Sadly, I didn't know anything about having a good connect, or better yet what the fuck a kilo was.

"How many zips is in a kilo?" I asked and looked back up to meet Leonard's calculating gaze.

He scoffed and got up from the table. "Thirty-six," he replied, and walked back to his bedroom. "It's thirty-six ounces in a kilo. If you can save up enough dough to get your hands on one of them, that'll probably change your life." I watched as Leonard disappeared into his bedroom and closed the door. All the stories he'd told me about his rise to power started with that one kilo. If he could do it, then I damn she' could do it!

"What up, O-Dawg? Is you rollin' wit' me or not?" I happened to look over just in time to catch O-Dawg giving Kathy the fuck face. He eyed her lustfully from head to toe all the while biting on his bottom lip.

She giggled.

"Nah, I'ma chill here until Stutter wake up." O-Dawg replied, while trying to conceal his lustful intentions by appearing to be consumed by something in the dining room. "Plus, Kathy got some important business that she need me to check out. Feel me?"

I looked at Kathy, then back at O-Dawg. "Really? You know y'all outta line. If Leonard come out here and catch y'all doin' somethin' crazy, you know what it's gon' be."

"Nigga, pleeeeeease," O-Dawg said. "I'll knock that nigga's top back if he ever try and step to me."

"Yeah, aiight," I said and walked to the front door. "It ain't no secret that he a stone-cold nut about fuckin' with Kathy. If you willing to play with fire and take the risk of gettin' burned, then who am I to try and stop ya'?"

**LEONARD**

"A thousand-eight grams. A thousand-eight muthafuckin' grams!" I strolled across my bedroom and plopped down at the edge of the bed. The subtle clawing sound I heard inside the bedroom's closet was but a reminder of the rat-infested motel that we'd created. To think about the dumb shit that just came out of Kevin's mouth was enough to make me question why I'd ever fucked with him. How could he fix his mouth to ask me for a connect, but don't even know what a kilo was? That's the dumbest shit in the world if you were to ask me.

As I sat listening to the murmur of voices coming out the living room, my room where I sat had stacks on top of stacks of dead presidents scattered about the floor. Back when my closet was stuffed with so many minks and furs, we literally had to use the rooms upstairs to hang up Momma's clothes. For me to think back to such a beautiful time in my life, yet have to look upon the dump that we'd turned this place into, was killing me. I was at the point in my life where I just wanted to end it. I wanted to put That Bitch to my dome and pull the trigger. But in the back of my mind I knew I couldn't. I still had one more thing that needed to be done before I left this earth.

I glanced over to the dresser as a mouse shot across the floor. I caught sight of myself staring back at me in the mirror. I'd been in the same clothes for the past three days. My hair hadn't seen a comb in probably just as long. If you were to say that the man staring back at me was once a self-made millionaire, most people would say that you were a got-damn lie. But in truth I was once that nigga.

Folks called me L back in the day. I controlled any and everything that had to do with dope being sold in my city. If you wanted to sell drugs, then guess what. You bought 'em from me. If you wanted to sell a particular type of drug that I didn't have, then guess what. You waited until I got it. If by chance you went behind my back to score, but I didn't get my cut, I'd send some killas to your Momma's front door. It ain't because I had a problem with her, either. I'd just be sending you a message. This is business.

Unlike these youngstas now days that don't value their position as a boss, I did. I valued my position because I knew what it felt like not to have anything.

My mother raised me and my older two brothers in a small two-bedroom house, not far from where I live now. It was one of those houses that was well beyond the point of being deemed as livable. But then again, back in those days, the white man didn't give a damn about how us black folks where living. As long as we stayed our black asses on our side of town, they ain't give a damn if we were dead or alive.

I never had a chance to get to know my father before he passed. The only time I ever really saw him was when Momma got some money, or when he'd wore himself down from running the streets and needed some rest. Both of my brothers, Kenny and Harold, had different last names than I did. When I was a kid, I didn't understand that that meant they had different Daddys than I did. I didn't understand why the milk man came by and only gave Harold money. Or, why the preacher only stopped by to pray with Momma whenever Daddy wasn't around.

I remember lying awake some nights listening to Momma cry her eyes out. My older two brothers would be sound asleep. Sometimes, even against Momma's stern instruction, I'd go in there to try and comfort her. Of course, I'd be met with a slew of curse words and promises about how she was gonna beat my ass, but I didn't care. If she was hurt and crying, then we were hurt and crying.

Regardless of how young I was, I still had an understanding of what was going on. I knew we had bills due that Momma couldn't pay. Hell, we barely had enough food in the house, let alone warm clothes that was adequate to endure the freezing winter that was upon us. Had it not been for my grandparents, I don't think we would've made it.

My grandmother was the backbone of our family. When all else failed, she was the glue that kept us together. Every time she came around she brought these delicious smelling pies that would light up the entire house. It seemed like, no soon as she stepped through the door, the smell of those pies would instantly do away with any negativity we were dealing with.

My grandfather, who was very poised and mysterious, kept a pocket full of money. Whatever bills that were due and Momma couldn't pay, my grandfather had no problem forking over the cash needed to get the bill paid. I used to daydream about how much money he must've had in those slacks of his. But if he ever caught me eyeing his cash too heavily, he'd say, "I went and got mine, now you get out there and get your own!"

I remember all the great stories that my grandfather told me, about when he was younger and smuggling moonshine with his friends. I have to admit, some of those stories sounded a tad bit far-fetched. While often times than not, he told me things and demand that I looked him in the eye. That's how I knew whatever he told me was the truth. He'd once told me, "If a man can't look you in the eye when he's got something to say, then either he got something to hide, or he a got-damn lie!"

Armed with the many things that my grandfather taught me over the years, it made me respect him more. Besides the fact that he was my only example of what a real man was, he taught me how to carry myself. When he walked into the room, people knew it. They might not have heard him when he came in, but they damn sho' felt him. My grandmother said, "Babe, everything your grandfather been teaching you, be sure and remember it. There'll come a time when he and I won't be around to help see you and your Momma through. You gon' have ta' know something up here." She tapped me on the head. "And have enough courage to stand up and be a man. If neither of your brothers will step up and help out around here, then it's gonna be up to you to look after ya' Momma."

At seven years old, I had no idea how soon that time would be upon me. But, by the time I turned thirteen— that time had come. I was doing everything under the sun to take care of Momma like she'd done when she raised me. My grandparents had already passed, and both of my brothers had moved out, leaving me and Momma to fin for ourselves.

At first, learning the ropes to the streets was downright frustrating. I didn't understand how I could take nothing and turn it into something. Once I figured out how the game was played; I was a hard-young brotha ta' deal with. Robbing and stealing were just a couple of tactics in my arsenal. I was running numbers, strong-arming other young hustlers, even extorting whomever I felt I could. The things I used to get away with, even I couldn't believe I did. I wouldn't dare tell another soul about some of the things I done out of fear that no one would believe me. I guess that's how my grandfather must've felt when he used to tell me stories. The only difference between him and I was he'd conquered his fears while I was still battling with mine.

As the years continued to come and go, naturally I grew stonger and wiser. But, while I gradually transformed into the man I was to become, the rock that I'd so long depended on started to wither away. There'd be times I'd come in from hustling and Momma would act like she didn't know who I was. She'd say, "Harold, is that you?" My initial thought was Momma was playing. Ain't no way I looked anything like Harold. Harold, was chubby, dark skinned, with a ton of bumps all over his face. I was slim, handsome and chiseled to perfection.

"Nah, Momma." I replied with a soft chuckle. "It's only me, Leonard." The expression that shown on Momma's face as she peered up at me from her rocking chair prompted me to rush over to her. "Momma, what's wrong?" I kneeled beside her and took her hand into my own. When she looked me dead in my eye then snatched her hand away, I knew then something was wrong.

After several mind-boggling episodes, I ended up taking Momma to see a therapist. The first couple of visits, in my opinion, they were only trying to swindle us out of our money. They'd run a few costly tests, give Momma a prescription, then send us on our way. But after a few visits, the results from those tests had finally came back.

"Alzheimer's disease!" I shouted, repeating what the Doctor had just informed me of. "But-But-But how is this even possible? Are you sure that that's what it is?"

The Doctor looked me dead in the eye and said, "Yes, Leonard. We're sure."

I peered over at Momma who sat cradling her purse as if it were a newborn baby, and I lost it. I fell out right there in that Doctor's office and cried like a baby. The only person on this whole got-damn planet that I loved didn't even know who the hell I was. I tried to force myself to believe that it was all a dream, but it wasn't. I wanted to hop up and make that white muthafucka fix her. I wanted to take all of my hate, anger and frustration, and wreak havoc on the world, but what good would that fucking do?

It took months for me to digest the weight of the burden I was to carry. Although Momma's mental state was fading in and out, her health was fading just as well. A time was coming when she too would no longer be with me. I wanted—no, I needed— to see her happy before she left me. I used to sit alone with Momma and tell her some of the stories she'd told me about herself, when I was growing up. That was my way of reminding her of the amazing woman she once was, and still was to me.

One day, while we sat having one of our many conversations, Momma said, "Leonard, when are you gonna buy me a new house? I've always wanted a new house you know. I asked your father to do it," she paused and shrugged, "but he dead now. I even asked your brothers, but they tol' me they can't do it!"

When Momma asked me to buy her a house, that almost made me cry. She hadn't ever asked me for something that I couldn't give her. We lived in the same two-bedroom house ever since I could remember. The brilliant white paint that once covered the outside of our home had long since pilled away; leaving dull, grayish, rotting wood exposed. I barely had five pair of pants, let alone five matching shirts. All of our clothes were hand-me-downs, just like everything else we owned. At the time, I had no idea how I was gonna buy Momma a new house, but in time I would.

# Chapter 6
# LEONARD

By the time I turned twenty-one, there was a new drug pouring into my city. Heroin was reigning king amongst other dealers across the nation, but in my city, cocaine was the new thang. Although, it took a while for me to work my way through the ranks, before I could get my hands on the good stuff. Back then, everyone didn't have access at buying large quantities of cocaine. You had to know somebody that knew someone in order to get your hands on the good stuff. And with me being in the business of dealing with everyone, well, that speaks for itself. I knew someone.

My rise to power was short and sweet. I practically took over my city in the blink of an eye. Anything you wanted, I could get it. Any shipment too large for the average crew to push, then I would push it. It didn't take long before my name started circulating in circles that I never knew existed. Instead of having to scour the earth in search of a connect, plugs came looking for me. I'd already established myself as a man of my word. So, when the time came to re-up, and I accidently stumbled in on my connect getting his head chopped off, by his connect. It was over. Nothing needed to be explained on my behalf. My connect's plug had already heard that I could handle the pressure of being a real supplier. And I did.

My new connect started me off with 1,008 grams. He told me how much money he wanted back, and gave me a few days to do it. I opened up a few dope houses around town and ran them bitches around the clock. Before I knew it, I'd moved up to selling weight. Packs started coming in, and packs started going out. I was picking up brand new cars loaded with bricks of the finest blow that money could buy. The only fear I had was if I'd be able to make it home that night. I didn't have any worries about putting the word out that I had the good stuff. The good stuff sold itself. People came from far and wide to buy as much as they could.

Before it was all said and done, I'd saved up enough money and bought Momma a two-story house. I plushed that thang out with everything luxurious that money could buy. Once everything was fixed up the way I wanted, I blindfolded Momma and drove her to her new home. Of course, I'd waited until one of those rare moments when she fully understood what was going on. So, when I finally removed the blindfold, she squealed, "Leonard, you did it!" She buried her face in my chest and cried.

Hell, I was so happy to see her happy, I started crying too. I think we must've stood outside for thirty minutes relishing what I'd done for her. But those gleeful moments of tears and joy would only be used as motivation. When I tasted the sweetness of success, I wanted more. I expanded my operation and started selling bricks to people in Arkansas, Nebraska, and even Kansas. I was bringing in so much money I'd fall asleep trying to count it all up. I didn't know anyone, at the time, that I felt I could trust to help me count up all that dough. It'd just be me and Momma, in her newly furnished home, with stacks on top of stacks of cash all around us.

Eventually, I invested in a couple of Doberman pinchers to help keep our fortune safe. Although, a few times I came home to find a trail of cash leading out the back door. My first thought was, we'd been robbed! But, when I followed the trail leading outside to the doghouse, come to find out, we hadn't been robbed at all. Momma was using my hard-earned cash as hay to help keep the dogs warm. I almost died laughing when I realized what she'd done. Just a few short years ago, we were struggling to keep food on the table. Now, even my dogs were rolling in dough.

It didn't take long before word reached my older brothers that I was making some serious dough. I'm sure they must've assumed that they'd be walking into a situation where everything would be laid out on a silver platter for them. But, that's only in a fairytale. In the real world, there's levels to this shit. That means, situations that will define how loyal you are. Situations that will either help make you a boss, or help me to decide if I should leave you dead and stanking out in the middle of nowhere. Out of the kindness of my heart, I gave both Kenny and Harold important roles in my organization. Kenny was in charge f distribution to the locals, while Harold simply collected money, and made sure our mother was straight.

During, or around, this time in my career, I had the streets in a mean chokehold. Nothing moved unless I gave the okay for it to. Because of this, there came a few instances when I had to pump lead in a few knuckleheads. But that's all a part of the game. People are gonna try your hand when you're on top. Some may come for your money, others for your spot. But always remember, when they come, kill 'em.

One evening, I was on the phone trying to explain to my connect that I needed a larger shipment. Talking in code to a person that barely spoke English was giving me the blues. Business was going too smooth for me not to double down. Everybody wanted a piece of the action. I had people coming from everywhere trying to buy kilos. The only problems I had were I couldn't keep enough product, and it was impossible to tell my plug what I wanted over the phone, without catching a conspiracy case.

By the time our conversation concluded, I'd agreed to fly out to his location and have a sit down. That was the only way to make sure he had an understanding of where I wanted to take our business. While I was to be away, Kenny and Harold were left in charge over everything. The Ghetto, which was where most of my dope was sold, would continue to be managed by Nate and his crew. Being that I had to meet up with the connect, I left Nate with enough work to handle the locals. Whenever anyone from out of town needed something, they'd simply call Kenny, and he'd deliver the pack.

It was a cold December night. Harold lay passed out drunk in the living room, while Kenny sat at the dining room table snorting coke. The meds the Doctor prescribed for our mother kept her out of it most of the time. She too was fast asleep in the back room. Business had been booming non-stop up the hill at The Ghetto. By the time Kenny received a call from Nate for a couple of bricks, he was too high and paranoid to move.

"Harold!" Kenny shouted over the hum of the 70's classic *Float On* playing in the stereo. "Harold! Come on, man. Wake up!"

Harold stirred on the sofa while mumbling various curse words. "What is it?" He asked. "Can't you see I'm trying ta' sleep?"

Kenny scuffed and shook his head. "Come on, man. I need you to do me a favor and drop these packs off. I'll stay here and look afta' Momma until you get back."

Harold bolted up into a sitting position. "It ain't my fuckin' job to drop that shit off! If you'd stop shoving that poison up your nose, maybe you'll be able to think well enough to do your own job." The continued clink from Kenny's razor hitting the plate was confirmation that Harold was right. "How much they want?" Harold asked, realizing that Kenny was in no shape to conduct business.

Kenny lined out two perfectly straight lines of coke, then snorted them through a straw. *Smmmmmmmmmmfffh! Smmmmmmmmmffffh! Smfh Smfh.* Kenny tilted his head back allowing the powder to drain down his throat and said, "That's what the fuck I'm talkin' 'bout."

"How you gon' ask me to do you a favor, but you too damn high to tell me what I need to do?" Harold asked.

Kenny's eyelids fluttered as a lone tear rolled down his cheek. "Oh, ummmmm. Just take three kilos up to The Ghetto. I think Nate said he was out. Plus, some other people supposed to be in town that wanna buy up the rest."

Harold glared at him momentarily, disappointed that Kenny had allowed the drugs to cloud his better judgement. "You need ta' leave that shit alone! If Leonard could see you now, your ass would be outta' here!" Harold marched through the dining room and into the back bedroom where their mother was sound asleep.

From the beginning, Momma was supposed to have the master bedroom upstairs. But, as her health began to deteriorate, we moved her downstairs. But that was after I'd already installed a hidden safe in the downstairs bedroom closet. It was impossible to tell it was there. I had to have a special crew come in and cut the closet floor out, then install the safe. The floor was rebuilt around the safe and concealed under plush, removable carpet.

After unlocking the safe and removing the three kilos, Harold put them into a brown paper sack, then put everything back the way he'd found it. Upon walking back into the dining room, he was met with the sight of Kenny still sitting at the table in a daze. "I'm warning you," Harold spat. "The next time someone calls, wanting you to bring 'em something, it's gone be on you to do it!" Harold marched out the front door and slammed it behind him.

Kenny glanced over to the door, just to be certain Harold had left. He then quickly lined out another hit and snorted it off the plate. *Smmmmmmfffh! Smfh-smfh.* "Damn, that's some good shit!" Kenny brushed at his nose, smacking his lips as the coke drained down his throat. When he leaned back forward, he caught sight of movement just outside the dining room window. "Harold?"

Kenny peered curiously into the night. He slowly inched forward, almost certain that he'd saw something. Although he hadn't seen any distinguishing features, or any clothing, just the dark outline of what appeared to be a face. Kenny cautiously rose from his chair and leaned closer to the window. But, the closer he drew near to the window, the more he began to realize someone was watching him.

*BOOM!* A bullet burst through the window and hit him right between the eyes. Kenny's body fell to the table where his brains oozed out of his forehead. Moments later, several masked men stormed the house. They went from room to room literally ripping the place apart. Finding nothing, they eventually ended up in the back bedroom.

"Who who's there?" Momma asked, squinting at the blinding light raining down on her face.

"Don't worry about who the fuck it is, ol' woman. Just tell us where the fuckin' money is at."

Momma propped up on her pillow and asked, "Where's Leonard? Where's Harold? If my son's find out that you're in here—"

*BOOM! BOOM! BOOM!* Three crimson patches appeared across Momma's chest as bullets ripped through her. Assuming she was being used as a cover to hide the stash, the masked men drug her lifeless body out of bed and tossed it on the floor.

"Find it!"

Several men commenced to butcher Momma's pillows, box spring and mattress in search of the hidden stash spot. Still unable to find anything, they were forced to make a critical decision. Either they could risk being caught if they stayed and continued to search for the stash, or take anything of value they could find and leave.

For seasoned Jackboyz such as these men, the latter would be their only option. They quickly gathered everything of value that they could find, and made a haste retreat back out the front door.

"Hey! Wha-Wha-What the hell are you doing?" Harold shouted, as he got out of his car, noting several men clad in black racing down his mother's porch steps. The masked intruders continued on their way, showing total disregard that Harold had returned.

The last man out the house spotted Harold and aimed his gun at him. "Gimmie your fuckin' money!"

Harold raised his hands high above his head and said, "Whoooooa, take it easy with that thing. Let's-Let's just talk about this, can we?"

The masked man cautiously inched toward Harold who stood by his car with the door open. "I'll give you five seconds to hand over that money," the masked gunman said. "You can either walk away from this thing alive, or be a dead man. Either way, I'm gettin' that money."

Harold peered down inside his car at a leather duffle bag on the seat. The bag contained money that he'd just made from the sale of two kilos. A brown paper sack containing the last unsold kilo sat next to it. "Listen, I gotta' bag full of money right here on the seat," Harold explained. "I'm going to slowly reach down in here and get the money for ya, but please *don't shoot*!" Harold reached inside of the car and grabbed the paper sack containing the kilo instead. He then dangled it over the car and said, "Here it is. Now what do you want me to do?"

The masked gunman eyed him skeptically. "Toss it over!"

Harold threw the bag several feet away, so that the man would have to step away in order to retrieve it.

Red and blue lights crested the top of the hill, just as another man yelled, "Come on! We gotta' get outta' here! The cops are coming!"

The man that held Harold at gunpoint ran, scooped up the bag and trained his sights back on Harold. It was obvious that he knew there was more cash around, but with bright, flashing lights now illuminating the front yard, he was forced to retreat.

I couldn't tell you how many times I've pondered that story over the years. I wanted to believe everything my brother said happened. It's just certain things didn't add up. The story he'd told me provided him with the perfect opportunity to take what he could; assuming because of the quantity that it'd be overlooked. But he failed to take one important thing into consideration. You'll never make it to the level of the game where I'd been overlooking the very things that got you there. Had that have been me that was sent to rob someone, I'd have been thorough in my search to find the loot. Ain't no way a muthafucka gon' just toss me a sack and I'ma leave it at that. Either he gon' show me where the rest of it was at, or I'ma rock his ass to sleep too. Don't make no sense to leave someone alive and take the chance of that shit coming back to haunt you. Sure, I understood that Harold said the police were coming. But once again I wanted to believe everything my brother had told me. It's just certain things didn't add up.

## Chapter 7
## LEONARD

Shortly after the funeral services that we held for our loved ones, Harold came talking about wanting out the game. He gave me some long, drawn out spill about how he'd been studying with some kind of witnesses. So, I asked, "Nigga, is you workin' with the police?"

Harold laughed and replied, "Come on, man. You know me better than that. This ain't got nothing to do with being a snitch. These kind of witnesses are Jehovah's Witnesses."

Being that I'd spent the better part of my life knee-deep in the streets, I had no understanding of the direction Harold wanted to go with his life. In my mind, his actions only added to my suspicions. It looked like he was using the deaths of our loved ones as a scapegoat to take whatever he had and start a new life. I may not have had any proof to back my assumption, but that don't mean I wouldn't find some.

As days continued to come and pass, my sanity slowly began to slip away. I found myself sitting alone at the dining room table, in the same spot that they'd killed my brother, staring out the window. Paranoia had me in a fucked up state of mind. I was seeing shit that wasn't even there. I suspected people were out to get me when it was all just in my head. Things got so bad that soon I started making all the wrong decisions. Petty beefs that should've been overlooked, I'd zeroed in on it and let bullets fly. Homicide Detectives practically lived on my doorsteps. Every time a body turned up around my city, they automatically assumed that I had something to do with it.

Finally, coming to the conclusion that things could no longer continue down the path they were on, Nate came to me with an ultimatum. Either I would fall back and let him handle everything, or he'd cut all business ties with me. Had that conversation not transpired over the phone, I'd have gladly shot his ass too. My ego was on King Kong status. I could care less about a muthafucka cuttin' ties with me. I was the one with the connect, not them. My money was gonna be straight regardless.

My plug must've caught wind of the mayhem that I'd been causing. He called me up and asked if I'd fly out to his estate. Naturally, I did. My connect was good peoples. He looked out for any and everything that was in my best interest. When we had our little sit down, he helped me to understand how my actions could hurt business. Lord knows I didn't wanna do that. I loved making money too much to wanna ruin a good thing. By the end of our meeting, I'd agreed to fall back and let Nate handle everything. Although I'd still be in charge, I needed a little time to get my mind right.

Harold moved out and bought himself a 3-bedroom brick home. That move only raised my suspicion a little more. I paid both of my brothers well when they worked for me, but neither one of them negros had discipline. They spent money just as fast as they could make it. Needless to say, I kept cool and didn't say a word. If it ain't but one thing I knew for certain, Harold couldn't outsmart me. Whatever he may or may not have done would soon come to the light. I didn't make it to Kingpin status without applying patience. Besides, Harold had a few other things going on, that I was slightly curious to see how they turned out.

Rumor had it, Harold had hooked up with a young lady at the Guthrie Job Corp. I heard he'd got himself a good paying job, and was supposed to be getting married. Around the time all those rumors were circulating, I'd also heard he was creeping with a strawberry named Special K. From what I was told, Harold would spend a couple hundred on some blow, hide out in a motel, and do his thing. I asked around trying to find out who would dare sell my brother some dope to get high. I'd already lost one brother because of that shit. I'd be damned if I'd lose another. But, no one would own up to selling Harold anything. Some claim they didn't know that he still had any dealings with drugs, while others just assumed that he bought all of his dope from me.

The thought to stop by and see how Harold was doing crossed my mind, but I quickly decided against it. Harold and I had fallen out on numerous occasions since the funeral. Our relationship had grown apart. We didn't even treat each other like brothers anymore.

The more he got involved with that Jehovah's Witness bull crap, the more he started to freak me the hell out.

One day, after being cooped up in the house for several weeks, I decided to break my cycle of depression. It was a beautiful Sunday afternoon with not so much as one cloud in the sky. Very seldom did I ever go out just to shine, but on that day that's what I felt like doing. Feeling a little sporty, I chose to take my '57 Chevy out and open her up. That car was my baby. It was cherry red with cocaine white leather guts. Every time people saw me coming, they'd stop whatever they were doing and wave.

After hitting a few corners, I stopped by the store to grab a few snacks. I pulled into the IGA parking lot and hopped out. As I strolled across the parking lot, I noticed an unfamiliar face watching my every move. Normally, I wouldn't hesitate to set a bitch straight for staring at me for too long. But, this fine specimen of a woman had me staring too. She wore a multi-colored head-wrap over hair that appeared to be done in a ponytail. Her blouse was bright yellow which complimented the tan and yellow skirt she also had on. Her eyes were so piercing that it almost felt like she could see my naked soul.

"Good afternoon," I greeted her as I approached.

"Hello," she replied, happily.

"You here waiting on someone?" I asked, noting several bags that she cradled while seated on a bench.

"Yes, and no," she replied. "I called a cab earlier, but I've been waiting for over an hour for them to get here. Now, I'm just hoping I can pay someone a few dollars to catch a ride home."

"Where you from?"

Her head slightly swayed back as if that were the wrong question for me to ask. "Oklahoma City, why?"

I chuckled. "I didn't mean to come off like I'm trying to pry all of into your business. But, if you're really looking ta' catch a ride home, don't you think the driver should know where to take you?"

The look on her face never changed. If someone were to tell me she was a mind-reader, I'd probably believe them. Those mesmerizing eyes of hers were unlike anything I'd ever seen. But when she stood up, I knew then I had to have her.

"So, you're going to give me a ride home?" She asked flirtatiously.

I shrugged and replied, "Yeah, I guess so. My name's Leonard, but folks 'round here call me, L." I extended my hand in greeting.

"You can call me Kathy," she replied as she accepted my hand with a soft giggle. "Don't you still have some shopping to do?"

I gave her a slow, lustful once over and said, "My shopping here is done! Come on so I can get chu' home."

From that day on, we were practically inseparable. Come to find out, Kathy had just moved to Guthrie and was living at a motel. She told me that her ex-boyfriend was very abusive, and she ended up leaving him on a spare of the moment. Being that my money was longer than I-35, I had no problem with welcoming her into my place. I never told her about what had happened where I was living, or anything about my brothers. However, I did let her know that I was heavy in the dope game. I figured, that was the least bit of information I could give her, for safety reasons.

Over time, I found out that Kathy was a real party girl. She liked to drink, snort coke and fuck until the sun came up. I think I must've fucked that poor woman every which way but loose. I say that I think, because half the time we ain't start gettin' busy until I was drunk out of my mind, and she was nice and toasty. I guess now that she knew that the coke I splurged on her didn't amount to a crumb from a loaf of bread, that made her go harder.

At first, I was a little skeptical of how reckless she was because of the amount of coke she consumed. But, baby girl knew what she was doing. She snorted that shit like a champ and rode my dick all the same. Kathy would get so wild when she was high off that stuff, before I knew it, I had to snort a line or two just to keep up. The first time I did it, I got so high my dick wouldn't go limp. I fucked her in every got-damn hole on her body. I saw the light then. I knew why I'd been getting so rich off that shit.

From my understanding, Kathy had some unfinished business going on back in Oklahoma City. Every now and then, she'd spend a day or two out of town. I never questioned her about her whereabouts, and she never questioned me about mine. I can't lie and say I didn't wonder what she was doing. Hell, it felt like the whole world had come to a stop whenever she wasn't around. As time continued to drift away like beads of sand in an hourglass, Kathy continued doing whatever it was that she did, and I continued to do whatever it was that I did. Everything was just perfect until she got pregnant.

"Leonard, I have to talk to you about something," Kathy cried.

I was in the bedroom half asleep, half watching television. Kathy had been gone for the past two days, and upon her return she'd come straight into the bedroom with a face streaked with tears. "What's wrong?" I flung the covers back and swung my feet outta' bed.

"I have something that I need to tell you," she said between sobs. "But, I don't want you to get mad at me."

1,008 negative assumptions instantly flooded my mind. I thought she was about to tell me that she didn't love me anymore. I thought she was going to tell me that she was leaving. I thought all kind of weird ass shit, but then she told me she was pregnant. If I could pause the hands of time and rewind them bitches, I would.

"I'm sorry, babe!" Kathy cried.

"Sorry about what?" I asked, trying my damnedest to figure out what so wrong with her being pregnant by me.

"I didn't know!"

"You didn't know what?" I got down on my knees between her legs, prying at her hands that were glued to her face. "Kathy, talk to me, babe."

Kathy cried yet a little while longer and said, "Why didn't you tell me?"

I frowned and thought about it. "Tell you what, babe! Kathy, you gon' have to come straight with me and quit jivin' me."

Kathy sat quiet for a moment and took a deep breath. "Harold is your brother."

At first it didn't register to me as to what she had been trying to tell me. Thinking, thinking, thinking. I looked over at the television,

Soul Train had just came on. Thinking, thinking, thinking. But when that shit finally registered about what she'd said to me, I folded that disloyal ass bitch up right there where she sat. *WHAP!* "Bitch, you pregnant by my brother?"

# Chapter 8
# The Present
# KEVIN

The patter of paws clicking across the floor is what stirred me from another peaceful slumber. I opened my eyes to see that I was in a room at the hospital. The first person that came to mind was the little boy down by the stream, he'd saved me.

I slowly sat up on a gurney and accidentally tugged the IV that ran from my arm. "Damn it!"

The clicking sound quickened. *Click-click-click-click-click!*

I looked outside my room into a nurse's station that was completely empty. Surprisingly enough, the entire floor felt like it was empty. All the lights were off except the emergency lighting, casting ghostly phantoms across the dayroom floor. A dull yellowish glow seeped through the blinds on my window. An exit sign could be seen reflecting off of the waxed white tile floor.

*Click-click-click-click-click!*

The clicking drew nearer, followed by a peculiar whimpering that only a dog would make. My eyes widened, literally glued to the hallway. Not only was there no one around to explain what was happening, but the exit sign reflecting off of the floor had suddenly disappeared.

*Grrrrrrrr!*

I gasped.

"I won't let him hurt you unless you want me to." The little boy said.

I damn near leaped off that gurney straight into that mutha-fucka's mouth. "Boy, you—" I looked back to the door, but it was gone. I heard the shuffle of paws making a quick retreat back down the hallway. I looked back at the little boy. He's just standing there; back against the wall, in the dark, watching me. "Say, turn on some damn lights!"

The little boy slowly shook his head and yelled, "You turn 'em on! All you do is sleep, sleep, sleep! You don't wanna do anything anymore! You don't even wanna try! All you want, is for someone else to do what you can do for your own self!"

I just mugged his punk ass. He had no idea how close I was to committing child abuse. "Check this out, Harry Potter."

"My names not Harry Potter."

"I don't give a damn what your name is. All this magical Reading Rainbow shit you done plugged me into has got to stop! You and all your little Pet Cemetery friends can go back to wherever the hell you come from. I'm good on that shit right now. I got too much other stuff going on." I looked around the hospital room again, hoping to see something that might help me understand what was going on. "Where is everyone?" I asked. "And why are you..." I pointed at him and noticed that my hand was covered in blood. I looked down at the sheets where I'd been shot. The bleeding was so severe that the sheets were soaked through with it. "Find a doctor! I'm bleeding."

The little boy calmly walked over to my gurney, unphased by the blood that he saw. "They're here," he said.

"I looked around the room again. "Where?"

"Here!"

I peered outside my room into the hallway. Everything was riddles with this lil nigga.

*They're here.*

*Where?*

*Here!*

Riddles.

Suddenly, the room had a fuzzy dream like haze to it. It felt like I was watching the world through a small. black tunnel, except the tunnel kept pushing the world away from me. "I feel..."

The little boy peered up at me expectantly. He'd leaned up on his tippy toes and gripped the bed railing as if he were holding the bed in place. "Sleepy," he said, completing my statement. "You always feel sleepy. That's what you do, you like to sleep. When you're asleep you can't see nothing. You don't know what's really going on. You don't understand. But I'll let you go back to sleep if you want me to." He paused and looked over at the door.

*Click-click-click-click-click.*

The little boy peered back up at me and said, "But, it'll be awhile before you wake up again."

The clicking brings with it an eerie, unsettling understanding. "I don't wanna die," I pleaded. "I have a little girl home, and she's only five!" The world was moving further and further away from me. With each passing moment, the tunnel that I viewed the world through kept getting smaller and smaller. Memories of my entire life flashed across my mind. Every lie I'd ever told. Every sin I'd ever committed. Every lesson I'd ever learned, yet never even tried to teach another. "Please, just give me one chance. That's all I'm askin' you for. Just one."

A cold darkness that could be felt, swept over my body, paralyzing it. I twitched, fighting fearlessly to hold on to what little life I had left. Tears raced down my cheeks and fell onto my pillow. My eyes rolled into the back of my head, forcing me to face the darkness that would soon consume me. My mind felt like it was being erased; erased of all my memories; erased of all the love, hate, understanding, and every other humanly emotion I had. Death was, and is, complete. It leaves no memories, no thoughts, no emotions, no nothing. As I lie drifting away into a never-ending abyss of darkness, the only glimmer of hope lie in a scripture that my father always used to quote. Proverbs 3:5-6. That's it. That's all I could think of. That's all I had to hold on to.

"I... trust you."

As if on cue, my leg began to burn like it'd caught fire. I barred my grill, fighting to suppress the scream threatening to explode from my mouth. The tunnel that I viewed the world through, slowly began to open back up. It felt like I was riding on a toe-curling, nail-biting rollercoaster. First came the chattering teeth, rumbling and shaking. Then came the monstrous gush of wind on my face. Next, came the sudden twists and turns, followed by a slow, antagonizing climb to the top. Just when I was certain that there'd be nothing else, that the ride would soon be over. I fell.

I screamed so loud and hard I could taste blood in my mouth. My hands trembled and my legs quaked. Just as my lungs had squeezed out the last bit of oxygen left inside of them, I bottomed out. My body jolted, convulsing until I begun to rise.

"Doctor Anderson!"

The world was just up ahead. I could see it. I could damn near touch it. All the familiar sights and sounds related to life came rushing back to me. People yelling and screaming, filled with excitement. People running around in a rush to save the world.

"Doctor Anderson!" A nurse yelled. "I need you over here, now!"

The loud commotion of people moving about didn't register to me as to what was going on. My eyes were still closed, and I had someone, or something wrapped up tight and I wasn't letting go.

"Get him off of her!"

People tugged at my arms, literally clawing at my fingertips, trying to pry them apart.

"I don't wanna die! I trust you! I trust you!"

Someone slammed me down on the gurney where I fought with my last ounce of strength to get back up.

"Hold him down!"

Several people took hold of me. Some gripped my arms and feet, others held my legs pinned to the bed.

"You've gotta' keep him still."

I heard my pants leg get ripped open, which only urged me to fight harder. I bucked, growled, surely foaming at the mouth, fighting to break free. With all of the yelling and screaming, and people constantly tugging on me, only put me in the mind frame of the devil trying to drag me off to hell. But I wasn't going. "Get the fuck off me!" I tried to kick, but they'd already had my legs strapped down.

"Ready?" Someone said.

I felt something sharp pierce my thigh. "*Sssssssssss.*" Instantly all of my fight was zapped out of me. My body fell limp. It felt like I was swimming in a whirl of bliss.

Giggles.

I opened my eyes to see white, sweaty faces huddled around me. Some filled with curiosity, others with care and relief. The tunnel that I viewed the world through was no more. Everything was vivid. I was alive.

Sleep.

**15 Years Ago**
**KEVIN**

Several days had passed since my run-in with Stanley and his crew. My Pops was on my back about sitting still long enough for my body to heal. Between him and the constant slew of calls from my mother, I almost thought I'd never see the light of day again.

The block had been popping non-stop, regardless of my spot being out of commission. That brought to mind something Leonard had told me. He said, "They ain't never stop doing what they'd been doing because I fell off. They just found someone that could do what I did, and kept it moving!" That was some real-life shit, no matter how you cut it. I'd applied that statement to 1,008 different situations. I thought so long and hard about it, until it finally dawned on me. If Justin wasn't going to produce the way I needed for him to, then I'd just have to find someone that would. On the real, fam had me feeling some kinda way. It didn't make sense for him to up and start giving me the runaround. I'd been copin' work from that nigga since I came into the game. He knew how much I depended on him.

I heard from a few of Justin's clientele that he still had plenty of work. They were still getting plugged for the low while I was stuck outta' commission. I guess now that I was able to see his true colors, it was time for me to devise a new plan.

Word on the streets, them cats up at The Ghetto, were making major moves. I heard they'd shut down every dope house on the eastside, and pushed everything out west. I suppose niggas from my city didn't want any problems. With the exception of a handful, everyone else either fell in line, or shut down shop. All the heat, and unwanted attention was drawn far away from whatever these new cats had going on. The way that they handled their business kept everything hush-hush. Nobody really knew what they were up to. All anyone could do was assume.

Although I had a pretty good idea about what was going on inside The Ghetto, I still needed to figure out a way in. The only problem with that idea was, those cats up at The Ghetto kept niggas at a distance. They didn't allow just anyone to approach them and talk about business. I ended up calling Leonard and had to tell him about my plan, to try and speak with them. He didn't seem too excited about it because he felt like I'd be walking into the unknown. Leonard was the type of dude that had to know who was who when it came down to doing business. I had to admit, his spill came off as hella tight. But, talking a good game and having one are two totally different things. I told him to holler at Nate and see if he could get me in.

Nate was the old head that owned The Ghetto. Anything that went on inside of that place, he knew about it. I'm sure whatever was going on, they must've been breaking him off real proper. Nate wasn't lettin' no other niggas set up shop. The only people that were allowed up at the spot, were those new cats. Lucky for me, I had an ace in the hole. Leonard and Nate went way back. Whatever work them fools put in together back in the day, made them niggas tight like brothers. It wasn't shit for Leonard to give Nate a call and ask him for a favor.

At first, I thought it'd be a mission in itself for me to get the okay to stop by. But, after one quick phone call to Nate, I was in. he gave me the green light to slide through around six that evening. But with my Pops still on my back hella' hard, I wasn't able to shake the spot until well after he'd gone to bed.

10:30 P.M.

I pulled into The Ghetto's parking lot, looking every bit just as excited as the first time I stepped foot in the complex. Shit was crazy. Accept now, there weren't a bunch of junkies huddled up smoking crack. Now, the back of the apartment complex had a real club vibe to it. I could hear music bumping inside the club and what sounded like a crowd of people partying. I even saw a few cats posted on the hood of their whips as if they were auditioning for the next Jeezy video. A handful of old school players, dressed in tailor-made suits kept a watchful eye on the traffic while several young hitters thugged out, sporting hoodies, skullies, and t-shirts, played the shadows.

The parking spot that I was parked in was the perfect spot for me to scope everything out. The way they'd set the place up, it was made to appear like they'd changed The Ghetto into an exclusive club. Many of the cars parked out front were foreign whips. My 1986 Cutlass looked so out of place I was already wishing that I would've left it at home and just walked.

A soft tap at my window stirred me from my observations. Some cat in a skully pulled down just above his eyes stood outside. I'd peeped him and several other dudes watching when I first pulled in, so I wasn't even sweatin' it.

"What up?" I asked, as I hit the button to lower my window.

"Da' fuck is you doin' out here, youngin'?" The man quipped as he stooped down to peer inside my car.

"Nate tol' me it was cool to stop by. I was supposed to come through around six, but I got a lil' caught up."

The man took a casual glance back to the old heads that were watching us. "Why Nate say that it was cool for you to stop by? Everything going on around here is already on lock; feel me?"

I flashed a half smile and said, "I ain't come here to step on anyone's toes. Nate just tol' me it was cool to stop by. We were supposed to chop it up about some business. Now, if Nate ain't the nigga that I need to be hollering at, then point me in the right direction and I'll be on my way."

The man looked back in the same direction as he'd looked before. All the ol' heads that were once checking me out, had spread out in the parking lot. There was one ol' head that still stood in the same spot. He hadn't moved an inch. He simply stood there, watching us.

"Aiight, get out and come with me," the man finally said, then flagged over two other men.

Instantly, butterflies swarmed to life in the pit of my stomach. I couldn't believe it. This shit was actually about to happen. All this time I'd been racking my brain on how to get a plug, come to find out, this was all I had to do.

As I got out, the man that I'd been talking to gave me a thorough onceover. I don't know if he was checking to see if I was strapped, or if he was digging my swag. I wore a pair of LRG denim jeans with a matching blue and black short sleeve button down. My fitted Kansas City Royals hat matched my black and blue Nike Air Max.

"You bang?" The man asked.

I looked down at my outfit trying to figure out what he could be talking about. "Yeah, only if it got something to do with my money."

Even in the dim light, I could see the sparkling diamonds in his grill. Although I could hardly see his face because of the skully he wore pulled down, I could still tell he was mugging me.

After a few moments, I guess he'd finally felt comfortable enough to lead the way inside. He led me across the parking lot where two other men fell in tow. But they didn't led me inside the club like I'd expected. Instead, they led me up a small flight of stairs to a section of The Ghetto that was never used. All the apartments in that section were empty. Most of them because the roof had caved in. Others, because the rats had literally taken over.

"So, what type of business was it that you needed to holler at Nate about?" The man asked.

I looked around the empty apartment that they'd led me to, broken glass lay scattered about the floor. A roll of carpet was propped against the wall in the far corner of the room. An old, dirty mattress lie in the middle of the floor. "Nate was supposed to introduce me to someone that might be willing to put me to work." I explained.

"Someone that might put you to work?" The man repeated. "What? You know how ta' fix up apartments or something?"

I had a weird feeling that these niggas were up to no good. The thought to make a run for the door danced around in my mind, but the fact that two other men were blocking my escape made it highly unlikely that I'd ever be able to make it. "Nah, I don't know shit about fixin' up no apartments. I'm out here trying to get mines however I can get it. You and I are probably in the same line of business. Judgin' by the way you move, I can recognize a real nigga when I see one."

The man laughed and looked back at his comrades. "Y'all hear this lil' nigga? He can recognize a real nigga when he see one." The man walked a few steps closer and lifted his shirt, revealing a gun. "Since you and me is possibly in the same line of business, I take it that you got one of these then, huh?"

The door to the room came open, drawing everyone's attention. It was the same old head I'd saw down in the parking lot. He walked in, eyeing me suspiciously. "What chu' young muthafuckas got going on up in here?" He asked. Everything about him reminded me of James Brown; from his feathered perm to his raspy voice. He wore a long sleeve burgundy dress shirt half unbuttoned, revealing 2 gold chains.

"Youngin claim Nate gave him the okay to stop by." The man that stood in front of me said. "I figured it'd be best to bring him up here and make sure he wasn't packin' or nothin'."

The ol' head eyed me curiously and asked, "What's your name, son?"

All of a sudden, my mouth felt dry as fuck. Whatever these niggas were up to, the only way I was walking out of there, was with the okay of the man in front of me. "Kevin," I finally managed to say. "My name's Kevin."

The man chuckled and looked around the room. "Okay then, Kevin... My Name's Kevin. What brings you to our lovely establishment?"

I had to take a deep breath to calm my nerves. Judging by the response I got moments ago, I was a little reluctant to say what I'd just said. "Nate said that it'd be cool to come through today. He also told me that he might be able to hook me up with someone that'll front me some work."

"Nah, that ain't what the fuck he just told me!" One of the men interrupted. "He told us that Nate was supposed to introduce him to someone willing to put him to work!"

"That's the same thing!" I exclaimed. "Maybe you took it the wrong way, but you can ask Nate and I'll bet he'll verify everything that I'm telling you."

The ol' head bobbed his head as if he were considering what I'd told him. He looked over my outfit, then stepped back and said, "Search him!"

They spun me around and slammed me against the wall. It didn't make any sense how rough they were handling me. They slapped at my thighs, snatched at my pants, someone even snatched off my hat.

After they were finally content that I had nothing on me, the old head said, "Turn around." I slowly spun back around and placed my back against the wall. The ol' head took one step closer to me and said, "If I take you downstairs and Nate tell me that he don't know you, you do understand that we're gonna have a problem, don't cha?" I nodded, but he just stood there with a funny look on his face. It wasn't the kind of look as if he were waiting for me to say something else, but as if he knew me. The ol' head opened his mouth to say something, but decided against it.

They led me back downstairs and inside The Ghetto. The inside of the club was just as I'd remembered it; sagging floors with lots of beaded strings concealing other doors. The club still had the same red light bulb in the middle of the room, and music still pumped out of an old house stereo.

"There goes my muthafucka!" Nate shouted, no soon as he saw us. He shuffled around the bar and came to embrace me. "I see y'all done met my hustlin' ass nephew, Kevin."

I had to shoot Nate a look that said now wasn't the time for extras.

"Oh, come on now!" Nate exclaimed, picking up on my expression. "This ain't my real nephew. I just call him nephew because his daddy, Harold, used to be like a brother to me. Harold was one hell of a muthafcuka back in the day. Kevin here done probably picked up on some of his father's tricks of the trade."

The ol' head gave me a questioning look as if he were trying to figure out something. If he knew anything about my father, then he'd know he was the furthest thing from a hustler that you could be.

"Have a seat, son." Old head said as he pulled out a stool from the bar and shooed his henchmen away. "Sorry about all the added precaution. Ya' can't ever be too safe these days." He dug into his pocket and pulled out a pack of Winston 100's and asked, "Do you need a smoke?"

"Nah, I'm good."

The man slapped the pack against the palm of his hand and shook a cigarette out and lit it. "The name's Cabbage. You'll find that I can be a very good person to have in your corner, or I can be your worst nightmare." Cabbage took a long, concentrated drag from his cigarette and released the smoke through his nostrils. "Do you see that crazy son of a bitch right there?" Cabbage went on to say while pointing where Nate sat. "I've known that negro for years. I got the chance to meet his parents before they passed. I also got the chance to meet a whole bunch of other people he hung out with back in the day. I knew his wife, his cousin; shit, I practically knew his whole got-damn family. But you wanna hear something crazy?"

I shrugged, having no idea where he was going with this.

Cabbage smiled and said, "I don't recall ever meeting your father." I opened my mouth to try and explain, but he stopped me. "No need for any explanations. I done already made up my mind that you must be alright. That shiner on your face tell me, either you done got cha' ass whooped, or you round here raising hell. And that's not to mention your face does look kind of familiar."

"I got a spot down the street that I be servin' at."

"Which one? I hope it's not the two-story house down there on the corner."

I nodded.

"Son, it's probably a good thing that you came by here when you did. I told some real good friends of mine to pay you boys a visit. Who's that staying there these days?"

I was so busy thinking about him paying us a visit, that I'd failed to hear his last question. "What were you gonna pay us a visit for?" When Cabbage didn't answer and just sat there with an ice-cold stare, I knew why.

"Hey, Nate!" Cabbage shouted. "Bring us over two double shots of that good stuff you've got back there."

Nate was seated a couple of stools over, giving us ample space for privacy. Occasionally, he'd walk by to appear busy, but that was just his way of checking on me.

"I hope you drink," Cabbage said as Nate placed two glasses in front of us. "A person can't even think to talk to me unless we done had ourselves a drank first."

I glanced down at the glass then back up at him. "Yeah, I drink. But right now, I'm trying to keep a clear mind so can stay on point."

Cabbage raised a brow and said, "You must gotta problem with listenin'. I just tol' you ain't gon' be no talk about business until we done had ourselves a drink!" He pushed one of the glasses closer to me and lifted his to propose a toast. "Here's to the future. May all our days be bright and sunny."

That was the first time I'd noticed Cabbage's hands. His fingers were swollen due to the lack of circulation. The gold nugget rings he wore were entirely too small. I couldn't help but to imagine how he'd ever be able to get those rings off, unless they were cut off.

"Ahhhhhhhhh!" I hissed while holding my chest after taking a drink. "What the hell was that?"

Cabbage laughed so hard that he had tears falling from his eyes. "That there is gon' put some hair on your chest, son."

I looked down at the empty glass and made a mental note not to ever drink shit that nigga offered me again. "Look, big homie, I done had my drink. I done almost got killed by your goons out front. What it's gon' take for me and you to start doing business?"

Cabbage chuckled and said, "Boy, you's a persistent son of a bitch ain't cha? What makes you think I have anything to do with the line of business that you're in?"

I flashed a weak smile and replied, "I'm from here. The talk of the town is how you niggas done took over the streets."

"Don't nobody listen to the streets anymore. Niggas lie, just like bitches do. The sooner you get that through your head, the better off you'll be."

I shook my head and sighed out of frustration. No matter what I said, this nigga wasn't trying to let me in.

"I'ma go ahead and give you a chance, youngsta." Cabbage finally said. "But if you fuck up one time, I promise you, you'll regret it."

I nodded, suddenly overwhelmed with excitement. I had a million of other questions that I wanted to ask, but being that Cabbage had finally softened up and let me in, those questions could wait. It was time to get money.

**O-DAWG**

*"Drank drank in my cup, cup in my hand! These hoes on my dick cause they know I'm da' man. Hoes hoes on my dick cause they know I'm da' man!"*

Every time I heard E-40's song it put me in a zone. I swear it had me trippin', thinking that the shit I done earlier made me the man.

"We gon' have to rewind that bitch!" I shouted to Uncle Tim over the music banging out his deck. But he was too busy trying to drive and get high to pay attention to what I'd just said.

The work I gave him from the lick I hit turned out to be straight drop. My pockets lumped up so fast after simply handing out a few packets, I was already plotting on how I could get my hands on some more.

Earlier that day, I was startled awoke by the sound of a car door slamming just outside our crib. It sounded like the police were about to raid with all the yelling and screaming I heard. I quickly grabbed my strap from under the sofa and took a peek out the curtain.

Stanley's car was parked in the driveway while my sister unloaded her bags out of his trunk. From what I could see, it looked like they'd been arguing. LaShura had that look on her face like she'd been crying. And Stanley looked like he was about to cry.

"LaShura, please!" Stanley pleaded. "Babe, I get it. You don't have to break up with me for me to see your point. I'll fix this shit, ASAP!"

I tucked my strap in the small of my back then stepped outside. "Wuz crackin', sis?"

LaShura sniffled, and shook her head. "Noth-Nothing," she stammered. "Will you just help me get my things inside, and I'll tell you everything later?"

I eyed that nigga Stanley something serious. I just knew he remembered all that slick shit he was poppin' the other night.

"Babe, listen," Stanley began by saying, as he blocked LaShura's path. "I was drunk when I said all that stuff. I know you know how much I care about you. I'll call Toyia right now and prove—"

"No!" LaShura shouted, and shoved Stanley out of her way. "You should've thought about that shit before you cheated on me."

As my sister stormed past me, leaving Stanley standing there with a sissified look on his face, I stepped to him. "Wuz crackn' wit' that shit that went down with the homies?"

A look of recognition, remembrance and malice flickered across Stanley's face. "What chu' want to be crackin'?" He fired back.

Uncle Tim swooped in from outta nowhere and snatched me up from behind. "Ain't gon' be no fightin' out here," he said.

"Fightin'?" I repeated mockingly. "Fightin'? I'm fixin' to burn this bitch ass nigga to the ground!" I easily broke free from Uncle Tim's frail ass and whipped out my burner.

Stanley smirked and peered down at my strap and said, "What? I'm supposed to be scared or something?"

I lifted it, aimed it, and fired. *BOOM!*

On God, Allah must've had plans for this nigga. Lucky for him, Uncle Tim

knocked my hand up just as I squeezed, causing me to miss. "James, are you crazy?" Uncle Tim asked while panting like a stripper fresh off stage. "Do you wanna go to jail for killing this boy?"

"Fuck that nigga!" I exclaimed. "That fool did the homie and Stutter in the other night. I'm trying to see if he can do me the same way."

LaShura ran outside at the sound of gunfire and saw Uncle Tim trying to hold me back. “James, what are you doing?” She cried. “Put the gun down and let’s go in the house.” She tried to step in and help Uncle Tim, so I shoved both they asses away and fired two rounds in the sky.

“Errbody, back the fuck up!” I pointed my gun back at Stanley and dared that hoe ass nigga to say something. My hand was shaking so bad I could’ve easily killed everyone out there.

“James, listen to me,” LaShura pleaded while slowly inching toward me. “Don’t do this, he’s not worth it. Just give me the gun and let’s go in the house.”

All that bullshit she was saying was going in one ear and out the other. My sights were dead-locked on blowing Stanley’s top back. The only one that could save him right now was Allah.

“James, wait!” Uncle Tim shouted. “The police are sittin’ down there on the corner.”

I didn’t wanna look, but unintentionally I did. A black and white police cruiser bent the corner several blocks down. The way they crept up the street toward us, it was obvious they were searching for where the gunshots came from.

“Gimmie the gun!” Uncle Tim spat.

I spared another peek down the street; them bitches were still coming. “Here,” I said, and passed off my strap. I immediately took my stance to get ready to box, but Stanley stood there lookin’ shook.

“See what the fuck you done did?” Stanley spat while looking back and forth from the police to me. “You done made this big ass scene for nothing! While you over here fakin’ like you ‘bout that life, I’m over here dirty!”

LaShura gasped and looked toward Stanley’s car. “What do you want me to do?” She said.

Stanley shook his head, realizing there was little time to do anything and said, “What can you do?”

The police cruiser came to a squeaking stop in front of our house. The police officer that got out was a black officer from the hood that nobody liked. “How’s er’body doing this morning?” He asked as he strolled around his car and walked up in the yard.

"We're fine," LaShura replied, trying to sound reassuring. "Is there something that I can help you with?"

The officer glanced from me to Stanley; from Stanley to LaShura, LaShura to the house. "Hmpf," he grunted and said, "Got a call somebody was shootin' out here. Y'all folks wouldn't happen to know anythang about that, would ya?"

I'm sure we all had to be lookin' guilty as fuck. LaShura looked like she was about to cry. I looked like I ain't give a fuck. And Stanley looked like he was ready to do what any real nigga would do. Run.

"Excuse me, officer," Uncle Tim said, as he rushed back outside. "This here is my sisters' house. While she's away, I'm in charge. If there's anything that you'd like to know, you can ask me. If not, and no one is under arrest, we'd like to continue saying our goodbyes to Mr. Exboyfriend."

The officer lowered his sunglasses to the tip of his nose. "Didn't nobody say nafin' about arrestin' anyone. I'm here to make sure you folks ain't seen nafin'."

Stanley took that as his cue to leave. "I'll catch up with you later," he said while calmly walking back to his car to get in.

While the officer had his sights locked on Uncle Tim, I saw Stanley stuff something in one of my sister's bags. "LaShura!" He called out. "Don't forget this." Stanley waved for her to come and get the bag, but unbeknownst to him, I'd seen the whole play.

"I'll take that!" I mobbed over to the car and snatched the bag out of his hands. That bitch ass nigga mugged me for a minute before reluctantly putting the car in reverse and driving away.

"I guess I'll be on my way as well," the officer said, now eyeing me suspiciously. "You folks be sure and give us a call if you hear anything."

Uncle Tim gave the officer a fake reassuring nod that he would, while I calmly strolled into the house. Whatever Stanley had stuffed in my sister's bag had to be important. I peeped how hard he was sweating bullets when Uncle Tim told him the police were coming.

I took the bag into my bedroom and quickly closed the door. When I opened the bag, I couldn't believe what the fuck I was looking at. Stanley had stuffed a whole bag of raw coke inside. The thought not to take the shit, no doubt popped up in my mind. But the more I stood there and thought about it, once word got back to Stanley's homies that I just tried to murk his bitch ass they'd surely be coming for me. The best thing I could do was be ready when they came.

My cell phone lit up in the console which caught my attention. It was a text from Kathy stating that she had some grip that she was tryin' ta' spend. "Stop by Stutters house when you get a chance," I informed Uncle Tim. "Kathy just hit me up talkin' 'bout spending some money."

Uncle Tim nodded and immediately busted a u-turn in the middle of the street.

We'd been riding, hitting licks like that all day. The work I took outta my sister's duffle bag came out to be four and a half ounces. I used a quarter piece of it as hush money to keep Uncle Tim quiet. And the rest, I planned to bleed the block and get my money up. My plan was to hustle only at night, that way it'd be harder for Stanley and his homies to find me. I needed to stay out of sight, out of mind long enough to make them niggas get tired of looking for me.

When we pulled up in front of Stutters crib, Kathy was already outside waiting. She walked out to the truck as I lowered my window. "Hey, babe." She greeted me and leaned up against the door. "Why don't chu' send your Uncle on home so you and I can go inside."

I swiped my hand over my face, trying to keep from smiling. One thang I knew about Kathy, if that bitch wanted me to go inside, what she really meant was she wanted me to *cum* inside. "Where's ya' mans and Stutter at?" I inquired, then guzzled down a nice portion of Ice 800 that I'd been drinking.

"They been gone since earlier," Kathy replied. "Do you think I'd be asking you to come in if my crazy ass husband was here?"

I couldn't help but bust out laughin' 'cause I already knew what this bitch be on. I gave my Uncle Tim some dap and said, "Come swoop me up in about forty-five minutes to an hour."

Kathy looked at me like I was crazy. "Boy, you need to stop playing! I'll have him give you a call whenever I get done with him."

Uncle Tim chuckled softly as I hopped out his truck and mobbed up to Kathy's house. "Don't be havin' me in here chillin' and your ol' man and Stutter walk in. I'd hate to have to pop one of them niggas 'cause they done found out that I'm fuckin' you."

Kathy giggled and closed the door behind us after we'd walked inside. "They probably won't be back until tomorrow," she explained. "Usually when the boys leave this time uh night, they gon' be gone until the next morning."

I strolled over to the sofa and got comfortable. For safety, I sat my gun on the coffee table, then quickly downed the last of my 40.

"Damn!" Kathy exclaimed. "How many of 'dem thangs you done drank tonight?"

I lifted the empty bottle and belched. "Three. But, that ain't shit, though. I'm fixin' ta' top this shit off with a blunt, while you take yo' ass back there and get freshened up."

"Are you sure that you gen' be able to handle all of this?" Kathy traced her fingers over her body, having no shame in the fact that she was still wearing the same clothes from yesterday.

"Let's not forget, you called me over here. Don't start playin' dumb like you don't know that I'll beat your back in!"

Kathy rolled her eyes and marched her ugly ass right back to the bedroom and slammed the door. Now was the perfect time for me to spark up my blunt, and set my mind at ease. I had so much ill shit going on in and around my life, really the last thing I needed to be doing right now was fuckin' Kathy. *I'm willing to bet Stanley and his crew were out combing the streets in search of me*. I figured I'd invest in a few straps and bring in a few homies from the hood. I can't say whether or not Kevin and Stutter is built for the shit that was comin' my way. But I had a few homies that I planned to pay a visit that are without question 'bout dat life!

Moments later, Kathy sauntered into the living room wearing nothing but a long, yellow YMCA t-shirt. She'd wet her hair and slicked it back. I could tell she was already horny because I could see her nipples bulging through her t-shirt. "I hope you brought something extra for what I've got planned to do to you." Kathy said as she came and sat next to me on the sofa. She folded one leg beneath her and left her other leg gapped open; giving me a clear view of that fat, pink pussy.

"See, there you go wit' that bullshit! If I show up after you done asked me to come through, you should already know, I ain't comin' half cocked." I pulled out my sample sack and watched Kathy's eyes get big. Everyone that I'd given a sample to loved my shit. I just knew once Kathy tried my shit she was about to act a fool on 'dis dick.

"Umpf." She grunted after hitting her pipe. "I thought you said this was some fiyah?"

I looked at that bitch like she was crazy and said, "I know my shit's some drop! Errbody dat's done hit my shit love it. What? You don't like it?"

Kathy hit her pipe again, swaying her leg; flashing that monkey, fanning that funky. "No, uhn-uhnnnnn." She mumbled as smoke trickled out of her nostrils. "This ain't it. Here... You try."

I tried to smack that muthafuckin' pipe down the street. "The fuck you thank this is, huh? Don't chu' ever come at a real nigga like that again."

"My bad," Kathy replied, with her hand still dangling in the air. "Don't get mad at me 'cause this dope ain't worth a damn. The only person it'll probably do some good for is you. I just thought you might need some help to keep your dick hard."

On me, I started to slap the shit out that dope-fiend ass bitch. "Do it look like I have a problem with keepin' my dick hard?"

Kathy rolled her eyes and got up to go pick up her pipe. Instead of bending over to pick up her pipe, she bent over and peered back at me. "Well, prove it."

## Chapter 9
## The Present

Glimpses from my past slowly came back to me, like droplets of water seeping out of an old, leaking faucet. Some of my memories helped to give me understanding about how I ended up where I was. Other memories were just careless mistakes that I'd made, stupid things that I've done that I wished I could take back.

I've heard people say they wouldn't change a thing about their past if given the chance. When I ponder a statement like that, I wonder if it'd be because their life would be different? If I was given the chance to change something about my past, I'd probably change everything. I wouldn't have ever brought my ass back to Oklahoma for starters. I would've just stayed with my mother and tried to figure out a way to reach my dreams. It seems like I'd been stuck in the same rut ever since I came back to Oklahoma. With all the chaos that surrounded my life, in a way, it made me feel like I was doomed from the start.

While most of my friends had both of their parents around to raise them, I didn't have that option. It was either one or the other. Pick a path, but choose wisely. A lot of times, people don't understand the pressure they put on their kids when they put them in situations like that. They don't take into consideration the possible consequences of what the wrong choice can do. The perks that came with living with my father outweighed the things I could afford to do while living with my mother. For a little kid, that made my choice easy, yet hard at the same time. Although, my life wasn't a financial struggle while I lived with my father, it became a spiritual one.

My mother used to tell me, "Pray, Kevin. Ask God to show you which path you should take, and I promise He'll show you the way."

No matter how many times I prayed that prayer, or how hard I begged God to show me which path I should take, nothing ever changed about me wanting to live with my father. The only thing that changed is that I didn't want to live with my mother anymore.

A gentle tap at the door prompted me to close my eyes and play sleep. I'd been harassed by one cop after another for the past two days. All of them armed with millions of questions, demanding answers, or accusing me of something. I swear if I had a way out of this fucking place I'd vanish in a heartbeat. Everyday felt like I was locked up in a prison cell all over again. They wouldn't allow me to make any phone calls because they claimed it was for security reasons. No one even knew where I was so there was no way I had a chance at seeing any one I loved. The only thing that they did allow me to do was think and be harassed by one cop after the next. If something didn't give soon, my next step was sneaking outta here.

"Kevin, how's it going today?" A man said. "I heard the television on, so I figured you were finally awake. I'm just stopping by to see how you're holding up."

I released a sigh of disappointment, remembering who that voice belonged to. He'd been by my room every day since I'd gotten here. He told me that he heard me yelling and screaming the night they brought me in. I guess whatever story I rambled off to the staff that night must've caught his attention. "I'm holding up just fine," I replied, while partially opening my eyes to look back at the television. "I'd be a whole lot better if someone would tell me when they're gonna let me outta here."

Pastor Johnson smiled, assuming because I was finally speaking to him that that gave him an invitation to come in. "Well, let's see," he began by saying. "You've suffered quite a few serious injuries. You have a gunshot wound in your leg that got infected. Another bullet went straight through your shoulder. Let's not forget about the blood transfusion. And to top it all off, you had a minor concussion. I'd say the least thing you need to be worried about is when they're gonna let you out of here. I think you should be more concerned about getting well again, don't you?"

I rolled my eyes and looked back up at the television. "You sound like my father." It wasn't that I didn't like Pastor Johnson. It was the unrelenting truth that he came to bear witness of that made it hard for me to be around him. And that's not to mention, he did remind me a lot of my father. My ol' man always wanted to talk about the Word, like him. He was there to talk about the Word.

Pastor Johnson was an older black man, possibly in his mid to late 50's. He was clean-shaven, chubby, with sagging cheeks that gave him the appearance that he was always sad. Every time he'd stopped by, he always wore the same thing. A black suit with a white dress shirt. He always carried a bible with him, that's it. No briefcase. No phone. Just a bible.

"Kevin, I know it must be hard dealing with the loss of your father, especially in the manner that he was taken from you."

"Try telling that to those damn detectives that blame me for everything that happened."

Pastor Johnson pulled a chair up alongside my bed and sat down. "I'm not here to place blame on no one," he said, while unzipping a black bible case and thumbing through the scriptures. "I'm here to try and get you to accept Christ as your—"

"Pastor, please! Now isn't a good time for all of that. I have way too much going on in my life to be distracted by talking about God. What I really need is some time alone so I can get my head right. It's too many people constantly messing with me. I need some time to think."

"Hmmmm, I see." Pastor Johnson replied softly. "How about you talk to me about what's going on. I'd like to be of some help to you if I can."

"Yeah, right. I doubt that'll ever happen."

"Why not? You don't think I can be a good listener? Or, maybe you believe that you're in this situation all alone, is that it?"

The things he was saying sounded good as hell, but that's exactly how the police work. They send someone to talk to you that says all the right things. Before you know it, you'll been done said the wrong thing and look up and find yo' ass in jail.

"What would you do if you were me?" I asked.

Pastor Johnson quietly pondered my question for a moment. "I don't know," he replied. "It depends."

"On what?"

"On what I've done. What I'm up against. Who I'm up against." He paused as if searching for the right words. "I guess I'd also need to know if things could be fixed. But, it'd be hard to give a more precise account of what I'd do, unless you open up and tell me a little about what's going on."

I sighed again, allowing my eyes to close. It seemed like every time I thought too much about the things that have happened, I saw my father staring back at me. I couldn't help but see his eyes just as a bullet ripped into his back. I relived that moment over and over again. I wanted it to stop, but I knew it wouldn't. "I saw them kill my father right in front of me. He didn't have nothing to do with nothing! They just gunned him down like he ain't shit. They didn't have to do him that way; he ain't ever hurt anybody."

"Calm down, Kevin, it's gonna' be alright."

"No, it's not! If I would've just stayed my ass away from him, they wouldn't have come looking for me."

Pastor Johnson placed a comforting hand on my arm and squeezed. "Don't start blaming yourself for what happen. You don't—"

"It's my fault! Don't you get it? If I would've never went back to my father's house, then none of this would've happened."

Silence.

"So, you knew whoever killed your father would go by his house looking for you?" I didn't have to say a word for him to know the answer to that question. "Kevin, I can't stress how important it is that if you know who killed your father, you should talk to the police. Who's to say that they're not out there still looking for you? Don't you have a family? Think about them. Think about your friends. Think about all the innocent lives that could be in danger if you don't step up and do the right thing."

I shook my head and swiped away the tears racing down my face, and said, "I can't. Whatever has been done, is done. Just like I gotta lay here and mourn the loss of my Pops, them muthafuckas is gon' have to do the same thang."

Pastor Johnson jumped to his feet. The stern look on his face was but a reflection of how disturbed he really was. "I'll be back tomorrow," he said while zipping back up his bible case. "I'll be bringing someone along that might be able to help you understand things better. I think the two of you may have a lot in common. Sometimes, when you're dealing with certain types of people, it takes people with a certain kind of credentials to get those people to listen."

"Nah, I'm cool on all that. I just need some time to think. That's it. If I come to the point where I feel comfortable enough to open up, maybe you'll be the first person I look up."

Pastor Johnson forced a weak smile before turning to leave. "Oh, and one more thing before I go," he said while peering back at me. "Don't allow yourself to be tempted into doing the wrong thing. Remember, the Devil is a liar, he is the master of deception. Everything outside of what is right, is wrong. Remember that. There is no gray area, Kevin. If it's not God's work that you do, then it is Satan's."

**KEVIN**
**15 Years Ago**

The next couple of weeks felt like time slowed down to a complete stop. Each day felt like one boring lesson of why not to be the low man on the totem pole. The place where Cabbage had hired me to basically live was on the westside of town. It was in an old ugly green house that reminded me of something I'd seen on Little House on the Prairie. There was no driveway leading up to the garage from the street; just a tire-worn path filled with bumps and broken glass zig zagging its way up to a hollow, wooden structure. The garage looked like it'd topple over at the slightest hint of a storm coming. Even now, as the wind blew, I could hear the wood crackling under pressure. Out of fear that one day the whole thing would come crashing down, I kept my car parked around back.

The inside of the house didn't look much better than the outside. Everything was old, dusty, and had long ago lost its vibrant luster. The walls were covered with faded flowery wallpaper. The floors were made of wood. Even the air had a funny smell to it. All of the household appliances were either rusted, broken, or too old to even work.

Lucky for me, I brought over a small flat screen television. Had I not, I would've definitely quit this fucking gig a long time ago. Not only did they not pay me enough, but living way out here all alone kinda gave me the creeps. Only a handful of people lived around me. There was an old white lady that lived next door. An elderly couple lived on the other side of her. And a grumpy, senile white man lived across the street. Everyone except for my neighbor stayed in the house for the most part.

Unlike the eastside, the westside had a bunch of racist white folks. These weren't the uppity rich kind. These were the kind that were stuck in a time warp; mad because black people had just as much as they did now a days. Most of the houses in the area weren't much better than the ones on the eastside. Except, nobody wanted to live in these houses. These shits were old; too old. There wasn't nothing out here but a bunch of old, dying white folks. Well, that and plenty of farmland. I'm sure the KKK was hidden out there somewhere. The closer to town you got, the more people there were. But, the further out you went, things were just the opposite. Wasn't nobody out here and I mean nobody.

My next-door neighbor was a fat, nosey woman. She'd been giving me dirty looks since the day I moved in. She had a white picket fence around her yard which was basically one big flower garden. Her dog was a furry little mutt named Panther; it was white too. I don't know why she gave it a name like Panther. He sure as hell wasn't quite like no damn Panther. He wasn't good for nothing but waking me up in the middle of the night with all that damn barking. I noticed that my neighbor kept two neatly tied pink ribbons in his hair. But there was something very wrong with that picture. Panther wasn't a female dog. I know so, because I'd saw him humping an elf statue in their front yard. Every morning I'd look out to see my neighbor waddling around, pulling weeds with Panther hot on her trail. Occasionally, I'd see her staked out in her garden trying to watch me. She made it perfectly clear that she suspected me of being involved in something illegal. But it was highly unlikely that she'd ever catch me doing anything. Cabbage was very insistent about the things that I was allowed to do while I lived at my new spot.

For whatever reason, Cabbage had zero tolerance for bringing new people around. He didn't give a damn who it was. Those niggas up at The Ghetto were so on edge about keeping things top secret, it almost made me think they were hiding from someone. They didn't want me talking to anyone that I'd been able to meet. And they didn't want me keeping nothing illegal at the spot. Basically, all I was allowed to do was sit around and wait on a phone call. Whenever I got it, I'd go pick up a bag and bring it back to the spot. Later that night, Cabbage would send someone over to pick up the bag from me. I don't know what they had stuffed inside the bag, although whatever it was kind of heavy. I tried not to think about trying to peek inside because I didn't wanna mess up anything.

Outside of a severe case of boredom, there really wasn't nothing complicated about my job. I lived in a two-bedroom house, rent-free and all I had to pay for was my own food. To the average person content on having nothing, my job would be considered as the shit. But for a young nigga trying to make his way up in the game, this just wasn't gonna cut it. They paid me $500 a week. I had to either come up with another way to make some more money, or save up as much as I could and get out there and find another connect.

"What up, my nigga!" I'd been sitting on the porch smoking a blunt when out of nowhere Stutter walked up. He looked tired and worn out. His clothes looked like he'd been in them for the past couple of days.

"Not-Not-Nothing," he stammered. "I just stopped by to see what chu' was up to."

I hopped down off the porch and gave the homie a quick embrace. "How you get way out here?" I asked, while peering back in the direction from which he'd came. "I know you ain't mobbed all the way out here from the eastside."

Stutter peered back down the road and said, "You know-know I ain't fucked up about doing no walking. I got tired of listening to

Moms and Pops fuss and fight. I called myself going out to get a little fresh air, but before I knew it, I was way out here!"

We both laughed as we sat down on the porch. But on the real, wasn't a damn thing funny about what he'd just told me. It saddened me to hear my nigga was still dealing with the same issues that he'd been dealing with since he was a kid. If it were up to me, I'd move him out here to the spot. I bet it wouldn't take us that long before we'd saved up a nice chunk of change to cop some work.

"So, what's all this I've been hearing about, O-Dawg?" I asked, trying to keep the conversation moving on a positive note. "I heard he over there doing the damn thang. I've been calling his crib everyday, but his Moms say she haven't seen him. I even blew up his cell phone, but now his shit keep sending me to voicemail. I don't know how I'ma be able to get in contact with him. You ain't heard nothing?"

Stutter shrugged and sparked back up the blunt that I'd just passed him. "You know I don't too much fuck wit that nigga," Stutter growled, while staring aimlessly into my neighbor's yard. "He be on too much scandalous stuff for me. One day, somebody gon' have to teach that fool a lesson." I didn't have to ask why he felt the way he did. By me knowing what type of nigga O-Dawg was, it probably had to do with Stutter finding out that he'd been fucking his Moms. "It's been all b-b-b-b-bad since you left the block," Stutter went on to say. "Leonard been havin' me out on some wild goose chase missions. I'm tired of putting in all the work and ain't reapin' no benefits. I wanna get on with them same niggas you fuckin' with. They don't even gotta pa-pa-pay me the same thing they giving you. All I'm looking for is a chance to make some money."

I flashed a weak smile, wishing like hell that it could be that easy. "Let me run it past my peeps the next time I talk to him. If them cats wasn't so spooked about meeting new people, I'd simply take you over there now!"

Stutter nodded and passed me the blunt. The look on his face told me that there was something else on his mind.

I'd noticed a small gash across his forehead when he first walked up. I hadn't spoken on it yet because I already knew how him and his ol' man be gettin' into it. "Tell me what's on your mind, bruh. I can tell when something is bothering you. You can run that drag about you'll mob anywhere in the country on somebody else. If you done walked way the fuck out here, then something's up. You and your Pops been fighting?"

Stutter smirked and said, "Fuck that nigga. I done told you what's on my mind, but I guess you ain't feeling me. I'm tired of putting in work to make some money, and Leonard ain't doing nothing but smoking that shit up. I'm too old to be living with my parents anyway. I should've been had my own place, I'm older than you. It's time for me to get on my grown man shit. If I ain't eatin', then what sense does it make for me to be living?"

I turned to gaze out into the endless rolling meadows just beyond my neighbor's backyard. I could feel my nigga's pain. He was starving with a voracious appetite. The bad part about it was, things had gotten so bad on the block that it damn near felt like drought season. The only people that I knew that had any work were them niggas up at The Ghetto.

"Fuck it!" I exclaimed. "I'ma hit Cabbage up right now, and tell him that we need to talk. If he try to get on some bullshit, I'll just tell him that I quit."

Stutter hopped down off the porch, eyes wide with excitement. "But, what if he say no? No, wait. Wha-Wha-What if he don't? What if-if he-he-he-he-he—"

"Fuck that shit, my nigga. You been like family since day one. If they ain't willing to do business with you, then they damn sho' can't continue to do business with me. We been rockin' this way for years; ain't shit changed. We in this together." I whipped out my phone and punched in Cabbage's number, but right before I pushed send, my phone rang. "Hello," I said, but the line was dead quiet. I had to look down at the phone just to make sure it was still on. "HELLO!"

"We need to meet in one hour," a man said.

I was slightly confused because I could barely understand what he said. But right before I could ask him to repeat himself, the line went dead. "That was weird."

Stutter peered over at me curiously and asked, "Who-Who-Who was that?"

I shrugged and replied, "I don't know. Whoever it was said that we needed to hook up in one hour. I guess it's got something to do with business, 'cause fam sounded like he was a Mexican."

Stutter went back up on the porch and sat down. He had a serious look on his face as if he were trying to figure out what was going on. "Tha-That-That's all they said? Did it sound like they was on some sna-sna-snake shit?"

I chuckled and dismissed his assumption with the wave of my hand. "This is pretty much how things go around here, bruh. I get a call, then go meet someone. They give me a bag, then I have to bring it back here."

Stutter sat silently processing what I'd just told him. It was obvious that something about what I'd just told him was bothering him. "You strapped?" Stutter asked.

I burst into laughter and replied, "Fuck I'ma need a strap tor? All I do is pick up a bag. Can't nobody jack me for nothing. The money I make is just to pick up a bag, I ain't selling no work."

Stutter bobbed his head, but I could tell he was still thinking. But whatever he was so worried about he'd soon be at ease. I figured I'd take him on my next run just so he could see how things work.

On the ride over to make the pick-up, I threw on some MJG & 8Ball and cranked the music up. The way them niggas sang on the track called *It's Real* had me on a whole other level. I could see myself really pushing bricks and having big money. The work I was putting in was just a process I needed to take in order for me to reach the top. Although, it was Kibble's and Bit's that I was actually making, in due time I'd be on top.

When I turned down a dark country road headed toward the meeting spot, Stutter leaned up and paused the music. "Why we me-me-meeting someone way out here?" He asked. "We could've just met who-who-whoeva back over by the spot."

I looked over at Stutter and shook my head. "We gotta do this because this is how they told me to do it. Ain't no telling why they got me doing this shit the way I'm doing it. I just do what I'm told and try not to ask too many questions. Don't forget, we ain't got no work so this is our only means to come up."

Up ahead, the chrome grill of a Chevy SUV shinned brightly in my headlights. The Suburban was parked on the wrong side of the road, facing us, with its parking lights on.

"Stay here while I go take care of this," I told Stutter as I parked and opened the door to get out.

"Wai-wai-wait!" Stutter exclaimed and grabbed my arm. "If all-all you doing is picking up a bag, then why it's two cars instead of one?"

I looked back to the SUV and sure enough, another car was parked behind it. I don't know how Stutter could have seen it from where he was seated. We were parked right in front of the Suburban, which was practically hugging a ditch. Lots of trees, tall grass and stubble stretched alongside the road.

"Bruh, you gon' have to chill with all that paranoid shit. I don't know why it's two cars instead of one. I do know that this is how I've been eatin' since I ain't had no work. So, if you'd just be cool for a second, I'll show you how this is done."

The driver of the SUV flashed his headlights, signaling for me to kill mine. I left my parking lights on and then hopped out. As I approached the Suburban, both doors on the passenger side came open. Two nicely dressed Hispanics slid out. The one in the front wore black square framed glasses with gold emblems on the sides. His clothes weren't the type of attire you'd expect to see worn on a dirt road in the middle of the night. He wore the type of garments that I'd expect to see on a Kingpin. The man behind him appeared to be much older. He was short, rather thin, with a sharp crew cut. Had I not have left my parking lights on, I'd have surely missed the menacing expressions etched on their faces.

"What is this, some kind of a joke?" The man dressed as a Kingpin said, sounding as if he barely spoke English. "Where is your boss, and where is my fucking money?"

The sound of two car doors slammed, which drew my attention to the car behind the Suburban. Two men silently approached. I couldn't get a good look at their faces, but judging by their size and demeanor, they weren't the kind of faces that I wanted to see. "I don't know nothing about no money," I explained. "I got a call to meet you here an hour ago. My job is to pick up a bag, that's it. Just pick up a bag and take it back to the spot."

The man laughed hardily and snapped his fingers, ordering his men to search my car. "You mean to tell me, you thought I give you more coca, but you no pay me for all 'de times before?"

I looked at him, then at his homie; then at the people searching my car. "Look, bruh, I don't know shit about no coca, no money, or any other kind of business that you and Cabbage done did. That nigga pay me five hunnit a week to pick up a bag. I've only been doing this shit for a couple of weeks. If you want me to, I can call Cabbage right now so he can straighten all this up."

The man that I'd been talking to peered back at the older man behind him. They spoke in a hushed tone before he turned his attention back to me. "Cabbage answer phone for you?" He asked.

I nodded acknowledging that he would.

"Well, call him!"

It didn't take me but a split second to whip my phone out and punch that nigga's number in. I couldn't help but think that Cabbage knew what type of fucked up situation that he'd put me in. Lucky for me, after a few brief moments he answered.

"What a surprise to finally hear your voice!" The SA said, after I'd passed him the phone. "I hope that you have the money that you owe to me, because I have some people that work for you."

Everyone stood deathly still, seemingly waiting on our verdict. I'm sure if Cabbage chose not to pay, somebody would stumble across our dead corpses face down in a ditch.

"Hmpf, si!" The Mexican said, then disconnected the call and shoved my phone into my chest. "And who might this be?" He asked and strolled past me to stand in front of Stutter. "Your boss say, no kill you. He pay. But, he no say nada about him."

"That's just the homie," I explained. "He wasn't even supposed to be here. I brought him along to show him how this shit work, then try to get him on working with me."

The man gave Stutter a thorough onceover, taunting him and asked, "What is your name, puto?" Stutter gritted on the man so hard I thought surely, he was about to snap. "Oh, so you tough guy, guy? You don't wanna answer me? You no scared to die?" The SA pulled out a gun and placed the barrel against Stutter's head and said, "I ask you for 'de last time. What is your name, puto?"

Stutter never flinched. He stood firm, ice-grilling the man and even went so far as to press his head against the barrel of the gun.

"ENOUGH!" A voice boomed. "I no come here to kill these children. I came here to get my money!" The older Mexican walked toward me. I could hear the crunch of gravel smashed into the earth with the fall of each footstep. "Let him go!" He ordered his men while peering back at Stutter. "And you." He nudged me in the chest with fingers covered in expensive jewelry. "Be careful who you choose to make your alliance with. Your boss no care if you live or die. These men were brought here to kill you tonight. Know who you're in business with, and never sell your soul for such a cheap price." With that being said, he spun on his heels and left.

**STUTTER**

On the ride back to the spot, all sorts of wicked thoughts ran ramped in my mind. I couldn't help but wonder would Kevin be dead if I hadn't have came along on this run. I think it was because of someone else being there, was the only thing that saved his life. Who knows what they would've done had I not been there. I can't speak for Kevin, but I'd had my fair share of guns being pointed at me. Two of those times happened while I was with him, but when my own flesh and blood tried to take me out, I knew then it was time to strap up.

The last few nights I'd been staying out later than usual to avoid being drug along on another one of Leonard's bogus missions. Ever since Kevin got on working for them dudes up at The Ghetto, Leonard been having me out pulling desperate moves. Smacking a nigga up outside the club, would be to say the least. We'd graduated and started pulling kick doors. Sometimes, we'd come out with two or three hundred. But never once had one red cent touched my pocket.

Leonard said, "We gotta' make sure to stack up every single dime we make. When we save up enough money to buy a quarter kilo, I'll get in touch with some old friends of mine. Maybe they'll front us an extra nine ounces, considering we done already bought nine."

The first couple of licks, I was like, "Hell muthafuckin' yeah, I'm wit' this shit!" I was down even though I knew damn well he was spending up our loot to get high. Every time we came home after hitting a lick, Leonard would up and disappear for about an hour. By the time he'd return, he'd have a 5th of Wild Turkey and a small sack of work. Sometimes, I'd just lie in the living room and watch him smoke up every last crumb of it. I couldn't help but wonder, what could possibly be going on in his mind to make him smoke up all that dope. All he did was smoke, smoke, smoke, and stare out the dinning room window. Every now and then, Momma would come in and massage his shoulders and neck. She may even whisper sweet nothings in his ear then leave him with a kiss.

I know whatever it was that was going on inside that head of his, Momma must've known about it. Whenever Leonard would get so high that all he did was stare out the dining room window, Momma would tell me, "Don't go in there messing with your Daddy. If you need anything, I'll be in the bedroom." Before she left, she'd always restart the music that Leonard had been listening to. That was some crazy shit to me. Who in their right mind could sit and listen to the same fucking tape over and over again?

Finally, I got tired of it. It was bad enough that both of my parents were strung out on dope. They didn't need me to help hide them form whatever demons they were afraid to face whenever they weren't high. So, before the sun set each day, I'd started sneaking out. I'd go up to The Ghetto and hide out in an abandoned house across the street. Since everyone was so consumed with whatever was going on inside the club, I was able to sneak up through the alleyway, duck off in one of the houses, and hideout for hours. When the sound of cars passing by had dwindled down to an occasional gust of wind blowing, I figured that it must be getting late, so I'd best be headin' home.

Normally, Leonard would leave the house about nine or ten to go on a mission. He'd rent the neighbors beat-up Lincoln, and wouldn't return home until he had whatever he'd went in search of. So, by the time that I got home and didn't see the neighbor's car I figured I was straight.

I mobbed up the porch steps and was just about to walk inside, then I heard my mother say, "It ain't my fault your dope is some bullshit. You could smoke this shit all night, and still not get high!"

Instantly my blood pressure shot through the roof. I already knew who it was, because nobody from the hood would dare step foot in our house while Leonard wasn't around. All I could think of was how that bitch ass O-Dawg was trying to feed my mother some dope so he could fuck her. Just as I reached out to open the door, I heard a car pull up.

*HUNK! HUNK!* It was Leonard.

"Stutter, did you hear what I just said to you?"

I blinked, squinted, blinked again, then peered over at Kevin. Unbeknownst to me, my face was still twisted into a menacing scowl. My mind was still on O-Dawg. I wanted that nigga dead!

"The fucks up with you, bruh?" Kevin said. "I'm over here trying to put chu' up on game, but you over there on some other shit."

Before I could even respond, I suddenly realized that we were back at the spot. A white Cadillac was parked in front of the house. I could see three people standing in the front yard, but it was hard to tell if they were people that I knew. The only light that shown came from a lamp post on the side of the neighbor's house. "Who-Who-Who's that?"

Kevin glared at me, then shook his head in disgust. "What chu' think I've been trying to tell you?" He snapped. "That's them niggas that I work for!"

We pulled into the driveway and killed the lights. Instead of pulling around back, Kevin threw the car in park and we hopped out.

"I thought you and I had an understanding about bringing new people around." A man said, while remaining concealed by the shadowy darkness that covered the front yard.

Kevin looked nervously over at me as I shuffled around the car to stand beside him. “I’ve been meaning to holler at you about that,” Kevin replied. “This is the homie Stutter. I’ve been meaning to introduce you to fam. He tryin’ ta’ start working for you. He the one I was telling you about, that I hustled with down the street from The Ghetto.”

“Funny,” the man said. “Now, what the fuck that got to do with what I’m askin’ you, slim? The rules for working for me are simple. I told you, no new faces, don’t shit where you lay your head at, and above all keep your got-damn mouth closed!” The man strolled across the lawn toward us. This had to be the same dude Kevin had been telling me about. Out of the three people there, he was the only one decked out in a suit.

“Listen, big homie. After what we just went through trying to pick up one of your bags, I think the least thing you could do was hire someone to watch my back.”

The man bobbed his head while slowly drawing closer. “I see somehow you’ve managed to get this whole thing mixed up. You came to me looking for a job, not the other way around. If I hire you to work for me, that means I call the shot! My rules, my fucking show!”

A set of headlights splashed over the yard as a car speedily approached. The neighbor’s dog went crazy at the sight of another car, and possibly more people. The white lady next door showed no shame by openly watching us through her screen door. There wasn’t a doubt in my mind, if things got outta’ hand, she wouldn’t hesitate to call the police.

The car slowed as it neared the front of the house. I sensed the tension rise as Cabbage and his men went on alert. While everyone stood anxiously awaiting the unknown driver to get out, I released a sigh of regret. This situation was bound to get ugly.

**Leonard**

I know trouble when I see it. I’ve been in these streets far too long not to know when something ain’t right. The white car parked in front of Kevin’s spot is the same one that I’d seen up at The

Ghetto. Kevin told me a lot about the man that owned that car. His name didn't ring a bell, although his name should've rang a bell. Hustlers don't just open up shop on somebody else's turf unless they know somebody that knows somebody. You at least gotta know somebody that can show you around. For a person not to take the proper steps to get your foot in the door would be an easy way to get your blocked knocked off. I have to admit, I've done some pretty bold things in my life but stupid shit like that, ain't one of 'em.

After Kevin told me everything he knew about Cabbage, I spent a little time letting it marinate. At best, these new muthafuckas would be the last people that I'd ever have to rob. The only thing I needed to do now was find out what Nate thought about the idea. Regardless of what a person may think, Nate was a loyal muthafucka to me. It didn't matter if he worked for Cabbage or not. If I told Nate that I wanted to rob Cabbage, then he'd help me out the best way he could.

The other day, I called him up to see what he could tell me about his boss man, Cabbage. I didn't know anything other than what Kevin told me. The first thing Nate said when I asked who those fellas were, was, "I can't believe you don't remember Cabbage and his older brother, what's his face?" He snapped his fingers while desperately trying to remember the man's name. "You know, the one y'all took out there to the country, but ain't ever bring him back."

I sighed into the phone and said, "Whole lotta' eats went out to the country and ain't ever come back. It's because too many of 'em was going out to the country, was the reason you had to start handling things, remember?"

Nate must've begun to get frustrated. He started mumbling various things to himself that I could hardly understand. "Where in the hell did I put my...?" I heard paper rattle around in the background. He struck a lighter, inhaled, and coughed. "Man, it's a damn shame you don't remember Cabbage and 'em," he continued. "If I remember right, y'all first started hookin' up, not long before that went down with your mother."

I sat there and thought about it hard. I mean, really hard. But, no matter how hard I thought about it, I couldn't remember him. I just couldn't put a face with the got-damn name.

"Kevin, Stutter, you boys alright over here?" I walked up the driveway, playing it cool like I knew to do. The wind snatched open my flannel jacket, conveniently concealing the little present that I had for the two other fellas in the yard.

"Yeah, we good." Kevin replied. "I was just talking with Cabbage about—"

"Wait wait wait! Hold the fuck on." Cabbage quipped. "How many mo' muthafuckas you got comin' around here? First you told me it was just your friend. Now it's him. How many more?"

"Won't be anyone else." I interjected on Kevin's behalf. "We're the only ones that needed to know where Kevin was, ya' dig?"

"And just who the hell do you think you are?" Cabbage asked mockingly.

"Excuse me?"

"Nigga, you heard what the fuck I just said."

This muthafucka had my trigger finger twitching like a son of a bitch. I don't know if it was because of his mouth, or that fucked up high pitched voice of his. All I know, I was about to rock his bitch ass ta' sleep. "The names, Leonard. But folks down this way call me, L."

"Well I'll be damned." Cabbage chuckled and started to approach me. "If it isn't the notorious L. Can't say that I ever expected to see you again."

I spared a questioning look from left to right. "Do I know you from somewhere?"

Cabbage smiled and replied, "I'm afraid so. You and my brother used to do a whole lotta' business together back in the day. That is until... Well, you know."

The way he said that shit didn't sound right. The way he stood there with his hands stuffed in his pockets didn't feel right. The way his crew had spread out in the yard when I first pulled up, didn't look right. So, I cocked the hammer back on That Bitch, just to let him know that I could make it right.

"That Bitch don't phase me," Cabbage spat. "I could care less if we turn this front yard into a graveyard, or a boxing ring. You done took all you gon' ever take from me."

My mind was reeling. No one except for my closest associates knew that I called my .38 special That Bitch. Cabbage and I stood face to face having a mean stare down. But, what I saw when I looked in his eyes went beyond anything that may have happen there that night. What I saw was hate. Not the type of hate tossed around having no plausible merit. This kind of hate had to be nurtured over time.

"I don't know what you boys got going on over there!" The next door neighbor shouted through her screen door. "I dun' already called the Sheriff, he should be here any minute. Won't be no congregating of you kind out here tonight!"

Cabbage didn't budge, and I didn't even think about it. I knew we were outgunned and outnumbered, but the irony in the way he spoke said to me that we still had some unfinished business.

"Don't chu' worry boutta' thang!" Cabbage shouted in response. "We'll be on our way now, Ms. Lady." Before Cabbage turned to leave, he looked me dead in the eye and said, "I'll be seeing you around. Don't chu' up and disappear like you did before. I'll be comin' for ya, so you best be ready." His last words were the underlining testament that we did know each other. I just needed to remember from where.

# Chapter 10
## KEVIN

The next morning, I was at Stutter's crib bright and early. I figured, in order for us to get the block back popping like we had it before, it would take some time and lots of hard work. With the exception of a few stragglers, the eastside was like a ghost town. The majority of niggas from my side of the city had either thrown in the towel, or hopped on the bandwagon working for them niggas on the westside. It was no secret that Cabbage and his crew had the city on lock. Whereas before, some dudes refused to shut down their spot and let other people from another city dictate how and when they made their money. Somewhere along the line, someone must've gotten served with that Act Right. I guess Cabbage's crew made a few examples, and niggas got the picture.

I heard several rumors that O-Dawg was still holding things down. Whoever he had backing him, must've sat him down and gave him the game. The homie was doing all his business on some next level type shit. However he made his money, it was hard for Cabbage and his henchmen to fuck with him. All of their threats and intimidation tactics didn't really matter now. It's hard to stop something that you can't see.

"Say, bruh, you wanna know what I've been thinking about?" I sat up on the sofa and peered over at Stutter. "I wonder how that nigga O-Dawg got on the way he is. Just a couple of weeks ago I was selling him double ups. Now, all of a sudden, he the man now?"

Stutter sat staring at the television like he'd been since I arrived. My question was left lingering in the air like a bad smell.

"Last night, when I talked to Justin over the phone, he seemed a little tight-lipped when I switched the conversation and started talking about O-Dawg. I think them two niggas got something going on. Justin say he gon' stop by and let me spend a little change with him. I guess we'll just have to wait and see how that plays out." Stutter didn't bat an eye. He sat silently watching the television. "Man, what's up with you, bruh? You've been acting weird ever since you showed up at the spot yesterday. I tried to give you the benefit of the doubt about you needing to come up, but I know you. Something's up. I peeped that crazy ass shit you did when that SA put his gun to your head. And that's not to mention, you've been spaced out."

Sutter laughed out loud and readjusted himself in the recliner. "I'm good," he said. "You-You gotta nigga high as a muthafucka this morning. I'm just waiting until your relative slide through like he said he would."

Not once had Stutter looked me in the eye. Not once had he ever looked in my direction. His father had always told me, "If a man can't look you in the eye when he got something to say, then either he got something to hide, or he a got-damn lie!"

"Come on with the bullshit, fam. You throwin' these curve balls like I don't know what you trying to do."

"Curve balls?" Stutter repeated. "What makes you th-thi-think I gotta lie to you? I'm telling you straight up... I'm good!"

I'd been fuckin with this nigga for too long not to know when something was bothering him. In the back of my mind, I figured he and his Pops got into it. Maybe that's how he ended up with that gash on his forehead. Maybe that's why he didn't wanna talk. But, whatever the case maybe, he was about to tell me what the fuck was going on. "How did you get that cut on your forehead?" I asked. "I guess you want me to believe that you slipped and fell down the stairs."

Stutter forced a weak laugh. "Nah, I-I don't want you to believe that. That ain't what hap-hap-happen."

"Well, what happened?"

For the first time since we'd been talking, Stutter looked at me. And whatever he was about to tell me, I could tell, would forever change the game. "Leonard, tried to kill me." Stutter said.

**STUTTER**

"What?" Kevin shouted.

"Shhhhh!" I shushed him while peering back to my parents' bedroom.

"When did this happen?" Kevin asked. "Does your mother know about this?"

I held out my hands to try and calm him down. It didn't matter if my Moms knew. It didn't matter who knew for that matter. I knew. "My-My Mom don't-don't know nothing about it. I-I don't even know why he did it either. One minute we was talking, and the next, he was shooting at me."

"He did what? Get the fuck outta here! That fool shot at you?" Kevin was on his feet, swinging his hands. He was clearly upset, clearly confused. He clearly had no idea as to what he should do next.

"Do you-you-you still want me to tell you what happened?"

Kevin looked at me like that was the dumbest question I could've ever asked him and said, "The fuck you mean, do I wanna still know what happened? Hell muthafuckin' yeah I wanna know what happened."

I gestured with a head nod. "Well, sit down."

The look he gave me was one for the books. Kevin looked back to the bedroom again, weighing options that we both knew he didn't have to make. There was always that chance he could go back there and overpower Leonard. There was always that chance that the element of surprise would actually work again. There was always that chance that Leonard would be sound asleep when Kevin burst through his bedroom door to beat his ass. But, there was always that one chance Leonard would be wide awake, laying there with That Bitch pointed at the door.

The house was dead quiet while Kevin stood, pondering his next move. I could hear the gas feeding the flames that lit the floor furnace. On TV, Bob Barker exclaimed, "Spin the wheel!" The crowd roared with excitement.

"Ke-Kevin."

He peered down at me and I slowly shook my head. Now wasn't the time or the place to address what Leonard had done to me. The best thing he could do was listen.

Normally, Leonard would leave around 9 to go out on a mission. He'd rent the neighbors beat-up Lincoln and wouldn't return home until he had whatever he'd went in search of. So, by the time I got home and didn't see the neighbor's car, I assumed everything was all good. I mobbed up the porch steps and was just about to walk inside, when I heard my mother talking to O-Dawg inside. Instantly my blood pressure shot through the roof. That nigga had no business being there. We didn't fuck with that nigga like that for him to be there. All I could think about was him trying to give my Moms some dope so he could fuck. Just as I reached out to open the door, a car pulled up.

*HUNK! HUNK!* It was Leonard. "Stutter, come on!" Leonard shouted through the passenger side window.

I peered over my shoulder, then looked back at the house. The sudden sound of the horn must've startled everyone inside. I could hear their feet shuffling around, obviously looking for a place to hide. Reluctantly, I walked back down the steps and out to the car. If my mother wouldn't have had to pay the same price as him, I'd have gladly run up in the crib and punished that nigga.

When I open the car door, the sound of Teddy Pendergrass' *TKO* whispered though the speakers. Disdain automatically registered across my face. I hated that song; it was on the tape. I'd heard Leonard play it more than 1,008 times, take the tape out, flip it over, press play; over and over and over again.

"Where the hell have you been?" Leonard asked.

My disappointment still showed clear as day across my face. I'd yet to even make eye contact. I'd yet to even speak. Any other time, I wouldn't hesitate to answer him, but that night, my mind was somewhere else. Not on Teddy Pendergrass. Not on where I've been. Not on some punk ass dope-fiend mission. The only thing on my mind was killing that bitch ass nigga, O-Dawg.

"Hmpf." Leonard grunted as he pulled away from the curb. "You grown now. I guess you ain't gotta answer to nobody." He twisted the lid off of a bottle of Paul Mason and took a swig. "Ahhhh!" He hissed. "The taste of sweet success. Here's to being a big, bad grown muthafucka!"

Leonard held the bottle out for me to take it, but I declined. "I'm co-coo-cool," I said.

"You cool? Ta' hell wit' all that! you a grown muthafucka now. This is what grown muthafuckas do. Gon' 'head and take it."

I peered down at the sparkling brown liquor illuminated by the soft green light glowing from the stereo. This was the first time he'd ever offered me something like this. I didn't know if it was a test, or some twisted toast to an unknown victory. I took the bottle and just held it. I called myself giving him time to reconsider. I already knew how precious his drugs and alcohol were to him.

"Gon' 'head now, drink up. You ain't got but a little while longer and we gon' be where we going."

I took a couple of quick sips, then swiped the hack of my hand over my lips. When I tried to hand Leonard the bottle back, he said, "Nah, gon' 'head and finish it off. Always finish what you start. If you gon' take something, be sure and take it all!"

I looked at Leonard skeptically, trying to figure out what he was getting at. "You tol-tol-told me to drink this. I-I ain't ever took nothing from you."

Leonard glared at me with the devil in his eyes. "You ain't never took nothing from me?" He spat.

I shook my head.

"Muthafucka', you did take something from me!"

I shook my head again and said, "I ain't took nothing from you."

The car swerved. "You calling me a lie?"

I shook my head. "I'm just-just—"

*WHAP!* I dropped the bottle, spilling liquor everywhere. I heard the bottle clang against the door. Teddy whispered, "*Looks like another love T.K.O.*" I leaned against the door trying to steady myself. The blow was vicious, it came from outta nowhere.

"You wanna' steal from me?" The car swerved again.

"NO!"

"Yes, you do. You think you's a slick muthafucka don't cha'?" Leonard slammed on the brakes and brought the car to a screeching stop.

*BAM!* My head slammed into the dashboard.

"How you like stealing now?" Leonard barked. *WHAP! WHAP!*

I covered up as best as I could, but the blows came raining down from everywhere. *WHAP! WHAP! WHAP! WHAP! WHAP!*

The next thing I know, he'd grabbed hold of my hoodie, and drug me out the driver's side. "You went all this time thinking you was gon' get away with it, didn't you?" Leonard drug me into the middle of the street and shoved me down on the ground.

"Wh-Wh-Why you doing me like this? I ain't done nothing, D-D-Daddy."

"Shut up!" He shouted, and whipped out his gun and aimed it at me.

"Dad, wait!"

*POP! POP! POP!* Sparks flickered around my head as I shielded my face with my arm. I didn't know what to do. I didn't know what to think. I didn't know if he was trying to scare me, or if he was really trying to kill me.

"Did you have something to do with killing, Momma?" Leonard asked.

I had no idea what he was talking about. I didn't know if I should try and make a run for it, or take my chances lying there and accept whatever happened next. "Da-D-Daddy, what are—"

"Call me that one mo' muthafuckin' time! One. Mo'. Got. Damn. Time!" Leonard kneeled beside me, and placed the warm barrel of his gun on my cheek. That's when I saw it. He wasn't looking at me. He saw someone else, not me; not his son.

"D-Don-Don't." That's all I could think to say. That's all that would come out. That's all that came out besides the tears racing down my cheeks, over the barrel of his gun. The only thing I could think to say, was. "Don't."

Recognition registered in his eyes as he snatched the gun away from my face. Leonard jumped to his feet and peered down at me as if I were infected with some sort of contagious disease. I watched as he back-paddled toward the car, seemingly terrified. He stumbled and almost fell, but caught his balance on the fender. I never moved, not once, not even an inch. Instead of him trying to make amends for what he'd done to me, he simply hopped in his car and sped away into the night.

"Damn!" Kevin solemnly stated. "That's deep. I'm surprised you ain't—"

The sound of footsteps drew our attention back to the bedroom. Leonard walked into the dining room, but never even acknowledged that we were sitting there. But I knew he knew we were there. I knew he knew, we were talking about him.

"Le-Let's go get something to eat." I told, Kevin.

He was so caught staring at Leonard that he failed to hear anything I said. Leonard calmly lit a cigarette and stood, gazing out the dining room window. Me knowing how Kevin was, I figured it'd be best to make sure I got his attention.

"Kevin! Let's go get something to eat." This time he heard me, so I gave him the eye to try and relax. If there wasn't but one thing a person should know if they ever decided to come at Leonard, he stayed ready.

"Yeah, y'all gon' and go get something to eat." Leonard said, then turned his menacing gaze upon us. "I'll be sitting right here waiting on y'all, so hurry back." He sat down at the table and draped one arm over the back of the chair. His shirt was off and he was barefoot, wearing a pair of jeans. He sat That Bitch on the table and just stared at us.

**LEONARD**

Just like any other tale, there's always two sides to every story. I can't say that what Stutter told Kevin was wrong; can't say it was right either. Hell, I can't say I even remember what the hell I did the other night. All I know is, I snapped.

I'm sure whatever I did to that poor boy will haunt me for the rest of my days. After all, we is blood. He might not have came from my loins, or saw things the way I saw 'em, but we still family. Can't take that away from him.

As I sat, gazing out the dining room window, I couldn't help but to allow my thoughts to drift away. That's what I did when I sat there. Drift away in time. My mind may drift away to a time when everything was simple. Wake up. Go to school. Come home. Eat. Go to bed.

Simple.

Looking back on life, it felt like everything was wrong. From the very start, it was all wrong. It almost felt like I wasn't supposed to be here. My prayers to Sweet Jesus weren't to give thanks. My prayers to the Lord were to ask him, why. Why am I here? Why do you keep putting me through this shit, day in and day out? Why? Why? Why? *Why do you hate so damn much?*

I've been waiting on His reply, but He still ain't got back with me yet. I even told Momma about how I felt, and she said, "Boy, God don't hate you. Just because life done dealt you a bad hand, that don't mean the Lord don't love you. The trials and tribulations that we go through, ain't to bring you down; they're to make you stronger!"

Those kind of talks with Momma always took a lot of stress off me. She helped me to understand things better, to see things clearer. Without understanding, I was lost. Like, stumbling through the woods in the middle of the night with no flashlight.

Lost.

Right now, I needed one of those talks with Momma. Right now, I needed to understand. I felt lost; lost in the woods in the middle of the night, with no flashlight. Nothing made sense anymore. Nothing.

I remember certain conversations with Momma gave me light. They helped me to see through the dark, through the confusion; the things that I didn't understand. When she gave me her wisdom, knowledge and understanding, she gave me light. Everything made sense. I needed things to make sense now. I needed to have one of those talks with Momma. I needed to have one of those talks so bad, I was ready to end it. Just take my fuckin' gun, shove it in my mouth and pull the trigger. End it. Done. Gone. That way I can be with Momma. That way we can talk.

Drifting. Drifting. Drifting away.

Just the thought of seeing Momma brings a smile to my solemn face. The thought of holding her in my arms is what keeps me pushing on. The thought of revenge on the people that took her away from, is the only reason I was still alive.

"Boy, let me go!" Momma squealed as I hugged her from behind, showering her with kisses. "Leonard, I'm not playing with you. You better get on now!"

I gave Momma one last kiss on the cheek, then hightailed it out of the living room. She hated it when I did that. When I snuck up behind her while she was knitting in her rocking chair, and showered her with kisses. I don't think Momma was used to receiving affection. Some people ain't used to folks lovin' 'em. I think Momma was one of 'em. Outside of Grandma and Grandpa, I can't recall ever hearing anyone tell Momma that they loved her. Not even my own two brothers. I don't know what their story was up until the day I was born. Maybe they weren't used to gettin' affection either. Maybe they was just like Momma; didn't know how to accept it when somebody love 'em. There's always two sides to every story, you know? Two.

"Leonard, come in here so I can tell you something." Momma said.

I was in the kitchen making me a plate of fried chicken, homemade biscuits, green beans, mashed potatoes, and corn on the cob. Whenever Momma got to feeling like her old self again, I'd always have us a meal fit for a queen prepared.

"Why you always sitting around this house doing nothing?" Momma asked, as I stood, finishing off the rest of a chicken wing. "There's more to life than just sittin' up under me all day. You can't live your life if you're too busy spending all your time, watching me live mine."

I thought about that for a second, but it was only for a second. I loved my mother too much to even think about leaving her alone for too long. I always had to have one eye on her. If I didn't have my eyes on her, then somebody I knew better have had theirs on her. "Ain't nothing out there in them streets that I want." I explained. "Grandmamma made me promise that I'd look after you before she passed. I gave her my word that I would, not to mention, you's my only Momma and I love ya'."

Momma had been knitting up until I told her about my promise to Grandmamma. "Family is always supposed to look after family!"

She stated sternly. "That's why I'm telling you, it ain't good to be stuck in this house all the time. You done moved both of ya' brothers down here to help out. You see what they've been doing. They out there living! It's time to get out and live a little. Have some fun for a change."

As much as I wanted to disagree, in the back of my mind, I knew she was right. For the most part, my every waking moment was spent with Momma. I took it upon myself to make sure she was straight. I made sure she took her medication, ate, and everything else in-between. Even now that I'd moved my brothers in and paid Harold to look after Momma, I still done it. If a business deal didn't have nothing to do with large numbers, then there was a good chance you wouldn't see me.

As I stood there thinking about what Momma had just said, I made up my mind to start living. It was time to get out and have some fun for a change, and that night, I was gonna start living.

"Damn, little brother, is that what you steppin' out in tonight?" Harold asked, while giving me an approving onceover.

"You damn right it is!" I exclaimed proudly. "Y'all must done forgot that I'm the big fish in this here pond. Ain't nobody in this city fixin' to outshine me. I'm steppin' out fly as E-muthafucka."

Harold laughed as he came alongside me. He draped one arm over my shoulder and we both stood, admiring ourselves in the mirrors that covered the living room walls. "You look good, lil' brotha." Harold said.

I looked over at him and replied, "Nah, we look good. We in this shit together, right?" I held out my hand to shake on it, but that's when Harold must've noticed my diamond studded bracelet and pinky ring. My hand must've looked like a light show, all courtesy of my connect.

"Sho' you right!" Harold exclaimed, while holding my hand and admiring the sparkling diamonds that covered it. "We in this shit together."

We shook on it, but suddenly something didn't look right. What I saw in his eyes didn't match the smile that was pasted across his face. What I saw, I'd been seeing more and more the more money that I made.

"I got some important people that I've been meaning for you to meet." Harold said.

I walked away from him, and stepped closer to the mirrors. I brushed at the invisible wrinkles in my tailor-made trousers. I adjusted my pants so that they fell just right on my custom-made gators. Everything had to be perfect. Everything was a statement. I was living. "You know how I feel about meeting new people. If it don't got nothing to do with big money, then it don't make sense for them to be meeting me."

Harold quickly stepped alongside me and said, "These the same brothers that's been spending a lotta dough with us. It'll only be right if they meet the man with the plan. Who know, that might make 'em wanna spend a few extra duckets the next time they come down."

I fiddled with my gold chain, making sure that it sat just right on my chest. The pendent dangling from it was a lion's head. Its eyes were made of diamonds; they sparkled brightly, seemingly captivating my gaze. "This is the only time I'ma do this," I finally replied. "I can see that whoever these fellas are must be very important to you."

Harold gave me a quick embrace. "Thanks, lil' brother. I've been promising these boyz for some time that I'd introduce you to them."

**Later That Night**

I hit the Deuce turning heads and soaking up the love. The Deuce was just a nickname we'd made up for 2nd Street. The Deuce had a small hole in the wall club on it called Deep Deuce. The Deep Deuce had been around since the late 70's. Folks still flocked to the Deep Deuce as if it was the only place on earth for us to go out and hang at. But, in a way, it kinda was. Racism was just as prominent in the 80's as it was back in the 70's. Ya' ass bet not get caught on them white folks' side of town trying ta' hangout. Them racist ass crackas didn't mind teaching yo' black behind the real meaning of hanging out. That's why we stayed in our area, and did our own thang.

The police didn't come down on the Deuce. Too many niggas, too many places to come up missing. Too many reasons we should catch they bitch ass slippin' and beat the dog shit out of 'em. We stayed on our side of town, and they stayed on theirs. That's the way it was.

Cars lined both sides of the small residential brick road. People that lived in the area didn't too much mind. Parties on the Deuce had been going on since the mid-70's. Wasn't nothing but a handful of folks that lived in the area no how. Most of the houses were vacant, damn near ready to come down. The Deuce was in a flood zone. It was one of only a few streets before you came to the viaduct, which you had to cross in order to go to the westside. But, regardless of how raggedy the area may have been, folks still came out. People pulled out their best threads when it was time to hit the Deuce. You may have seen someone looking ashy and nasty just hours before the club opened. But, when the time came, they came out ready.

"Hey, L! You show is looking mighty fine tonight." A group of women greeted me no soon as my feet hit the bricks.

I stepped out looking so fly, I saw a young lady miss her step because she was checkin' for me so hard. Of course, I played it cool. That was one thing I was big on. Playing it cool. I don't believe in showing too much emotion while I'm around other people. Emotions can get you killed. Some people see them as a sign of weakness. Give cats a weapon that they can use against you.

If people find out you're easily entertained by folks doing stupid shit, then guess what. You'll have a bunch of clown ass niggas around you. If women find out that you be lustin' after 'em, you gon' look up and find a bunch of women around you. Now, don't get me wrong, having a bunch of women around you ain't no bad thang. But understand, 95-percent of them bitches are fake. They do fake shit. They wore fake shit. Hair fake. Eye-lashes fake. Smile fake. Daddy fake. Momma fake. Fake, fake, fake! I don't do fake. All that fake shit is in the name of scheming on your bankroll.

My grandfather once told me, "Respect a woman. That's the one that has morals and values. A woman takes care of business and has respect for herself and her man. But a bitch? Don't ever take your foot off her neck. Treat a bitch like a bitch. If you treat 'em like anything else, they'll hate you for it."

"What a surprise to see you! Did you come down here by yourself?" That was Tammy, and what a fine young specimen of a black woman she was. Tammy was one of those black women that was so pretty that you had to check her out twice. She couldn't just walk past you and you'd give her a simple glance. No, sir, not with Tammy. Tammy was too thick for that. I'm talking the kind of thick that made you wanna feed her spicy chicken wings smothered in ranch dressing. Thick. Tammy had long beautiful hair. She wore gold looped earrings and her skin was the color of butterscotch candy.

"I'm looking for my brothers," I finally replied, trying to appear consumed with finding them. "I thought them negros would already be here by now. They told me before I left the house, that they were on their way down here."

Tammy spun around an began scanning the crowd. The room was dark, but not dark enough that we couldn't still see. There was a small stage across the room where the DJ booth was set up, and the bar sat next to it. "Is that them over there?" Tammy asked.

I was so busy checking out Tammy's backside to even notice that she was standing there looking at me. Tammy wore a black miniskirt that hugged her hips perfectly. Everything was just right. Perfect. To avoid the sudden awkwardness of being exposed, I simply trained my sights in the direction that she was pointing. "I don't know," I replied. "I really can't tell if it is or not."

Most of the people she was pointing at did look like guys from my circle. I say that, although the room was dark. The guys from my crew were always the loudest ones in the room. Anywhere there was a crowd, you were subject to find my crew. Kenny, on the other hand, was different. Kenny didn't do crowds; especially when they consisted of people he didn't know. I'd noticed that about him by how standoffish he was when we went to take care of business. If the deal didn't require for him to be there, then he wasn't.

"I'll walk with you back there," Tammy offered. "A fine man like you ain't got no business wondering around a place like this alone."

I laughed because that was something else that I liked about Tammy. She knew what she wanted and wouldn't hesitate to go and get it. Not only was she soothing eye candy, but everything about that woman lined up to match. Had I not already been madly in love with the streets, I would've probably given us a chance.

"Nate, my main man!" I exclaimed as we walked up on his table. "Man, ya'll over here doing it big ain't cha'?"

Nate hopped up, excited to see me and gave me a quick embrace. "Come on, man— have a seat," he said. "The party is just getting started over here. I got a table full of pretty girls and some fire ass blow that'll rock your world!"

I peered down at the pile of coke he had on the table, then at the women crowded around. Some of them were jittery, anxious, high, no doubt waiting on their turn to snort some coke. I glanced back at Tammy; she wasn't feeling that setup one bit. She nervously looked from face to face, while hugging ever so closely to my side. "I think I'ma pass on that tonight," I shouted over The Gap Band's classic, *Outstanding*, pumping through the speakers. "I'm looking for my brothers. You wouldn't have happened to have seen them, would ya'?"

Nate was having such a good time he was too busy worried about trying to get his freak on. He quickly bent down and buried his face in the pile of coke. When he came back up, he went straight into action. "Gon' get after it!" He commanded one of the women that had been waiting her turn. When she bent over to take a sniff, Nate slid his hand under her skirt, and finger fucked her from behind.

I was so shocked; I couldn't help but to stand there, mouth agape.

Tammy tugged at my arm and whispered in my ear, "Let's go find our own table. We can wait over there until we see your brothers." I didn't even get a chance to protest before she'd led the way over to an empty table in the corner. We sat down and placed our backs to the wall so we could see everything going on around us. "I hope you don't be foolin' around with that stuff." Tammy said, after she'd slid her chair closer so we wouldn't have to shout over the music.

"I don't do anything but make money," I assured her. "If my Momma found out I was snorting that stuff, she'd probably beat my ass like I was a kid again."

Tammy giggled. "I guess, since you're the youngest, you're gonna always get treated like a baby."

"I guess so. Because Momma sure in hell ain't playing no games when it comes to me!"

We both had a good laugh and settled in to relax. Tammy ordered drinks and we continued to flirt until the buzz started to kick in.

"Why don't you wanna go out with me?" Tammy asked and placed my hand on her lap. She gently rubbed the back of my hand, forcing me to feel her soft skin.

"What man in their right mind wouldn't wanna go out with you? It's not that I don't wanna go out with you, it's just hard to divide my time between my mother, business, and a relationship. A beautiful woman such as you deserves all of a man's time, not just some of it."

Tammy moaned. "Ain't nobody ever told me that before, L."

"Well, they should've. Most of these girls in here ain't worthy of my time. I need someone like—"

Tammy slid my hand further up her thighs, all the way up to her feminine folds. Her panties were wet, soaking wet. "I wanna be with you, L. But I want you to feel the same way about me." Tammy opened her legs wider allowing my fingers to slip inside of her panties. Her pussy was tight. Real tight. Her pussy was so tight, I was only able to get one finger in before she'd started moaning. "Mmmmmm, Leonard."

I wasn't about to play no games with her. If one finger had her acting like that, I had to see what two was gonna do.

"Shit, babe!" Tammy clamped her legs shut. "You gon' make me scream up in here, L."

Ta' hell with this. I scanned the room trying desperately to find us some place to go. Finger fucking was cool, but fucking felt a whole lot better. I ended up taking Tammy to the back of the club where the ladies' room was. We anxiously rushed inside of it, like two high school kids experiencing love for the first time. I couldn't get the bathroom door shut fast enough, Tammy was all over me. She pinned me against the bathroom stale, groping, kissing and sucking all over me.

It wasn't until someone juggled the doorknob that I'd decided to take control. "Turn around."

Tammy peered up at me as if I was trying to get away. Her fingers worked feverishly trying to unbuckle my trousers.

"I said, turn around!" I snatched her hands off of me and pinned them against the wall above her head. "You gon' get this dick how I'm givin' it to ya'; ya' hear?"

Tammy's eyes narrowed, seemingly begging me to fuck her. She squirmed beneath my grasp, panting, moaning, groaning. We kissed. Our tongues intertwined, fighting fearlessly to claim victory over a battle that could never be won.

The doorknob jiggled. *BAM! BAM! BAM!* "Open up!" A woman yelled. "Y'all need to take that shit somewhere else. I gotta pee!"

Tammy spun around and removed her panties in one swift motion. She hiked her foot on the toilet, while using the wall to steady her balance. I quickly positioned myself behind her and didn't waste no time easing up inside of her.

"Mmmmmmmmm," Tammy purred, trying her damnedest to stifle an outcry.

I slowly moved in and out, nice and easy. *Smth Smth Smth Smth Smth.* Pussy juices smacking, the sweet smell of sex filled the air. Our bodies' rhythmic motions searched for harmony as I started to pound on that ass. *CLAP! CLAP! CLAP! CLAP!* I fucked her like she wanted to be fucked. Balls slapping against her ass, ramming my dick as far as I could get it inside of her. With each back-breaking thrust, I could feel her pussy getting wetter and wetter. Tammy's pussy juices smeared across her butt cheeks, oozing down over my balls where they dripped down to the toilet. I knew I shouldn't have been fucking her like this. Not here. Not now. Not like this. I wanted to pull out and save some of this good loving for later, but it was almost like I could hear her pussy calling me.

*Smth Smth Smth Smth*

"Yeah, I hear you," I replied, and I couldn't take it back. I know what I heard. I know what it asked me to do.

*Smth Smth Smth Smth*

"That's right. L gon' fuck you real good, babe."

Tammy's pussy felt so amazing, I was already about to bust a nutty. I tried to pull out to keep from cumming inside of her, but she wouldn't let me. "Uh-uhhhhhhnnnn. Don't stop," Tammy moaned.

*BAM! BAM! BAM!* The doorknob jiggled.

***

"Nigga, did you hear what the fuck I just told you to do?"

Harold chuckled and tried to lighten my mood. "These are the guys that I was telling you about, lil' brother. This here is Fast Eddy from Oklahoma City. He—"

The look I gave Harold was mean enough to stop a lion stone-cold in his tracks.

In fact, Nate peeped how I was muggin' everybody and was at my side in a flash. "There a problem over here?" Nate asked, and lifted his coat to reveal a chrome .357. Harold knew what time it was with Nate. Nate was just like me—not to be fucked with.

"Everythings cool, man." Harold explained. "We just had a small misunderstanding about some seats, that's all." Harold bent over and whispered something in Fast Eddy's ear. Moments later, everyone reluctantly stood and moved to the next table.

Fast Eddy made sure that he and I made eye contact before he moved. His eyes undoubtedly told the same story that mine did. He didn't like me, and I didn't like him either. "My mistake," Fast Eddy said. "Your brother brought us over here to this empty table. We didn't know someone was already sitting here. But, check this out.

I've been hearing a lot of good things about you. I thought it'd be in my best interest if I came down so you and I could have a sit down."

I smirked and brushed past Fast Eddy. It ain't hard to distinguish between what's real and fake. Fake got a funny feel to it. You'll know it when you feel it. I led Tammy to an open seat and pulled the chair out for her to sit down. "Tonight, is all about living," I informed Fast Eddy. "When it's time for us to talk business, we'll talk business, ya' dig?" I sat down next to Tammy and draped my arm around her.

Fast Eddy just stood there tugging at his suit jacket as if he still had something to say. I'm sure he wasn't used to folks talking to him in the manner that I had. But, in my city, if a person don't like the way I do things, the best thing for him to do is move the fuck around.

"I don't like him," Tammy said as she watched Fast Eddy walk over to his new table. "Did you see the way he was looking at you?"

I simply nodded, and played it cool. Sometimes, exposing how you felt about things could be like tipping your hand in a Poker game. Folks know when something big is about to happen. "Don't chu' worry about a thing," I told Tammy. "Let me be the one ta' deal with all the bullshit. People gon' always have a negative attitude when you're doing good for yourself. It's when you don't give 'em nothing to hate on, when you should start worrying."

As the night drifted away into the wee hours of the morning, the crowd inside the club dwindled down to a handful of drunks and a few lovebirds slow dancing on the floor. Of course, my crew was still in the mix, and every last one of them had a lady friend or two. I found myself still catching eyes with Fast Eddy. I couldn't help but think he had some ill shit on his mind. Not too many people had the nerve to stare me down. He must've thought shit was sweet, but I had every intention on proving to him that I wasn't.

"I have to use the ladies' room," Tammy whispered in my ear. "Don't chu' dare think about running off and leaving me."

I chuckled and snuggled up close to her ear and said, "I ain't going nowhere! Ain't a man a live that can make me walk away from all this good lovin'."

Tammy got up from the table and strutted off toward the restroom. I couldn't help but smile, while envisioning all the freaky things I had in mind to do to her. As I sat thinking what the near future had in store for us, my attention kept being drawn back to Fast Eddy; he was watching me. We stared each other down as if we were trying to kill each other with only our eyes. It wasn't until someone started shouting, that I realized the grave mistake that I'd made.

"Woooooooweee! Look at the ass on this pretty little lady."

Tammy had yet to make it to the restroom before she'd been stopped and harassed by one of Fast Eddy's men. I was already kicking myself in the ass for showing her so much affection in public.

"Where you off to in such a hurry?" The man asked her, while blocking her path. "Whoever your old man is, must be crazy to let all this thickness outta his sight."

Tammy shoved at him, trying to break away. The handful of people left inside the club looked on in utter surprise. Everyone knew how me and my crew got down. If you fucked with me, or anyone in my circle, there would be consequences.

Tammy peered in my direction, obviously trying to gauge my reaction. She shoved at the man again, but this time she managed to break free. I shot Nate a look and gave him the signal to clear everyone out. My brother Kenny was already rounding up the crew. I figured I'd best try and buy some time for a better situation. We didn't need no extra witnesses.

"Steebo!" Fast Eddy shouted. "You leave that pretty woman alone before you start some mess up in here. Her old man is sitting right over there watching you." Fast Eddy must've thought it was funny because he laughed mockingly then looked at me and said, "Try not ta' get upset at ol' Steebo. He don't know no better."

His crew erupted into laughter, causing my blood to boil. Instead of getting up and beating his got-damn face in, I just sat there and stared at his dumb ass. That muthafucka really didn't know when to shut up. The envy he had in his heart must've been so overwhelming that he couldn't stop the shit from coming out.

"Mr. L." I looked up to see a younger version of Fast Eddy peering down at me. I don't know where this muthafucka came from; just up and appeared out of nowhere. "I've been waiting all night to come back over here and properly introduce myself. I know my brother and his friends might be a little too wild for your likin', but they don't mean no harm. If you'd just give 'em a chance, we can sho' make you a lotta' money."

I liked this cat; didn't care too much for his hairstyle. It reminded me too much of Fast Eddy's— shaved on both sides with a curl at the top. He was definitely younger than I was. Hell, he was probably the youngest person in the building. If I'd have given him a chance to speak when he first tried to introduce himself, things might've gone over a lot smoother. "What's your name?"

The young man nervously peered over at Fast Eddy, and wiped his sweaty palms on the side of his pants. "I'm Eddy Harding the third," he said. "And, my brother, Fast Eddy, is Eddy Junior. You can call me, Eddy, Eddy number three, Eddy the third, or just plain ol' Eddy."

"Damn, all these Eddies. You ain't got no other name that folks can call You? You know, like a nickname or something?"

His eyes fell to the floor, darting from one spot to the next. This negro was crazy; had to be. Couldn't keep still; kept shifting from one foot to the next. Must've been high or something. "Cabbage!" He stated confidently. "My Daddy call me, Cabbage."

I laughed and said, "You shit'n me."

"No, sir. That's what Daddy call me. He like to call me that 'cause I used to eat up a bunch of cabbage when I's a baby. I guess, even though I done got older and don't fool with that stuff no mo', the name still kinda' stuck."

I chuckled and began to relax a little. This nigga might've been a little weird, but he was alright with me. While Cabbage and I continued to converse, Tammy came strutting across the room captivating everyone's attention, including mine.

"I'll leave you two alone and grab something to drink," Cabbage said.

"Aiight, cool. Get up with me later on. I might be able to throw a little something your way."

Cabbage smiled and did some ol' weird shit that I'd seen on, Enter the Dragon. The nigga bowed.

"Hey, babe!" Tammy said. "Are you ready to go?"

I scanned the club looking for Nate, didn't see him. Didn't see his lady friends either. I looked for my brother Kenny, didn't see him either. The owner of the club was just about to lock the front door. "Yo', hold up!" I shouted, causing everyone to stop and look at me. I quickly pulled out my car keys and handed them to Tammy. "Here. Take these and wait for me in the car."

Tammy looked at the keys, then back at me. "Nah, uhn-uhn-nnnn!" She exclaimed and shook her head. "I ain't going nowhere unless you coming too! I know what y'all up to. You ain't foolin' nobody."

I chuckled. "Tammy, you gotta get out of here. It's some shit 'bout to go down and I don't want you to get caught up in the middle of it."

Tammy stood defiantly with her hand resting on her hip. I started to pick her ass up and carry her out the front door, but it was already too late. Kenny and several guys from my crew bum-rushed the club. "Ahhhh!" Tammy screamed.

"See, that's why you should've done what I told you!" I grabbed Tammy by the arm and literally had to drag her across the room. She fought with me the whole way, yanking and pulling, pulling and screaming. She did everything in her power to try and break free, but I was just too strong. "Tammy, chill!" I shouted, but she wouldn't quit screaming. "Tammy!" I shook her ass a few times and forced her to look at me. "You've gotta' cut out all that damn screaming, okay?" She nodded. "I ain't gon' let nothing happen to you, okay?" She nodded again. "I need you to stay here while I go over there and take care of this business. Can you handle that?"

"Babe, let's just go," Tammy cried. "You don't have to do this. Let's just gooooo. Let's just goooooo. Let's just gooooooo."

I shook her ass a couple more times. She was stuck on repeat. “Shut up!” I forced her down into a chair and looked her dead in the eye. “I tol’ yo’ ass to leave and you didn’t listen. You should’ve done what I told you to do. Now, I want you to sit right here and shut the fuck up. Do you understand?”

She nodded.

When I turned around, all I saw was niggas getting beat to fucking death. I could see why Tammy was doing all that damn hollering. The lights were on now. Niggas were sprawled out on the floor, some begging for mercy, others were already dead. I looked over just in time to see a guy get smacked with a crowbar so hard that the end of it got stuck in his head.

“Leonard, come on, man. Why you gotta’ do ‘em like this?” The sound of Harold’s voice instantly struck a nerve.

“Nigga, you brought these low budget muthafuckas to my city, sit there and let them disrespect me, and you don’t think I’m supposed to feel some kinda way?”

Harold rushed across the room and fell in stride beside me. “They was drunk, L. I know you know what it’s like to get drunk and get beside yourself.”

I mugged that stupid muthafucka so hard, there shouldn’t have been no doubt in his mind that nothing he said even mattered. “Give me your gun.” I said.

“Wh-Wha-What?” Harold stammer.

“Bitch, you heard what the fuck I just said! Don’t make me tell yo’ dumb ass again.”

Harold’s face drained of all emotion. My words must’ve cut him deep, but I didn’t care. Brother or not, he, they, anyone could get it. Harold handed me his gun, but not before giving me a mean stare down.

I lifted his chrome snub-nosed .38 Special to inspect it. “Cute,” I said. “Now get the fuck outta my face before I have to use it on you.” I crossed the dance floor over to where they had Fast Eddy pinned against the wall. I wanted to make sure that they saved the best for last. I wanted Fast Eddy to see his whole crew get whacked before I blew his fucking head off. "Didn't anyone ever teach you about respect?" I asked.

"Nigga, fuck yo' respect," Fast Eddy spat. "You doing all this over a bitch? You caught up in yo' feelings over a bitch? I thought you was supposed to be a real muthafucka. I thought you was the type of nigga that was all about his paper. Nigga, you ain't nothing but a *bitch*!" This negro was crazy for real. Can't take that from him.

"I'm a bitch?" I asked while slowly moving closer; close enough that I could smell his breath, close enough that I could feel his heartbeat. Close enough that I could put my gun on his dick and blow that piece of shit clean off. "I can't hear you, nigga." I went on to say. "I'm a bitch?"

Fast Eddy smiled and leaned his face closer to mine. "That's right," he said. "You a stone-cold bi—"

*POW!* I blew that stupid muthafucka's dick smooth off, and when he open his mouth to scream, I put one in his dome too. *POW!*

Tammy yelled.

"Now see what you done did?" I spun around and trained my sights back on Harold. "You got me in here killing people and today was supposed to be my day off!" Movement out the corner of my eye caught my attention. I looked over and saw Cabbage standing at the back door watching me. Not the Cabbage that didn't know if he was Eddy, Eddy number 3, Eddy the 3rd, or E-E-Eddy. This was Cabbage. The one that would come back for me. "Get him!"

Everyone immediately jumped into action to chase Cabbage down, but it was already too late. Cabbage had a nice size lead on them, and he was already out the back door.

"Fuck!" I stood in the middle of the floor shaking my head, unable to believe that we'd somehow overlooked Cabbage. As I began to take in the extensive clean up that we all had ahead of us, I heard Tammy crying behind me. "Damn, you alright?"

She didn't look good, and she damn sho' didn't look like the same woman that I was in the ladies' room with earlier. "Get away from me!" Tammy screamed.

I kneeled in front of her and sat my gun on the floor. "Tammy, calm down. Everything's cool. The shits over, aiight?"

Tammy shook her head, folded her arms, unfolded them; covered her face, trying to block the images, the bodies, the dead bodies. They were everywhere. "You killed them!" She cried. "I can't believe that you did that, Leonard."

"Babe, I ain't killed nobody."

"Yes, you did! I saw you. I saw what you did to him. I saw you take that gun and shoot him in the head. I saw you."

"Tammy, you scaring me."

"You killed them! I watched you kill them, Leonard." I reached out to try and touch her hand, but she snatched it away from me. "Don't you touch me! Don't you ever put your filthy fucking hands on me again!"

"Hmpf." I stood up, and swiped away any wrinkles on my tailormade trousers. I adjusted my pants so that they fell just right on my custom made gators. My chain. Can't forget about my muthafuckin' chain. I straightened that bitch up so that it sat just right on my chest. "Look at me."

Tammy sat with her arms folded across her chest. She stared out at the dance floor crying, legs crossed, lips tight, no doubt unable to believe what she was looking at.

"I said, look at me!" Tammy jumped, and peered up at me. "I want you to know that I really had a good time tonight. I needed for you to know that, okay?" She nodded. "I also needed you to know that I liked you. I liked you a lot. I liked you so much that I was gonna take you home so that you could meet my mother, okay?" She nodded again.

*POW!*

# Chapter 11
# KEVIN

The smell of bacon frying is what awakened me to my growling stomach. I was hungry as shit. I almost forgot what it felt like to wake up and smell a homecooked meal. I quickly slid out of bed and threw on a shirt and pair of sweatpants. I could hear my father talking to someone in the other room, but I could only hear him; which could only mean he was on the phone. I open my bedroom door and moseyed on into the dining room.

My father stood at the stove cooking with the phone to his ear. "Good morning," he said.

"Good morning." I replied.

"You hungry?"

I walked into the kitchen just to see what all he'd cooked. My father had just dropped a half stick of butter in a pot of Cream of Wheat. A plate filled with eggs, toast, and bacon sat next to the stove. "Yeah, I guess I'll have a bite." I finally replied.

My father smiled and said, "Well, gon' and get washed up. Breakfast will be ready in just a minute."

The first thing that came to mind, was what was the special occasion? Normally, Pops would be getting dressed to go to the Kingdom Hall on Sunday mornings. Today, he was dressed in faded blue overalls with a long sleeve white shirt. I knew if he wasn't attending the meeting that morning, then something must've been up.

Shortly after I'd washed up, I strolled back into the dining room to find that my father was still on the phone. Whoever he was on the phone with, it had to be about something important. Pops didn't like to talk on the phone, plus, I noticed that all his responses were short. His facial expression was serious, and occasionally he'd shift his gaze to me, then back down at the pot of Cream of Wheat that he'd been stirring since I came out of my bedroom.

"Let me get off of here and fix this boy a plate," My father said into the phone. "I'll give you a holla back in a minute." Silence. "Okay." More silence. "I will." Silence again. He hung up.

"So, what's got you at home on this beautiful Sunday morning?" I asked. "It must've been last year around Christmas that I recall you missing a meeting."

My father shuffled around the kitchen making plates. Never once did he look up from what he was doing. "I figured I'd stay home and find out what you've been up to." He replied. "I haven't had the chance to talk to you in a while. I needed to see what's going on inside of that head of yours." My father brought a plate over to the table and sat it down in front of me.

"Thank you."

"Would you like milk, juice, or water?" He asked.

"Ummmm, let me get some milk."

Pops spun around and headed back into the kitchen, but stopped just short and said, "I'll have some milk, *please*!"

I chuckled. "Oops, my bad. Can I have some milk...*please*?"

My father shook his head and went to make me a glass of milk. "I've been hearing a lot of strange rumors around town," My father began by saying. "The strange thing about 'em is, either your name keeps coming up, or it's got something to do with the people that you choose to hang out with."

I shrugged and dug into my food. "People are gonna talk. Half of 'em don't know what they're even talking about. And the other half don't know the half."

My father walked over to the table and sat down across from me. His facial expression was blank. I couldn't read him. I couldn't tell whether he was happy, mad, sad, or simply probing for more information. "I gotta friend down at the police department, that say you've been hanging out with them boys 'round there at The Ghetto. He tol' me to tell you them boys ain't nothing but trouble."

"Since when did you start having friends at the police department?"

My father dropped his fork and snapped, "When I figured out that I was grown, and I can be friends with whomever I wanna be friends with." I smirked and kept eating. "Besides, this here is a good guy. I met him a few years back at a car show. He gotta Sixty-Seven Gouger like mine, but his ain't got no engine in it. I told him about a few places where he could go and get him some parts. After that, well, he took a likin' to me, and we been friends ever since."

Ain't no way I would dare venture down that road of talking about cars. My father could go on for days, if not weeks talking about cars, car shows, car parts, and anything else that had to do with cars. The best thing I could think to do was finish eating and get the hell outta there. My cell phone rang in my bedroom, so I excused myself and got up.

"Why don't you give all that a break for now," my father said, stopping me before I reached my bedroom. "Sit down and enjoy your food. Them streets ain't going nowhere. I'm sure they'll be right there waiting for you when you get done eating."

I flashed a weak smile and walked back over to the table. "Might've been about something important." I said.

"Oh, yeah, like what?"

I sat down and tried to appear busy trying to eat. "Let's just forget about it, okay? Our food's getting cold, plus, you'll never understand."

"Wh-Wha-What makes you think that? You think 'cause I'm getting old that I don't know what's going on? You don't think I'm hip ta' what you youngstas is out there doing?"

I shrugged and tried to ignore him. I could always tell when my ol' man was getting upset, he started stuttering. Sometimes, his stuttering would get so bad that he wouldn't say anything else, he'd just sit there and stare at you. "Dad, you ain't in the streets to know what it's like to have to be on point. I have to know what's going on around me at all times. But, you'll never understand that. All you do is work, work, work. You don't have to know what it's like to be on point, 'cause you ain't out there in it! Being in them streets ain't nothing like working a nine to five. You gotta be on point to work on the block."

"Boy, you's crazy, you know that? Them people done really screwed up your head. Don't chu' know, being on point is going to work? Them people you hanging with done tricked you into thinking sitting around waiting on the police ta' come get cha is staying on point. Let me tell ya' something. I done been there, done that. I was out there in them streets when it wasn't nothing but dirt and rocks on 'em. They hadn't even put the pavement down when I started running the streets. I was out there fooling around, back when something might jump out the bushes on the side of the road, and bite yo' whole throat off 'cause you was out too late at night."

I sighed, but held my tongue. Just like every other old head, Pops was coming with these lame ass stories just to help me see the trials he'd had to overcome. My cell phone rang again. We both looked at each other.

"Dad, I really need to get that. I've been expecting an important phone call."

My father dabbed at his mouth with a napkin, then tossed it down on the table. "Tell me why, when the streets come calling, you always gotta go ta' running? But, when I try to get you to sit still long enough so you can hear me out, you ain't got time. Don't that sound a little strange to you?"

I took a deep breath and tried to block out the sound of my phone ringing. "You're right," I conceded. "Whoever that is calling can wait. It's obvious that you've got something very important that you need to tell me."

My father bobbed his head, then folded his hands on the table. "I'm trying to get you to slow down so I can save your life. Ain't nothing out there in them streets. Don't you see that, Kevin? The things you chasing after comes at a price. Ya' behind gon' end up dead or in jail. That's the price. Dead. Jail. That's it. The devil set the price. He use all that glitz and glamour to draw you away from doing what's right."

"Dad, I understand what you're saying. But just because I choose to make a living by a different means than you, don't mean you any better than me. Whatever is the devil's, is his no matter if I get it working or hustling."

"Boy you is... umpf. Your head is really messed up. You call yourself making a living? This here is my house! I pay the bills here. Them my eggs and bacon you eating. That's my toast and Cream of Wheat. I put the butter in that. You see the color of it? I did that. You think 'cause you done moved to the Westside for two weeks, you gon' come up in here telling me about how you making a living? Boy you is out cho' mind."

"How did you know that I moved to the Westside?"

"I told you! I been out there in them streets long before you. I know things, Kevin. I know more than you think I do. I even know you."

"You might know me, but you don't know nothing about them streets. Things done changed since the eighteen hundreds."

"Who tol' you that? I ain't never told you that thangs done changed. Ain't nothing changed in them streets but the people in 'em. Ya' behind gon' either end up dead, or in jail. That's the price Kevin. So, what it's gon' be?"

I couldn't do nothing but sit there and look at him. Everything he'd said had me feeling like he thought he was better off than me. Maybe if he would've been more supportive of the things that I wanted to do with my life, then I wouldn't have chosen to do the things I was doing.

"Kevin, I know you hear me talking to you," My father said. "So, what it's gon' be?"

I still didn't say nothing. I just sat there staring at him like he was staring at me.

"Don't make me ask you again."

That made me laugh. "What? I'm supposed to be scared like I'ma get a whoopin' or something?"

My father shook his head and said, "Nope, but you can sho' get knocked out!"

I got up and mobbed straight into my bedroom. Fuck sitting around listening to idle threats all day. I had other things that I needed to be doing.

"I've tried everything I can think of to get you on the right path, Kevin. I see you're stuck on doing what Kevin wants to do."

"I'm not a kid anymore, Dad. I'm grown now. You can't dictate what I do, what I choose to believe in." I heard the table creak as my father pushed against it to get up.

I was so busy changing my clothes that I'd failed to notice that he was standing in my doorway. "That's right, Kevin. You're grown now. You're not a little kid anymore. That's why it's time for you to get your own place. You won't have to worry about me telling you what to do as long as you got your own place."

"Oh, so you're kicking me out?"

He shrugged. "Didn't have to. You put yourself out. You chose to run the streets instead of doing the things that I ask you to. I'm just making sure you get whatever it is that you're out there looking for."

**HAROLD**

It hurt me to tell my only child to find him some place to go. I never thought in a million years that it'd come to this. Guess that's what I get for thinking. His mother told me to ask him if he'd like to stay with her for a while. I told her that I'd run it past him and get back with her about it. But, Kevin had walked out of the restroom earlier like he knew we were on the phone talking about him. I didn't want him to jump to any conclusions about what I was trying to do, so I simply ended the call.

Even as I washed up the few dishes left over from breakfast, I thought about asking him just to see what he'd say. I didn't wanna see my only child out there in the streets, but I didn't wanna see him living in Miami, either. All that shootin' and carryin' on down there. I didn't wanna see my boy get caught up in that mess. At least, as long as he lived in Guthrie I could keep my eyes on him. I couldn't keep my eyes on him way down in Miami. I wouldn't know how I could help him if he ever needed me.

After finishing up with the dishes, I threw on my jacket and hopped in my truck. I needed some time alone to get my thoughts together. Plus, I didn't wanna end up telling Kevin that he could stay. Sometimes, people need to bump their head before they realize life's not a game. I think Kevin needed that. I figured, a nice little drive out to Langston and back would give him and I exactly what we needed. Him ample time and space to pack his things and move out, and me enough time to think.

Langston is a small town about 15 minutes outside of Guthrie. The town ain't nothing but another small country town, except it got a lotta black folks in it. The drive out to Langston is what I liked the most. Ain't nothing but a bunch of hills and countryside. Often times, I'd pop in my Anita Baker CD and ride out to *Body and Soul*. I could listen to that woman sang and she'd put my mind in another place in time. Sometimes, I found myself getting lost in my thoughts while I listened to ol' Anita. I literally had to change up the music because I didn't want to dig too deep in my twisted memories.

Before I hit the road, I stopped by the filling station across the street from the Masonic Temple. My gas tank was almost on empty, so I figured I'd drop twenty in the tank and grab a few other items that I needed. "How ya'll doing this morning?" I waved, greeting the two cashiers working the register.

"Hey, Harold!" Pat exclaimed. "I just made a fresh pot of coffee. You betta hurr' up and get 'chu a cup before Bright Eye drank it all up." Pat was a curly haired white woman. She was at work almost every time I came into the store. The other person working was old man Bright Eye. He didn't do too much talking, he'd just sit there staring at you with them funny colored eyes of his.

"Not today!" I replied with a chuckle. "I just stopped by to grab a few things and I'll be on my way." I ambled down the aisle and allowed my eyes to roam over all the delicious candies— M&M's, 3 Musketeers, Mr. Goodbar. My favorite. I grabbed two of those jokers, one for now and one for later. Don't make no sense to play with your sweet tooth. When you feel like snacking, *snack*!

As I moved down the aisle, I stopped in front of the motor oil. I'd been thinking about changing the oil on my truck. The weather was changing, so I liked to stay ahead of the game. Seem like my truck ran better on Penzoil during the winter, but ran even better off Quaker State in the summer. May as well gon' and get ready for old man winter, 'cause he sho' as heck was comin'.

The sound of bells ringing announced yet another customer. Pat exclaimed, "Good morning!" But her greeting was met with silence.

I saw someone headed in my direction out the corner of my eye. I moved closer to the rack hoping to give whomever it was, enough room to walk by.

"Been a long time since you and I bumped into each other," a man said. "You'd think we didn't live right around the corner from each other. Or, better yet, live in the same town."

I didn't have to look to know who that voice belonged to. It wasn't nobody but Leonard. He was probably high off that stuff just trying to distract me. He must've known I was thinking about changing my oil. He ain't nothing but a distraction. But, I ain't gon' let him distract me. I'ma keep right on doing what I was doing and act like I hadn't heard a thang.

"Saw a few new faces around town," Leonard went on to say. "I thought it was kinda strange considering what they's doing and all. Turns out, they ain't no new faces at all. Them boys are some old friends of yours. I thought I should prolly stop by—"

"You stay away from my house; ya' hear! I don't won't none of that foolishness that you off inta' anywhere near my house." I looked Leonard straight in his eyes to let him know I meant business.

Leonard chuckled and threw his hands up. "I can respect that. Don't make no sense showin' up at 'cha door and you ain't done nothing, right?" He turned like he was about to walk away, but stopped and said, "I hope for your sake everything that you've told me over the years is the truth. Because, if I find out you've been lying to me and had something to do with what happened to Momma..." He pointed his hand at me as if it were a gun. "Bang! You're dead."

I walked off and left his spooky lookin' behind standing there. He'd allowed them drugs to eat him up, now his face was all sunk in. He kinda reminded me of a giraffe when I looked at him. A black one.

"That'll be thirty-eight dollars and fourteen cents." Pat said, after she'd tallied up my total for gas, oil, and candy. I took a deep breath and tried to relax. I'd been through enough nonsense for one day. "You have a nice day," Pat said cheerfully after I'd paid her.

I nodded and scooped up my bag, and walked outside into the cool morning air. I hurried over to my truck and hopped in. I couldn't get that joker started fast enough. I needed to get out of there, ASAP. The sound of my 350 engine roared to life, caused Pat to look. She waved, and I waved, then I pulled off.

As I drove up to the stop sign on the corner, I noticed Leonard standing on the side of the building. It was something about the way he was looking at me; something I could sense in his presence, something that made me feel strange, that continued to make me sit there and look back at him. I can't say if it was because of the stress that I'd been under, or if there was something more to it. All I could say was something was different.

Leonard and I haven't always been on the best of terms. I guess it's safe to say it's been that way since he was a baby. Leonard always got all the attention because he was a Momma's boy. Everything was about him— Leonard this, or Leonard that. It seemed like ever since the first day he was born my relationship with our mother went down the drain. Momma would always find some reason to fuss at me about something or another, even things that I didn't do. Like the time she got mad at me because someone drank up all the milk. She accused me of doing it, even after I told her who I thought had done it. Now, I've never been one to be a liar, or disobedient to my mother, but after that day, our relationship took a drastic turn for the worse.

"Who done drank up all the milk?" Momma yelled, while standing in front of the refrigerator with an empty milk carton. "I know one of you done did it. This empty carton ain't just up and emptied itself out. Now, who done it?"

I know I wasn't about to own up to it because I didn't do it. I'd been sitting in the living room watching TV all day. I hadn't eaten nothing outside of what Momma cooked for us that morning. I know my big brother Kenny didn't do it, 'cause he didn't even like milk. And my little brother Leonard was only three years old. He couldn't reach the door handle to open the refrigerator. The only other person that could've done it was Dorcey. Leonard's daddy. Dorcey would come home every now and then, eat, sleep, do the number two and leave again. Seemed like before he'd leave, he'd always manage to stir up some kind of mess that I'd be the one blamed for.

"Maybe it was Dorcey." I reasoned with Momma. "I saw him come in earlier and eat a big bowl of cereal. You was back there sleep, so he told me not to wake you up. He tol' me he'll be back later this evening. But I know it must've been him, 'cause he the only one I saw drank some milk."

Momma didn't like for anyone to accuse Dorcey of wrongdoing. Dorcey's name was like Jesus in our home; thou canest not throw dirt on thy name. Even Momma's friends would try and talk some sense into her about the stuff Dorcey was 'round town doin'. But Momma wouldn't listen, she put every last one of them out and told 'em not to come back. I don't know what Dorcey done did to my Momma, but whatever he done, he sho' had his hooks in her.

"Get up and bring yo behind in here." Momma growled.

I'm sure she was probably mad, probably wanted to give me a whoopin' too. But I didn't care. I was twelve years old. Whoopings didn't hurt me. I may have been a little on the chubby side, but I was way bigger than Momma. Sometimes, she'd give me a whoopin' and I didn't do nothing but stand there.

"Why you always doin' stuff, then turn around and blame it on Dorcey?" Momma asked.

I looked at her like she was crazy.

*POP!* She hit me on the arm.

"Ssssss."

"Straighten up your face!" Momma barked. "I'm sick of you always doin' stuff, then try to blame it on Dorcey. Dorcey ain't done nothing but be a good father to you."

"Dorcey ain't my daddy."

*POP! POP! POP!*

"Shut cho' damn mouth, and don't ever let me hear you say some shit like that again. If it wasn't for Dorcey, yo' behind would still be sitting in there staring at the wall. Dorcey bought that television set. Dorcey even bought them there shoes you got on your feet. Now, take your ungrateful ass back there and don't let me see your face no more tonight!"

I stormed off to our bedroom, stomping so hard I could hear the plates rattling in the cabinets. Momma had me hot, real hot. All I did was tell her the Gods honest truth, but she got mad at me. I couldn't wait until I got older so I could get the hell outta there. My big brother Kenny was seventeen. I knew he was about to move out. I figured I's gon' be just like him when I turned seventeen. I was gon' save up some money, pack my things, and move out.

"Kenny, wake up!" I hissed sternly after I'd clicked on our bedroom lamp.

Me, Kenny, and Baby Leonard all slept in the same bed. Kenny slept on one side of the bed, I slept on the other, and Baby Leonard slept in the middle. I hated to sleep in the same bed as Baby Leonard. Sometimes, he peed in the bed. Baby Leonard would still be asleep with a stupid little grin on his face. I told Momma that Baby Leonard needed to be sleepin' in the bed with her; let him piss on her night gown and see how she liked that. Of course, I got a whoopin' 'bout that too. She tol' me that I had a smart-ass mouth. I tol' her my mouth ain't smart, I'm smart.

"Kenny!" I shook him so hard that I could hear the bones pop in his neck. "Kenny, wake up!"

Kenny bolted up and flung the sheets off of him. "Huh? What? What's wrong?" He mumbled.

I plopped down on the edge of the bed and looked at him seriously. "When you supposed to be moving out?"

Kenny whipped his eyes and yawned. "Why you wake me up asking me all these stupid questions? Ain't nobody going nowhere but back to sleep!" Kenny lie back down and pulled the sheets over his head.

I'm sure he must've thought that no one knew of his plan to move, but I did. I knew everything that went on in our house. I knew Kenny snuck out late at night to go see girls. I even knew he had money stashed under one of the loose floorboards under the bed. I also knew Kenny's daddy wasn't really praying with Momma, although they tol' us they was going off to pray. And I also knew I was gon' tell on everybody if this negro didn't get to talking.

"Kenny, I overheard you tell your friends that you were moving out. I heard you tell them about the money you've got stashed under the bed. I also heard you bragging about your daddy doing the nasty with Momma!"

"Shhhhhh, nigga!" Kenny shushed me as he flung the covers back and held one finger to his lips. "Why you gotta be so loud? Do you want Momma to come in here fussing and we both end up in trouble?"

"I want you to tell me when you moving out."

"Why? Tell me why, Harold. You can't go. You gotta' stay here and help look after Baby Leonard."

"I ain't lookin' after Baby Leonard, 'cause Baby Leonard is a punk!"

"Shhhhhhhhh! Do you wanna die tonight? 'Cause that's sho' what's gon' happen if Momma hear you talking like that."

"I don't care what Momma try to do to me, it ain't gon' hurt! She done already whooped me once today; she hit me four times." I lifted my sleeve to show him there were no bruises. I needed him to know I could take a beatin' and keep on ticking.

"Harold, you talkin' crazy now. Momma gon' get ahold of yo' behind and it's gon' be something amazing. That there she done to yo' arm ain't nothing compared to what she's capable of doing."

I rolled my eyes refusing to give into the fear that he tried to instill in my heart. "Why I'm supposed to be scared of Momma? 'Cause I called Baby Leonard a punk? It's the truth ain't it? Momma know it. His daddy know it. You know it. All Baby Leonard do is cry, cry, cry. He get on my dang nerves with all that crying. Somebody is gon' have to toughen him up."

The door to our bedroom slowly crept open. Baby Leonard peeked in and said, "I she you!"

"See what I'm talking about?" I said. "He don't even know how to say *see*. He say *she* 'cause he a punk!"

Kenny lie back down and covered up. "When ya' behind end up in trouble for messing with that boy, don't say that I didn't warn ya'."

I looked at Baby Leonard and mugged him. He looked just like his daddy, and I couldn't stand that negro. For some reason, Momma had allowed Baby Leonard to run around the house that day in a stinking sagging diaper, no shirt, with one sock that barely hang on his foot. He stood in our doorway watching me, waiting, pissing me smooth off. "What chu' looking at?" I hissed.

"Bubba!" Baby Leonard howled with excitement. He stomped his feet and clapped his hands thinking that it was time to play.

"Shut up! I ain't cho' dat-gum brother. Come here."

Baby Leonard's celebration came to a screeching halt. His hands were still suspended in midair, his foot still dangled in between stomping the floor. His eyes were filled somewhere in between excitement and fear, his mouth gapping. "Bubba?"

"Negro, I done tol' you. I ain't cho' dat-gum brother. Now, come here!"

Baby Leonard cautiously opened the door all the way and timidly crossed the room. He wrung his fingers together, his eyes shifting from me to Kenny, Kenny to the floor.

"Harold, I'm warning you, this is not a good idea." Kenny said, while peeking from beneath the sheets. "You better leave that boy alone. If you keep messing around and make that boy start crying, it's over for you."

"Shut up! How you gon' tell me what to do? Ain't you plannin' on moving out? You sound like Baby Leonard with all that crying. All I'm 'bout to do is prove to you that he's a punk!" I peered down at Baby Leonard as his eyes searched my face for the slightest hint of danger. "Cry!" I snapped. "Cry like the crybaby we all know you is." I nudged him in the chest and accidently caused him to fall down.

"Oh my God!" Kenny gasped. "You done did it now. Once that boy start crying..." Kenny covered up and tried to play sleep.

I didn't care if Baby Leonard started crying. In fact, that's exactly what I wanted him to do. I needed for Kenny to see why I couldn't stay there and look after Baby Leonard. If Momma came in there asking what happened, I'd simply say I didn't know. It wasn't like Baby Leonard knew how to talk well enough to explain what happened. All he knew was a few words. *Bubba, I she you, Momma*, and *peek-a-boo*.

Baby Leonard's stomach started to jiggle.

"Look Kenny! Look!"

Baby Leonard's eyes filled up with tears as he started sniffling. When he opened his mouth, all that came out was one long hissing sound that eventually turned into a well. "Wwwwhhhhaaaaa!"

I burst into laughter and pointed at Baby Leonard as he cried. "See. It's just like I told you. Baby Leonard is a punk!"

"I sho' hope you's right with the Lord," Kenny whispered. "I'll see you in the next lifetime."

"Baby Leonard!" Momma called out. I could hear her running through the house in search of him. "Baby Leonard, where you at, babe?" Momma burst through the door immediately scooped him up into her arms. "Oooooh, babe. What's wrong?" Momma cooed, while patting Baby Leonard on his back as she bounced him around.

But Baby Leonard couldn't see me because she had his back to me. I could tell he was looking for me, because he kept turning his head from left to right. "Bubba!" Baby Leonard cried out.

"Your brother been in here being mean to you?" Momma asked, then turned Baby Leonard so that he could see me.

"I-she-you!" Baby Leonard growled as he pointed at me.

"Harold, I'ma beat cho' ass!"

"But, Momma, I ain't done—"

"I don't wanna hear it! I doooooo not wanna hear it. You been in here messing with my baby, now I'm fixin' to mess with yo' ass!"

Since that day, nothing was ever the same between me and Momma. Now that I knew, *I she you*, translated into, I've been messing with Baby Leonard, I had to reevaluate a few things. There was no telling what *Bubba* might mean. And God forbid the day when I was accused of *peek-a-boo*. Lucky for me, Kenny had decided not to leave. He decided to wait until I got a little older, that way we could move out together. Really, I gave him no choice but to wait. He couldn't move out unless he could afford to, and once I'd stolen his stash from under the bed he simply couldn't afford to. Now, I haven't ever been no liar or a thief, but after Momma put that whoopin' on me for making Baby Leonard cry, I was against the grain from that day on.

Up ahead a sign read, *Langston University Next Right*. I hit my blinker and exited the highway. Sometimes I wished I'd have gone to college. I think, maybe, I would've had I not been in such a rush to grow up. I think that was Kevin's case too. In a rush to be grown. Just like I couldn't stand Dorcey and Baby Leonard, I guess that's how he felt about me and my rules.

**KEVIN**

One hour later, I was at O-Dawg's Mom's house eager to see him. Both phone calls earlier were from the homie. He left me a message to meet him at his Mom's house ASAP. It'd been a couple of weeks since we'd last had the chance to talk with all the things that I'd heard about him. I was anxious to see if the hype was true.

*BAM! BAM! BAM!* The burglar bars on Ms. O'Dell's front door rattled as I beat on them. It was cold as shit outside, and I wasn't nowhere near dressed for the weather that had swept over the city. Oklahoma's weather was funny like that; hot as fuck one minute, and freezing to fuckin' death the next. *BAM! BAM! BAM!*

"What?" LaShura snapped when she snatched open the front door.

"What chu' mean, what?" I snapped back. "I know you ain't still trippin' about that shit that went down at my birthday party."

LaShura rolled her eyes and put her hand on her hip. "Whatever, Kevin. What do you want, 'cause my brother is not here?"

I looked at that bitch like her pussy stank. I just wanted her to know that I felt the same fucked up way that she was feeling. "That's all you had to say!" I rudely replied. "You know I don't come through—"

*BAM!* She slammed the door in my face. It took everything in me not to cock back and kick that fuckin' door of its hinges. Out of respect for Ms. O'Dell, I decided to give her ass a pass.

A silver Nissan Maxima pulled up just as I mobbed back out to my car. The windows on the Maxima were tinted so it was hard to see inside. The way the driver of the car had parked, partially blocking the driveway, I braced myself for drama.

I stood slightly startled, expecting to see Stanley or one of his homies hop out when the passenger door opened. It was O-Dawg. "Damn, my nigga. I was shook! I thought you was that fool Stanley pullin' up like that."

O-Dawg chuckled and strolled up, then said, "That lame ass nigga know better than to fuck around over here again. The way I put the check down on that nigga, he know what it's gon' be if we bump heads again."

I laughed, but gave no real thought to what O-Dawg just said. On the real, I was taken aback at how hard the homie was shining. He wore a gold chain with a big ass cross that was flooded with diamonds. I don't know if them shits were expensive diamonds, but I do know they were real. The designer jeans that he wore, coupled with the Polo boots and black leather jacket was a major indication that the game had been treating him well. "Who's that you riding with?" I asked. "You out here balling so hard that you got a driver now?"

O-Dawg laughed and spared a peek back at the car. "That ain't nobody but this white trick that I been fuckin' with. Her peeps got that paper. They own the Whites Jewelers downtown and a few restaurants in Edmond. Babe bought me this chain in exchange for a real nigga's loyalty." He held it up and the diamonds sparkled in the sunlight.

"I wish I could know me a chick like that. I bet I'll come through stuntin' in all the latest shit. What chu' think niggas gon' be sayin' if I hopped out Gucci down, with a chain that's bigger than yours on?"

We both shared a brief laugh as O-Uawg posted up on the trunk of my car. "What's with all the bags in the back?" He inquired while peering through my back window. "I told you to meet me at my Mom's house, not for you to try and move in!"

"It ain't nothing like that, bruh. Me and Pops had it out this morning. He told me that I had to move out and find my own place to live."

"Damn, for real?"

"For real, my nigga. I guess I'll be staying at Stutter's crib until I get on my feet. Ain't no way I'm trying to move back to Miami with my mother. Them niggas down there be on some whole other shit!" O-Dawg nodded and we both stood gazing down the street. "I heard you was on deck with that work now." I went on to say. "I also heard that you was the man to see if a nigga tryin' to get one."

O-Dawg smiled. "You know I ain't fucked up about pluggin' you in. What type of nigga would I be if I don't look out for you like you used to do for me?" I reached out to give the homie some dap, but right before our fist touched he said. "But I'm taxin'."

"You what?"

"I'm chargin' a little more than what you'd usually pay. It ain't much but that's what I gotta do if a nigga gon' be able to eat out here."

"How much for a zip?" I asked.

"A rack."

"You chargin' a thousand dollars for an ounce?"

O-Dawg shrugged and ran his fingers over his mustache. "Yup, but my shit's some drop though. You can either keep pushing that blow up that's gon' keep you out here starving, or you can pay a little extra and win!"

I had to think about that for a moment. A thousand dollars for an ounce was the most that I'd ever paid. Niggas be frontin' all the time like they had that drop, but once the truth hit the fan— they ain't have nothing but some bullshit. "Fuck it, I got five hunnit right now and I'll pay you the rest when I'm done."

O-Dawg smirked and said. "Don't sweat the small stuff, Kev. This me you talkin' to. Just hit me up in a few days with the rest of what you owe me and there won't be no problem for us to keep doing business."

Fam had no idea how glad I was to hear that That'd give me just enough room to pay Leonard a little something for allowing me to crash at his crib. and I'd still be able to front Stutter a quarter to get on his feet. "Aiight, bet!" I exclaimed, "What chu' need for me to do?"

O-Dawg looked back at his mother's house, then carefully scanned the block. "I don't need you to do nothing." He said. "I got the merch in the car; hop in the backseat and we can handle this right now."

We mobbed out to his car which sat blocking the driveway, I hopped in the back and he hopped in up front. Once inside, O-Dawg pulled out a purple Crown Royal bag and slid it back to me. "That's you right there," he said over the Brother Lynch playing in the deck. "I already weighed everything out before I left the tilt. I was supposed to drop that shit off to somebody else but it is what it is. I put my niggas over everythang! You straight?"

I opened the bag to take a look inside and instantly the smell of powder hit me. "Yeah, I'm straight. I can't wait to whip this shit up and see how those fiends react to it."

O-Dawg bobbed his head to the beat all the while dumping the guts out of a blunt into a bag. "You trying to get high before I roll out?" He asked.

I saw the white chick that was driving pass him a fat sack of weed. "Hell muthafuckin' yeah! You know I'ma need to have my head right before I gotta' go deal with Stutter's peeps!"

Over the next 45 minutes we chopped it up about everything that had been going on. O-Dawg told me about how he'd checked Stanley which led to him stealing the work out of his sister's duffle bag. He even told me how he'd linked up with Justin and started coping work. On the low, I was feeling some kind of way. How the fuck my relative gon' plug him but not fuck with me? Sure my paper was never on baller statues, but if he'd told me a number to reach for, I would've tried.

By the time we finished smoking a blunt, I was more than ready to hit the block and get my chips up. I still had a lot of shit to do, including whip up the work, unpack my things, and put the word out that I was back on deck. "I'ma hit chu' up in a few days when I'm ready," I said as I tapped on the front seat and opened the back door. "Don't start acting brand new when you see my number come across your screen."

O-Dawg burst into laughter and said, "Nigga, you'll be lucky if you don't see me calling you first!"

Just as I began to get out, something inside of me said, *look up.*

*BOOM!* The window next to my head exploded. I fell back into the seat and ducked for cover. *BOOM! BOOM! BOOM!* Slugs hammered into the trunk of the car, rocking it with each devastating blow. I braced myself, expecting to feel something hot rip right through my chest, but instead I heard O-Dawg's girl screaming. She screamed like I've never heard a woman scream before. She screamed so loud that her cries nearly blotted out the sound of more gunfire.

*Packa! Packa! Packa! Packa! Packa!* Bullets burst through the back window causing it to cave in. Cold air poured inside filling my nostrils with the smell of smoke. One minute the car was dim, shadowed by tinted windows, the next thing I knew I was nearly blinded by sunlight.

Suddenly a car engine roared to life as tires squealed away into the distance. I opened my eyes and prayed silently that the madness was finally over. My ears had a terribly loud ringing sound in them, and the only other thing I could hear was O-Dawg's girl screaming.

"Kevin!"

I slowly looked around. It sounded like someone had called my name from hundreds of miles away.

"Kevin!"

I was trembling; my whole body was trembling. I was scared to fucking death; too scared to think about getting up.

"Kevin, are you aiight?"

I followed the sound of the voice until I saw O-Dawg standing at the back door. He held his gun down along his side as if he were trying to keep it out of sight. "I'm good," I replied, but really I wasn't. I don't know what I was. Everything happened so fucking fast. I slowly sat up, finally having the courage to look around.

There were people outside pointing at us as if they couldn't believe we were alive.

Ms. O'Dell rushed over to the car in a mad frenzy. "James, what happened?" She cried.

O-Dawg glared over his shoulder and spat, “What it look like? Somebody shot at us!” Ms. O’Dell felt over his body, checking to make sure that he wasn’t hurt. “I’m good, Mom. I’m good! Why don’t you check on Kevin while I go try to calm Courtney down.”

Ms. O’Dell looked in the backseat and noticed that I’d yet to move. “Kevin, are you okay?” She asked, then kneeled and placed her hand on my thigh.

I nodded like I was cool, but my shit just keep bobbing and bobbing. I don’t think my brain was even working right. All the while I sat there listening to Courtney scream, my shit just kept bobbing and bobbing.

I didn’t realize my shit was still bobbing until O-Dawg barked, “Quit doin’ that shit!” I stopped and looked up at him slightly confused. “Take this and go hide it in the backyard,” he went on to say. “Make sure to hide that work too. The Rollers are gonna be here any minute.”

# Chapter 12
# LASHURA

I don't know what has gotten into everyone around here these days. Every time I look around, it's always something. First, Kevin pointed a gun at Stanley. Then I found out that Stanley had been cheating on me. Next, my own brother felt the need to try and kill Stanley. And now this. I hate that what happened today, happened here at my mother's house. Don't get me wrong. I hate that it even happened, but I hate it even more knowing that my mother had to see everything that happened. I'm sure that it hurts her to know that my brother could've been killed today; to know that this was the path that he'd chosen to go down with his life. Although I've yet to include myself into that same equation, I very well know that I should.

My life hadn't been squeaky clean, void of any wrongdoing. I was just as guilty as my brother was. I'd been involved with a man that sold drugs for the past few years. I may have never sold drugs a day in my life, but he had. I'm sure that I encouraged him to keep doing what he did every time he came home and saw how happy I was in the environment that he created for us. My mother always tried to get me to look at things from that perspective, but I wouldn't. I couldn't. I couldn't see beyond my own selfish desires until now.

I sighed heavily while tossing and turning in my bed; trying to find that comfortable spot where I could fall asleep. The past couple of weeks have been just like that. Miserable. I couldn't do anything without thinking about Stanley. Everything revolved around Stanley. Stanley, Stanley, Stanley.

I overheard my brother tell some of his friends that Stanley was behind what had happened to them this morning. I immediately had to step in and clear that accusation right up. Just because no one knew who shot up James's girlfriend's car didn't give him the right to falsely accuse anyone. Stanley and I were arguing on the phone when the first shots rang out. The last thing anyone needed, in a time like this, was to be falsely accused of something. It doesn't take long for the wrong information to reach the wrong set of ears. The police in Guthrie loved to harass us as it was. But armed with false information, now they could harass us and say that they had probable cause.

After the shooting, I spent the remainder of the day trying to talk some sense into my brother. I thought about renting a hotel room just so I could try to get some rest, but that wouldn't be fair to my mother. I couldn't leave her alone to deal with a yard full of nosey neighbors. After all, this very well could've been a problem that I helped to create.

I ended up deciding to stay until everyone had gone home. Now, it was just me, silence, and loneliness. I miss him. Stanley. I miss him so much that I couldn't even eat. All I did was mope around the house, reliving those blissful memories when I felt happy. I wonder how I ended up there; the place called happy. What made me so content with being with someone knowing that the things he did to provide for us were wrong. Maybe it was designer names of the gifts he showered me in. Although I've never considered myself to be the materialistic type. I had to question my intentions, because of what I chose to accept to achieve a sense of happiness.

The phone rang. I rolled over and looked at it. The alarm clock telephone read, 11:45 P.M. I lie there staring at the clock, listening to the phone rang. "Hello."

"LaShura, please." Stanley said. "Just hear me out for a se—"

*Click.*

I can't do it. I can't do this anymore. I can't listen to all his lies, play his games, or do anything else that may push me further down this lonely road of depression that I've been on. I flung the covers back and sat up. I had to find something to do; something to stay busy, something to keep my mind off of *him*.

Unconsciously my eyes drifted back to the clock. 11:46 P.M. Minutes clawed at the hands of time, anxiously awaiting to change the hour. The hands of time not ready to relinquish their hold on the hour. Time felt like it stopped. It was at a standstill.

If my mother was home, I'd go in her bedroom and sulk until I felt strong enough to face sleep again. But my mother worked the night shift at a nursing home. She wouldn't be home until in the morning. When my parents got divorced, my mother battled her dreadfully lonely moments with addiction. She'd drink until reality wasn't so hard to deal with, then go clock in at work and work until sleep had finally found her.

I wondered if I was addicted to Stanley. I wondered if there was a difference between being in love with someone, and being addicted to them. What does it feel like? Would I know the difference? I wondered if Stanley used Louis Vuitton and other brand name gifts to trap me in his web of love, or addiction. Or, maybe my attraction to Stanley ran much deeper than the finer things that he provided for me. Maybe in order for me to understand why I ended up with him, I needed to understand what attracted me to him in the first place.

I clicked on the lamp; 11:48 stared back at me in big red numbers. I slipped on my shoes and headed toward the restroom. But right before I walked out of the bedroom, the phone rang.

"Shit!" *Fight it*, I told myself. *Don't answer the fucking phone. Don't give into the desire just to hear his voice; to hear the lies that sounded so believable; the pleas ending with us both in tears because neither of us wanted to let go.*

I rushed into the restroom and splashed my face with cold water. "You've got to get over him!" I wiped my face with a towel then peered intently at myself in the mirror. My hair looked a mess—tiny strands dangled from the side of my head. The rubber band that held my ponytail together was barely hanging on. I even had bags under my eyes now.

Having had enough of looking at the mess that I'd made of myself, I retired into the living room. The family portraits that decorated the walls brought a smile to my solemn face. I reached under the coffee table and pulled out a photo album from beneath it. *O'Dell Family* read across the front of it in big gold letters. When I opened it, I began to understand happiness. I began to understand what brought me happiness and how I ended up in the place called Happy.

"LaShura! Come give Daddy some suga." The sound of my father's voice instantly filled me with lots of excitement. He was my everything— my protector, my provider. My friend. Everything.

Being raised in a household with a male sibling, you'd think I'd be prone to be under my mother, but I wasn't. I was a Daddy's girl. Wherever I was hiding, or whatever I was doing, whenever my father called my name, I'd race into his embrace. Momma would always try to convince Daddy that he was spoiling me, but Daddy wouldn't hear of it. I was their first born child and Daddy adored me.

Life was like it should be while I was a child. In fact, life was so good I find myself always trying to get back to that perfect space in time. The love that my parents expressed toward one another was like no other. They couldn't get enough of each other. No matter where they were they showered each other in tender, loving affection. But somewhere in between the good times and drowning each other in loving affection, the devil came knocking. I don't know who let him in, but when he came in he destroyed everything.

Often times, my brother and I were sent outside to play as if we had no idea about what was going on. James could probably care less. He was always too busy sneaking around with the neighbor's daughter. Seemed like I was the only one that was genuinely concerned about what was happening. I'd sit next to my parents' bedroom window and listen to them yell at each other which tore me apart inside. I couldn't imagine what may have happened to make them express such hatred toward one another. We were just one big happy family. Life was perfect.

After my parents spent the better half of an hour trying to diminish the other's self-esteem, my father would always leave. Soon as I heard his car start up, I'd run as fast as I could to try and stop him from leaving. Often times than not, the only thing I'd be fortunate enough to see were his taillights barreling down the street. Confused with a face streaked with tears I'd sit right there in the driveway and wait for his return. Sometimes I'd sit there so long I may doze off and wake up to my mother telling me it was time to eat.

Sometimes, I'd wake up to my father carrying me back inside. Sometimes, I'd wake up and my father had yet to return.

As weeks turned into months and months turned into years, my little brother Calvin was born. I just knew he'd be just what our family needed to make us perfect again. Calvin had a smile that was infectious; he could make the meanest person smile. I knew in my heart that his birth would bring us all close again, and give us a reason to be happy, but it didn't. For some reason or another, my parents grew further apart and soon after got a divorce. Why? We were never told why. All I knew was whatever happened between my mother and father was too much for Daddy to handle.

I was right there watching as my mother begged for his forgiveness and tried to stop him from leaving. Daddy literally had to pry Momma's hands off his thigh just to get out the front door. I didn't know what to think when I saw that. I hadn't ever saw my father treat my mother that way. My father was my hero, my provider. My protector; our protector.

"Momma!" I raced across the living room to where she lie drowning in her own tears by the front door. "Momma, don't cry. It's gonna be okay! It's gonna be okay!" I cradled my mother in my arms, rocking her as if she were my own child. I'd never seen her cry like this; not Momma, not like this.

Even as Momma lie crying her heart out, Daddy walked back and forth caring his bags out to the car as if we weren't even there.

"Daddy, why are you doing this?" I cried. "If you're leaving because of something I've done, then I'm sorry. I promise that I won't do it again."

Daddy peered down at me with a look torn between enraged and heartbroken and said, "It's not your fault, LaShura. Your mother and I just need some time apart so that we can iron out our differences."

As if his final words were my mother's last chance to save their marriage. she lunged for him. "Maurice, don't do this!" She screamed. "I'm begging you. Please!"

I held on to Momma with all my might. She clawed at the air, hoping to latch on to him; hoping to latch on to the hands of time and rest them; one minute before disaster, one minute before they hated each other. Back when they were happy. But Daddy was gone.

It took weeks before Momma had the will to step outside the walls of her bedroom. Her nights were spent with muffled cries into her pillow. Her days spent staring at a blank television screen. Everything that she couldn't do for us, I did it. I made sure we ate, showered, got ready for school and everything else in between.

Things got so hectic due to the weight of my new responsibilities, my teacher started to notice a change in me. I wasn't the same happy, energetic person that I'd always been. I remember the principal called me into his office to find out what was going on. But I wouldn't dare tell a soul what was going on at home. We already had enough problems as it was. When my principle asked me was there something going on that I wanted to talk about, I simply said no. I told him the reason why I'd been acting the way I had was because my period had me feeling extra irritable. He offered me some after school counseling I suppose because he knew I was lying to him. But I assured him that everything was fine, and promised that I'd get back to acting like my old self.

When my mother's side of the family caught wind of how bad things had gotten, my Uncle Tim offered to move in. I figured that'd take some weight off my shoulders with the presence of another adult. I'd be able to live up to my promise. Come to find out Uncle Tim was drowning in his own pool of misery.

Amongst whatever secrets him and my mother confided in one another, some of those secrets crept out in the open for all to see. Their secrets could no longer just be a discussion held behind closed doors or shrouded by ignorance. Some secrets are easily hidden; you can hide them forever. But some secrets aren't so easily hidden. No matter where you hide them they'd eventually make their way to the light.

I sensed something was wrong with Uncle Time the first day he moved in. His gaunt face and clothing that no longer fit because he was too skinny was a tell-tale sign of a sickness I'd come to learn about through watching television. When I finally figured out that Uncle Tim had been battling with drug addiction, I made up my mind that I had to go. I refused to sit back and watch my family destroy themselves. It was bad enough that my mother was an alcoholic. Now this.

I used all that negativity happening around me as incentive to push me through high school. I kept my head in a book and plowed through school like a mad scientist. I graduated from Guthrie High School with a 4.0 GPA, and immediately enrolled at Langston University.

I remember the first day of school like it happened yesterday. The positive energy buzzing through the campus was intoxicating. The feeling of just being there felt utterly amazing. Besides the thrill of finally being out on my own, I was amongst people like me; people that wanted more for themselves; people that hadn't given up on life; people that didn't mind taking the extra step to get what they wanted out of life.

When I enrolled at Langston University, I signed up for a 2-year program to get my Associate of Science. I wanted to become a Registered Nurse. My mother was a Certified Nurse's Assistant. I wanted to take it one step further than she did. I didn't want to look up twenty years later with no one to confide in, but a drug addict for a brother, or a bottle.

I took to my school work with just as much vigor as I'd used to push me through high school. All I did was work and study. I had no life outside of making a better future for myself. The job that I had paid just enough to keep me from asking my mother for money. I worked at a small restaurant inside the school's cafeteria. It really wasn't nothing to be proud of, but it wasn't something to be ashamed of either.

Occasionally I'd look up and see James and Kevin sneak into the cafeteria. Back then, those two were inseparable. Whenever my dad went to visit my brothers, he'd allow James to use the car for a while. I'm sure Kevin had something to do with them ending up at my job; him and the slew of girls running around the campus.

"What do ya'll want?" I asked, and swiped my bangs across my forehead. I was tired. My feet hurt. All I needed to do was clean up and clock out.

"What chu' mean, what do we want?" Kevin quipped. "You know the drill. Let me get a Double Whopper with a large order of French fries."

"And don't forget my strawberry shake with that," James added.

I just looked at dumb and dumber like they were crazy. I knew they didn't have any money; they never did. They called themselves hustling, slash pimping, but neither one of their occupations was working. To keep from causing a big scene that would ultimately end with me being fired, I went ahead and made their order. "Here!" I slid them a tray of food across the counter, causing French fries to spill out.

"Nah, where's the homie's milkshake?" Kevin snapped.

Lord knows I wanted to snatch his boney ass right over that counter, but no one knew James was my brother. I didn't want to raise any suspicion that I was giving them free food. Had my boss not been watching me from her office, I'd have cussed both they asses out. "Sorry about that," I said and forced a weak smile as I handed James his milkshake. "You two have a nice day." I busied myself wiping down counters while Kevin and my brother sat down at a table nearby.

I couldn't help but notice how hard Kevin was sweating me. Every guy that walked up and placed an order, Kevin was checking to see if he was trying to holler. I knew then I'd have to put a restraining order on his young ass. He'd been a serial stalker since I was in high school. The only difference between then and now was that we were getting older.

As the hands of time continued to wind around the clock, days flew by turning into weeks. I started dating a guy named Darrel. I met him by chance when I accidently bumped into him in a rush to get to class. Darrel was the captain of the basketball team. He'd enrolled at Langston to get his bachelor's in business administration. He was a senior with half of the campus vying for his attention. I suppose you could consider me lucky to catch the attention of such a prominent person. All the stories he'd told me about girls swinging off his coattail sounded ridiculous. We hit it off instantly. I can't say if that was more so because of me, or the other way around.

We went out on a few dates to the movies, out to dinner, typical things that people do during courtship. After a while, I began to feel as if we were a couple. Darrel became the only person who I felt comfortable enough to confide in. I didn't have any friends at the time outside of a girl named Nikki. I wasn't the type of chick that liked to deal with other females. Either they were too messy, conniving, or flat out just the kind of bitch that I don't fuck with. But Nikki, she was cool. Nikki was a devote Christian and her favorite response to anything bad that I said, had something to do with her belief system.

"Nikki. Look at that print in his pants."

"Girl. God don't like ugly."

"Nikki, why you don't have a boyfriend?"

"God will give me just what I need when the timing is right."

"Nikki, you gon' work yourself to death with all that studying you doing."

"I rebuke that in the name of Jesus! It was Gods Will for me to study and learn. Why do you think he allowed me to enroll in collage?"

Not long after Darrel and I started dating, homecoming came around. I was finally able to pull Nikki away from studying long enough to go to the game with me. It was the Langston Lions against Washburn University. The Lions had yet to win a game that season, but that night, they were dead locked at 88 points and the Lions could see their first victory on the horizon.

"Jump ball!" The referee shouted as Darrel and another player fought for possession of the ball.

Half of the crowd cheered with excitement, the other half booed and cursed the official for his judgement. Darrel took his position in front of his opponent. They stared each other down while anxiously awaiting the tossup.

The ref took his position between them and spared a peek from left to right. "Ready?" He asked, and blew the whistle.

Darrel got a hand on the ball first and done a shuffle pass to the point-guard; who dribbled down court and dumped it off to the center. The center was a tall, lanky sophomore that went by the name Smiley. Smiley had yet to score any point all night, yet decided to go up for a dunk.

"Uhhh!" The crowd exclaimed in utter disappointment as the ball bounced off the rim.

Number 3 of the Washburn's Ichabods grabbed the ball and barreled down court. He spied his teammate cut across court and threw a no-look pass. Deflected. Darrel broke away with the ball, headed the other way. The clock was winding down. There wasn't but a few more seconds on the clock and the Langston Lions would be forced into overtime.

The crowd chanted, "Ten! Nine! Eight! Seven!"

Darrel dribbled between his legs, shook an opponent; almost lost the ball, but managed to maintain.

"Six! Five! Four!"

Darrel ran up to the 3-point line looking for an open shot. Washburn players were all over him. It was now or never. He found an opening. He shoots. He scored. The crowd went crazy. Langston students poured onto the floor celebrating our last-second victory. I was so excited that all I could do was scream.

Nikki jumped up and down, shouting, "Jesus! Jesus! Jesus!" Her eyes were wide with excitement. Her glasses were one bounce from slipping off of her nose and falling to the floor.

"Come on!" I took her by the hand and led the way into the electrifying frenzy.

People were yelling and screaming everywhere. I had to be sure to keep a firm hold of Nikki's hand. She was way too little to get stranded in the middle of a crowd that big. People would surely walk right over her. By the time we'd elbowed our way through the crowd, I was worn out. I saw Darrel with the rest of his team shouting and jumping all over the place.

"Hey, babe," I cooed, while congratulating him in a sweaty embrace. "I can't believe you made that shot at the buzzer."

Darrel froze and looked surprised. His eyes darted from me to Nikki. Nikki to the group of girls celebrating behind us.

"What's wrong?" I asked and swiped my hand over his face, then held his cheeks.

"Nothing," he replied. "I'm just a little tired, that's all. Are you ready?" I nodded and he took me by the hand and led the way.

The crowd was unrelenting in their celebrating frenzy. We may have had to fight to reach Darrel and the rest of the team, but we had to fight just as hard once everyone realized that the star of the night was leaving.

Shortly after the game there was a homecoming party at The Lion's Den. The Lion's Den was a club that looked just about like everything else in Langston or Guthrie; everything was old, unsafe, or moments from falling to the ground. The parking lot was partially gravel, mostly dirt, weeds and potholes. The inside of the club didn't look much better, yet students still flocked to the place.

"When do you think he'll be here?" Nikki asked, while peering up at me curiously. "We've already been here for over an hour. How much longer do you wanna wait?"

I shrugged and looked around the room. Darrel told me to meet him there instead of wait around for him to get ready. He told me that he and his friends made plans to meet up at the club at the same time. At first, I didn't give any real thought to something may have been up. But the later that it got, the more I started to feel as if I'd been stood up. "I don't know," I finally admitted. "What do you say we stop waiting around for him? How about we have ourselves a drink and spend the rest of the night trying to enjoy ourselves?"

Nikki rolled her eyes, openly expressing her discomfort with my idea. She made it perfectly clear that she was pissed.

The DJ played one of my favorite songs by Guy, titled *Piece of My Love*. Instantly, everyone swarmed the dancefloor. People were bumping and grinding so hard it looked like they were making love on the dancefloor. "That's my jam!" I shouted, and swirled my hips to the beat.

Nikki looked at me like I was crazy. She wouldn't do anything that may imply that she wasn't being Christian-like.

"Do you mind if I have this dance?" A dark skin brother with pearly white teeth asked Nikki.

"Jesus, Jesus, Jesus, Jesus, Jesus." She whispered.

"Nikki, stop it!" I nudged her with my elbow and almost pushed her into the man's arms. "Gon' on and have some fun. The bible don't say that it's a sin to dance with someone."

Nikki's eyes wandered over the gorgeous man in front of her. He was nicely dressed in black slacks with a purple button-down shirt. He seemed to be just the type of guy that she'd be attracted to. "*One* dance." Nikki stated firmly, and held a finger in the man's face.

"One." He agreed, then took Nikki by the hand and led her to the dancefloor.

As I stood by the bar, trying my damnedest not to appear left out, my attention was drawn to a guy that I'd been noticing around campus as of lately. I really couldn't see him that well because he was across the room in the DJ booth. But I could see him well enough to know that he was looking in my direction. I'd asked Nikki about him on several different occasions, but she'd only say he was bad news, and leave it at that. Mr. Mysterious.

"Excuse me, are you waiting for someone?"

I looked back hoping to see Darrel trying to be funny, but it was Kevin. "What are you doing here?" I asked.

Kevin licked his lips and eased closer to me. "I'm here to see you," he replied smoothly.

"Nigga, if you don't—" I had to catch myself. Kevin wasn't nothing but a child. "This is a collage homecoming party for students only! How did you get in here?"

"We were invited."

"Boy, stop lying! And what do you mean, we? Is my brother in here with you?" I looked just beyond Kevin and saw James hugged up with two girls. "I'm going to give y'all five seconds to get outta' my face. If y'all still standing here by the time I get to five, I'ma go over there and tell those guards that you're not supposed to be in here."

"Damn, it's like that?"

"One."

"But I thought you loved me."

"Two." I didn't have to say anything else because they'd reluctantly walked away. Just as I was about to turn around and order a drink, I saw Darrel headed over to VIP.

"Darrel!" I shouted as loud as I could, but he didn't hear me.

The music was loud as hell, not to mention everyone had transformed into the next Aaron Hall set. I instantly recognized several of the starting players simply by how tall they were. They even had the nerve to have their own fake ass security detail as if they were famous. By the time I'd made it through the club they'd already roped the VIP section back off. No one was allowed in unless you had a pass or someone in VIP gave you the okay.

"Hold up." A guard sassed while holding me back with his arm. "Where the fuck you think you're going? I can't let you through here unless you've got a pass."

I saw Darrel seated on a big red sofa with several of his friends. It wasn't until they lifted their glasses to purpose a toast that I noticed the chick seated next to him. I recalled seeing her after the game earlier. Then, it didn't resister to me that something may have been going on, but now it did.

"That's my boyfriend right there." I explained, and yelled, "Darrel!"

This time we made eye contact. This time a look of surprise showed clear as day on his face. This time he began to get up, but the chick beside him pulled him back down and kissed him.

"Oh really?"

I stormed off steaming hot, but I'd be damned if I wasn't coming back. This was exactly the reason I don't deal with bitches; they're too messy. Men can be just as conniving and sneaky as the next bitch. They know how to play the innocent role to the tee, all the while they're creeping around town with the next bitch.

I trusted Darrel with all of me. I never lied to him. I never cheated on him. I never did anything outside of be the best woman that I could be for him. If he thought for one second that I was about to settle for being humiliated in front of the whole club, he was in for a rude awakening.

"Can I get two bottles of Budwiser please?" I was at the bar trying my best to appear calm, but I couldn't stand still. I didn't know whether to cross my arms, lean on the counter, or rest my hands on my waist. I was doing all kinds of weird shit. I'm sure to anyone that may have been watching that I was up to something.

"That'll be seven dollars." The bartender said.

My mind was so consumed with beatin' a bitch's ass I didn't even think to protest that overpriced beer. I quickly pulled out the money and slammed it down on the bar.

"Aye yo! I saw how them dudes strained you up in VIP," a man said behind me. "I got all access passes to every room in the building. If you still trying to fall up in there, you can roll with me."

I spun around and it was Mr. Mysterious. I have to admit, the brother was fine as hell. Had it been another time and place, I may have entertained his feeble pass at me. "I don't think it'll be a good idea for you to be over there when I get behind those ropes." I said as I pulled my hair up into a ponytail.

"Word? You gettin' down like that. Ma? Sound like you about to go start a bunch of shit."

I snatched the bottles off the counter and said, "Best believe I ain't the type that's gon' start nothing, but I'll damn sho' finish some shit." I struck out through the crowd. Anyone that didn't move, although they knew damn well that they saw me coming, I walked straight into them and dared them to say something.

I guess Mr. Mysterious wasn't done talking yet. He quickly caught up to me and jumped in my way. "Yo, chill!" He exclaimed.

I looked at him like his breath stank. "Nigga. Move."

"Don't call me that."

"Well. Move!"

"I can't do that. You about to go over there and do something that'll probably get you thrown outta school. You might even fuck up this bangin' ass party, and for what?"

I was in no mood for anyone's pep talk. I tried to walk around him but he grabbed me by the waist. "Negro, if you don't get cho' hands of me."

"My name is, Stanley."

"Do it look like I give a damn?"

"I know you don't, but that don't mean I'm fixin' to let you keep disrespecting me. I'm trying to do you a favor. You about to do something that you'll later regret. Not to mention fuck off all the money I spent to throw this party."

I forced a weak laugh. "Figures." Not only was Stanley not about to let me go anywhere, but somehow, Darrel managed to slip out of my sight. I stood on my tiptoes and scanned every inch of the room. I was so upset that I already had tears racing down my cheeks.

"My bad, Ma." Stanley said apologetically. He stepped in my line of sight and brushed away my tears with his thumb. "I ain't mean to make you cry. I just wanted to get your attention. I don't want you to do something that you'll later regret. Whatever whomever did to piss you off, take that as confirmation that you don't need 'em."

The truth is a hard pill to swallow. One minute I was clutching two bottles, ready to set this bitch off, the next I'd hurled them to the floor and lost it. I thought surely Stanley would have his security escort me out of the club, but he didn't. He gently pulled me into his arms and just held me. I cried and cried. I cried like there would be no tomorrow.

The next thing I know, I heard Nikki yelling my name. "LaShura!"

I felt her tug at Stanley's arms trying to unwrap them from around me.

"You need to fall the fuck back, shorty." Stanley growled. "I got this."

Just like that, several linebacker built security guards surrounded us.

"She's with me!" I shouted and shoved Stanley away from me. When I jumped in front of Nikki to protect her, she draped her arm over my shoulder and guided me outside.

The cool night air was exactly what I needed. I felt like I was about to suffocate inside that building. I fanned my face and lifted my ponytail so that I could feel the cool night air on my neck. We were just about to walk over to Nikki's car when I spotted Darrel's blue Ford Tempo. While Nikki's attention was consumed with trying to figure out what happened, my sights were dead locked on Darrel's car. Someone was in it.

I took off full speed across the parking lot and almost broke my neck. I tripped over something that was sticking up out of the ground and went airborne, but lucky for me, Stanley was right there to catch me.

"Slow down, Ma." He said. "Where you off to in such a hurry?"

I heard him, but I wasn't trying to talk. I saw how he'd managed to block my view of Darrel's car, but I'd already seen all that I need to see. I shook free from Stanley's grasp so fast, all that I could hear was him calling my name behind me. I ran up to Darrel's car door thinking I was finally about to check his ass; I was finally about to know the truth.

Who was she? Were they fucking? How long had he known her? 1,008 questions ran through my mind, but suddenly the world stopped. Maybe not the H-Town I heard rattling his trunk. Or maybe not even the fact that his car kept rocking. Just my world, my heart. I think that's all that stopped. Darrel didn't have any tint on his windows. Although the driver's side back window was partially foggy, I still had a clear view of Darrel's naked ass. He was fucking.

*BOOM!* "Open this fucking door!" I kicked his door so hard that I'm surprised my foot didn't go straight through it.

Darrel looked back, seemingly startled. He had a girl's leg pinned back and was in mid-stroke. When I saw his ass cheeks tighten as if he'd decided to push deeper inside of that girl, I snapped.

*BOOM! POW! PING-TING-TING-TING-SPLASH!* Glass flew everywhere. The next thing I knew, someone picked me up from behind and was trying to carry me away. They'd pay for it.

"Ahhh! Shit!" A man howled out in pain. I'd kicked him in his chin, clawed up his arm. I think I may have even headbutted him a few times. By the time the man finally put me back down, he was hurt.

"Hel-Hel-Help me get her in my truck," Stanley stammered.

I peered over the hood of Stanley's red Chevy Trail Blazer that he'd managed to pin me to. Nikki was standing there looking scared to death. I knew she would not be helping him put me in his truck.

"Let me go!" I yelled.

"No, uh-uhn. You trippin', LaShura," Stanley said. "I'm trying to do you a favor, Ma."

This negro was not gon' learn until I fucked his ass up too. I squirmed around a bit and somehow managed to get us off the truck. When Stanley went to try and pin me back against the truck, *BOOM!* I kicked it. Why did I do that?

That negro squeezed me so hard that my whole body went limp. I tried to tell him that I give; I'll get in the damn truck, but Stanley had already got the door open and sat me inside. I just sat there like the good little girl I was and cried until he'd buckled me in. I saw Nikki peek over Stanley's shoulder, shocked to see me acting that way. But, to hell with her. I was hurt. I was crushed. My whole world felt like it had come to a screeching halt, but really it was just about to began.

"Bitch, you busted out my window!" Darrel quipped. He mobbed up to Stanley's truck with several people in tow.

"I sure did!" I screamed at the top of my lungs. "You lucky I didn't bust you and that damn bitch's head in, bitch!"

Stanley had just buckled me in, but I was fighting with all of my might to get that seatbelt off of me. I was just about to pop off with something else slick when I saw Stanley pull something from under the seat.

"I know y'all better get the fuck from around my truck!" Stanley growled.

"Or what?" Darrel snarled. Darrel was so busy playing tough that he didn't notice that Stanley had a gun. He didn't see him when he'd cocked it back. He had no idea who he was dealing with.

Several of Darrel's friends began to press in on Stanley, preparing to jump him. I reached out and tried to pull Stanley back in the truck, but someone swung. *POP! POP! POP!* Stanley opened fire sending people scattering everywhere. I heard car alarms going off. I heard people screaming. I heard people yelling. I heard cars start up. I heard cars speed away. When the dust had finally began to settle, I saw Nikki. She'd been shot. The phone rang.

"Shit!

I didn't want to answer it, but in a way I did. All that time I'd sat there flipping through old photos brought back a lot of memories. Some of which made me happy, while many made me sad. When it was all said and done, I knew why I loved Stanley so much. There wasn't a person in this world that sacrificed what he had for me. I was ready to hear his lies. I was ready to try and believe them. Whatever I had to do to get us back to that happy place where we once were, I was ready to do it.

"Hello."

*Clickety-click-click-click-click. Clickety-click-click-click-click. Clickety-click-click-click-click.*

I peered down at the phone trying to figure out what in the hell that sound was. "Hello!"

*Clickety-click-click-click-click. Clickety-click-click-click-click. Clickety-click-click-click-click.*

I hung up.

# Chapter 13
# The Present
# KEVIN

I woke up this morning with tears in my eyes. Everything that I dreamt about was the type of things that should keep the average person up at night.

Yesterday, a nurse came in to change my bandages and noticed me staring in a daze out of my hospital room window. She asked me if something was wrong, did I need any help? I simply played it off like everything was cool and told her that I was just thinking; thinking about the boy; the coyotes; the birds that I'd sed down by the stream. I asked her was I crazy for thinking that I'd saw what I'd seen. She laughed and assured me that I wasn't. She told me, when we see things that the mind doesn't understand, our brain goes to work trying to break down the unknown, into something that we do understand. When I thought about it, it made sense. What I'd seen down by the stream didn't.

Several taps at my door drew my attention toward it. "Kevin, how are you feeling this morning?"

I sighed and swiped one hand over my face. Pastor Johnson returned, except he'd brought someone with him. "I'm still here," I replied. "And the way things are looking, I probably won't be getting outta here anytime soon."

Pastor Johnson nodded in understanding and looked at the man standing next to him. "This is Deacon Jenkins from the church," Pastor Johnson went on to say. "I told you that I'd be bringing someone with me the next time I stopped by."

Deacon Jenkins walked up and extended his hand for a handshake, but I just looked at it, then looked up at him. Cats like him I don't too much fuck wit'. He reminded me of that snake ass nigga Cabbage, except this dude wore dark tinted glasses which made it hard for me to see his eyes. He had several gold teeth and wore a suit that was jet black, just like Pastor Johnson's.

We shook.

"The Pastor has told me a lot about you," Deacon Jenkins began by saying as he pulled up a chair alongside my bed. "I figured it must be God's will that I stop by and have a word with you, especially being that it was on my heart to do so."

I shot Pastor Johnson a sideways look before returning my gaze to Deacon Jenkins. "I told the Pastor that I wasn't ready to meet with anyone," I replied. "If he told you anything about me, then you should know that now wasn't the time for this."

Denkin Jenkins smiled and sat down, despite what I'd just told him. Pastor Johnson strolled across the room and sat down in a chair by the window. I looked between they asses like they were crazy.

"Every day is the time for what I came to bear witness of," Deacon Jenkins went on to say.

"Haven't we all heard that one before," I stated sarcastically. "Don't get me wrong, I ain't knockin' nothing that y'all are trying to do. I get it. I'm going to hell if I don't do what y'all tell me to."

"Who told you that?"

"Deacon, please. I have too much going on to be playing these games with you. I got the feds snooping around, asking questions. Detectives stop by here every hour on the hour. I have problems sleeping at night, and now this."

"I'm not here to do what those other people have been doing to you, Kevin. I'm here to help you understand why you're here. You're in a dark place; a state of confusion. I want you to see the light. I want you to understand."

I slowly shook my head and replied, "And just how do you think you're going to help me understand? I guess you're going to open your bible and read me some ancient ass story about some shit that don't have nothing to do with me. Then, I suppose you're going to take that same story, turn it around, and make it out to fit the situation that I'm dealing with?"

"No, I'm going to tell you a little about me. I'm going to use my trials and tribulations; my triumphs as a testimony of God's Grace. We have a whole lot more in common than you think we do, Kevin."

"Oh, we do? I don't think you have people chasing you around trying to kill you. And I damn sure don't think you had to stand by and watch someone you loved get gunned down."

"I might not have people trying to kill me, now. But that's not to say that I haven't dealt with that problem in the past. Do you think that you're the only person in the world that has had something tragic happen to them, because of their dealings with the streets?"

I simply sat there and mugged his ass. I already told these dudes that now wasn't the time. The fuck I look like being nice and entertaining his sarcastic remarks?

Deacon Jenkins chuckled and said, "Sadly, if you think you're the only one that has been victimized because of your dealings in the streets, then you've been mistaken. When I told you that we have a lot in common, it's because we do. We both chose to go through this thing we call life the hard way. We chose the streets. But what you've failed to understand is when we chose the streets, we chose everything that comes with it."

"I didn't choose the game; the game chose me! If my father would've—"

"Your father didn't make you chose a life of crime." Deacon Jenkins stated sternly. "You made that decision, not him. That choice was yours for you alone to make. Although we both made the choice to learn life the hard way, I'm going to show you why that choice wasn't in vain. I'm going to help you understand why you're still alive. I'm going to help you see that God had a plan for you."

"Here we go with this bullshit again," I groaned.

"Yeah, that way!" Deacon Jenkins fired back. "Why do you think that you're still alive, Kevin? If what I heard, and what you say is true, then what makes you so special? People die every day, Kevin. Every. Single. Day. You've got people chasing you around trying to kill you; yet, here you are talking to me."

On the real, I was ready to check the shit outta this nigga. Being nice to these dudes had done nothing but made me more pissed off. Although part of me wanted to set these fools straight, the other half of me wanted to hear what he had to say. "Okay, look," I finally said. "I don't know why I'm still alive. I just am. If everything you've told me is true, then why are you still here? You claim to have been in similar situations as me, then how did you survive?"

Deacon Jenkins peered over at Pastor Johnson and smiled. I could tell by the way he was acting that I'd probably asked just the question that he'd been waiting for me to ask.

**15 Years Ago**
**O-DAWG**

*Clickety-click-click-click-click. Clickety-click-click-click-click. Clickety-click-click-click-click. SHRK! Thump.* "Ergh...mmmmh." *Shrk. Thump-thump.* Whatever the fuck that noise is, it's about to make me lose my fuckin' mind. Just when I'd finally got comfortable enough so that I could go back to sleep, I heard it again. *SHRK! Thump-thump. Shrk. Clickety-click-click-click-click. Clickety-click-click-click-click. Clickety-click-click-click-click.*

The chattering sound of my own teeth isn't what bothered me. It's not even the fact that it's freezing fuckin' cold and I can't feel my hands or my feet. It's that *SHRK* like when a spade hits the ground. Moments later that unnerving sound is followed by a dull *Thump* as if someone is stomping the spade into the ground. If only I had the strength to get up and put an end to that irritating noise, I would, but I felt weak, tired, and all I wanted to do was sleep.

***

Everyday felt like my inner glow was shining brighter and brighter. While the rest of my hood felt the chill of winter in its wake, I was the hottest thang movin' in the streets. It seemed like doors opened after I stole that work outta' my sister's duffel bag. People that never would've looked my way for anything were now faithfully swingin' on my nuts. Like that fat ass nigga Justin. He must've heard I was making moves and pulled up on me while I was bustin' a swerve.

"O-Dawg, wuz poppin', kinfolk?" Justin exclaimed.

I peered though the side mirror on Cortney's car as Justin strolled up. Cortney had been driving me around all that day bustin' swerves. I got a call from a nigga named Daz, and he asked me to stop by his crib. When I pulled up, I noticed all the niggas standing in the yard gettin' faded. I thought Daz would most definitely be trying to spend a little gwop wit' a nigga, but when he walked out to the car, all he was talkin' about was would I front him something.

"You know me," I finally replied to Justin. "I'm out here trying to get it, but it's all these buster ass niggas in the way. But, peep game. I'ma need you to move your load 'cause you blockin' us. My girl is ready to bounce, plus, these niggas ain't got no money."

Justin chuckled and seemed to pay my request no mind. "I've been hearing a lotta' good thangs about you, kinfolk," Justin said. "I heard that you was out here puttin' it down like a one-man army. I also heard how you handled that bitch ass nigga Stanley, and how you've managed to side-step the ops up at The Ghetto."

I took his little compliment as if it were a grain of salt. Can't no nigga butter me up just to get gobbled up. "Yeah, I did that," I replied. "But, I'ma still need for you to move your car. I don't like being boxed in, especially when it's so many mark ass niggas out here hatin'."

Justin nodded as if he understood, but said, "I'm the real reason why you're here, not because of Daz. I told folks to have you stop by so we could talk."

"About what?"

"Business."

"What kind of business do you need to holla' at me about?"

Justin looked at Daz then back at me, and smirked. "I don't *need* to holla at no nigga about nothing! I'm a boss, which means I do whatever the fuck I wanna do. I told Daz to have you stop by so I could present you with a proposition."

I sized Justin up for talkin' that slick shit. If it ain't but one thang I live and die for, a muthafucka gon' respect me. "What kind of proposition do you have to offer me, Boss?"

Justin chuckled, picking up on my sarcasm and said, "The kind of proposition that's gon' keep yo' black ass alive and still getting money." Justin walked up alongside Daz and pulled out a wad of $100 bills. "Do you see this?" He went on to say. "This is What gettin' money looks like. That comment you made about my niggas not havin' money was the furthest thing from the truth. We out here papered the fuck up. Daz, show 'em what it look like to have knots."

Daz pulled out a knot; the niggas in the yard pulled out even more knots.

I was so throwed off to see all that money, I was starting to get curious as to what Justin was trying to say. "So, you called me over here just so y'all can stunt on me?" I asked.

Justin laughed and said, "The fuck you thank this is, kinfolk? I wanted you here to see if you'd like to be a part of this. I know what kind of obstacles that you're up against. And I know that it's only a matter of time before the dirt that you've done finally catches back up to you. I want you to understand, any muthafucka that's down with me, I'ma make sure that the whole 'hood got cho' back. That little situation between you and Stanley is over the day you choose to get down with us."

The longer I sat listening to what Justin had to say, the more he'd helped me to see the advantages of being down with his team. Sure, I knew that Kevin copped his work from Justin, but Kevin was too careless. Justin needed somebody he could count on; someone that was an asset not a dependent; someone that was down to take it there and that person just so happened to be me. Needless to say, I chose to get down with Justin and his crew. The way I saw it, it didn't make any sense to face all of these obstacles alone. As long as I copped my work from Justin and continued to be about my paper, I had a clique of die-hard riders at my disposal.

I guess when Cortney realized that I was officially apart of a clique that was really gettin' money, her position as the side bitch had magically transformed her into my main chick. There wasn't nothing that I couldn't ask shorty to do that she wouldn't do. Within a few short days, Cortney asked me to move in with her. She lived in a two story wooden shake just outside Langston. Cortney's parents bought the house to use as rental property, but Cortney was insistent that we'd be the ones staying there for a while.

I used to count up stacks of dough in Cortney's living room. Sometimes, I'd leave it in bundles, then make shorty put on a show for me. Cortney would do all sorts of freaky things. Most of the time, she'd like to dance in front of me naked, but if I'd had a good day on the block, Cortney's favorite treat was to suck my dick all night long.

Cortney had a six-year-old daughter named Saira. Half the time Saira would be with her grandparents, but whenever shorty was at home, she made it hard for Cortney and me to get our freak on. Every time I looked up, Saira would be running through the house.

*Doom-doom-doom-doom-doom-doom-doom!*

"Saira, stop running in the house, honey!" Cortney yelled.

Although Cortney was a stone-cold freak, she was still a good mother. Between Cortney and her mother, Saira wasn't wantin' for notin'. On the cool, I could tell Cortney's mom felt some kinda way about me and Cortney being together. Every time she came by the crib, she'd always have something to complain about.

"Who's been smoking weed in my house?" Cortney's mom quipped.

I just ignored her dumb ass. I know she saw me sittin' there lookin' high as hell. But it never failed.

When Saira was home, she'd run her snitchin' ass in there and tell it. "Grandma Grandma!" Saira cried out. "James been smokin' that stinky stuff in the house."

Cortney's mom spun around and glared at me. I guess she thought because I lived in one of her rental houses that she was gon' be able to tell me what to do. *Wrong.* "James, I don't want you bringing all of your drugs and bad habits around Saira," Cortney's mother snapped.

"And I don't want you thinkin' just because you own this place that I'ma do whatever the fuck you tell me to do."

Cortney's mother gasped. "Excuse me? If you can't respect me by following my rules, then I have no problem with calling the police and having you escorted outta here!"

Instead of going back and forth with her about something that wasn't gon' ever change, I just left the conversation alone. Nothing good was gon' come from me makin' her see things my way. She'd already threatened to call the police on me. What more did I need to hear?

*Clickety-click-click-click-click. Clickety-click-click-click-click. Clickety-click-click-click-click.*

"Bring his ass on over here so we can get this shit over with!" Someone shouted.

I felt someone grab me by the shirt and started dragging me across the ground. I opened my eyes to see Cortney cradling Saira, just a few feet away. We were in the woods. It was dark, cold, and I couldn't stop shivering. The only thing illuminating our surroundings was a set of headlights from a car parked several yards away.

"Leave him alone!" Cortney cried out. "You don't have to do this. You've already taken his money, his jewelry, all of his dope; everything! Let him go!"

A man kneeled next to Cortney, just as I was drug on top of a mound of dirt and left there. I tried to move my arms and my legs, but I couldn't. I couldn't feel the rest of my body. I heard a terribly loud ringing sound in my ear. It just kept ringing-ringing-ringing.

"Hello."

My sisters voice sounded so real; so close, I could hear it; it was right there.

"Hello!"

LaShura's voice echoed in my ear causing me to wince. My head throbbed. I was freezing cold; so cold that all I wanted to do was sleep.

Several of the homies had decided to link up and get faded tonight. Although Cortney's car had just got shot up, that didn't mean I was supposed to stop shinin'. The way I figured it, as long as I kept that thang nearby, and the homies was watchin' my back, couldn't nobody fuck wit' me.

I called Kevin up and asked him if he was down to join in on the festivities. Not only was the plan to get faded, but I had about five bad bitches slidin' through. Being that Cortney was bisexual and all the way wit' it, ain't no way the night could go wrong.

As it turned out, Kevin wasn't doin' no fakin' about gettin' his bread up. Bruh wasn't tryin' to shake the spot; he was out there tryin' to get it for real. When I asked Kev why he couldn't just come kick it for the night, bruh replied with, "I'm tired of being broke.

I'm tired of askin' niggas for shit. I'm tired of goin' through all this bullshit with my ol' man." I couldn't do nothing but respect that shit.

Naturally, I still needed someone around that I semi trusted, so I asked Stutter if he was willing to come through. Would you believe that goat-mouth ass nigga wasn't tryin' to shake the spot, either? Stutter gave me some lame excuse about havin' to go put in some work with his Pops. Now, with two of the only muthafuckas that I trusted stuck handlin' their business, I decided to kick it solo-dolo. I still had a bad bitch slidin' through that was down for the threesome. All that was left for me to do was get rid of Saira, and stop by the liquor store.

*Doom-doom-doom-doom-doom-doom-doom!*

"Saira, stop runnin' in this muthafuckin' house!" She'd been doin' that dumb shit all day. I had the music up bangin' *Uncle Sam's Curse* by Above The Law. Being that the floors inside the crib were all wooden, every time Saira came running through, she'd caused the CD to skip. "You know you need to beat her little ass for being so hardheaded," I said.

Cortney sighed heavily and quickly finished braiding the last cornrow at the top of my head. "Do you like it," she asked.

I hopped up off the toilet seat where I'd been seated to inspect my hair in the mirror. The parts looked straight. The braids felt tight. My edge-up was clean. "Yeah, you did aiight," I replied. "But, how much longer do you think it's gon' be before your mom picks up Saira?"

Cortney stepped alongside me in the mirror, then pulled her long blond hair into a ponytail. "Up, or down?" She asked.

"Do what?"

"Do you think I should wear my hair up, or down?"

"Cortney, you need to stop trippin'. Why you streesin' about stuff that don't even matter? Ol' girl that's down for the threesome is supposed to be here in a hour."

Cortney seemed to ponder what I'd just said, and let her hair back down. "James, I know that I said I don't really mind if we have a threesome, but I'm only willing to do this under one condition."

I sighed. “See, there you go being extra’d out again. You gon’ wait until the last minute to hit a nigga wit’ some stipulations.”

“Ain’t nobody being extra’d out,” Cortney assured me. “I just don’t wanna look up one day and this girl is pregnant by you. I think it’s only right if you’d use a condom.”

Something just outside the bathroom window drew my attention toward it. I peered curiously through the window on the shower wall. Although it was pitch dark outside and I could hardly see beyond the cosmetics aligned on the ledge of the window, I had a strange feeling we were being watched.

*Bam! Bam! Bam!* A knock at the front door startled me and I spun around.

“Are you just gonna stand there looking scared to death, or are you gonna go and answer it?” Cortney sassed.

I don’t know what the fuck this bitch was thankin’. I had too many niggas combin’ the streets in search of me. “What I tell you about not thinkin’ before you speak?” I replied. “Instead of tryin’ to figure out what I should be doin’, you could’ve already went and done answered the door yourself. It probably ain’t nobody but your hatin’ ass moms anyway. The fuck I look like answerin’ the door for her?”

Cortney glared at me momentarily then snatched her brush off of the counter. “If it is my mother,” she began by saying, “I still have to do Saira’s hair. If I wasn’t so busy tending to your ungrateful ass, Saira’s hair would already be done!” Cortney stormed out of the bathroom and went to answer the front door.

I could hear Saira in the other room yelling for no apparent reason. I think she was just doin’ that dumb shit to try and get on my nerves. But then again, who knows? Saira had two invisible friends that she constantly stayed in arguments with. I’d told Cortney to have that little girl checked out, but she simply dismissed the idea.

“Who is it?” Cortney shouted over the music.

I was just about to walk out of the bathroom when I spotted my Bluetooth earpiece behind the toothbrush holder. “How my shit get behind there?” The first person that I thought about was Saira. She was the only person that took my things and hid them from me. I quickly picked up the earpiece, inspecting it, then put it in my ear.

*BOOM!* Cortney screamed.

The sudden crash of the front door being kicked in sent my heart racing. I quickly hit the lights and pushed the bathroom door partially closed.

"Get your fucking hands off me!" Cortney yelled.

My eyes darted from one corner of the shadowy darkness to the next. I needed to find something, anything, to fight with.

*Doom-Doom-Doom-Doom-Doom-Doom-Doom-Doom!*
"Mommy!" Saira cried out.

"Hurry up and grab that lil' bitch and shut her fuckin' mouth!" A man barked.

The solid thud of several footsteps racing down the hall sent me into a panic. I rushed over to the bathroom window and knocked everything off of the ledge. My fingers worked feverishly to try and get the window open. Just as I'd finally managed to lift the window a few inches, I was met with a harsh reality. The window was too small for me to fit through. I'd still have to find another way out.

"James!" Saira cried out. *Doom-Doom-Doom-Doom-Doom-Doom-Doom-Doom!*

Wide eyed with fear, I spun around and braced for the unthinkable. Saira burst through the bathroom door and raced into my arms.

"James!"

I quickly scooped Saira up and tried to comfort her.

Moments later, the man chasing her entered the bathroom. "Just the muthafucka' that I've been lookin' for." He snarled.

I knew in that very moment that it was over. There was nothing I could say, do, or pray for that would save me from what was about to happen. "Pu-Pu-Put the little girl down so we can finish this."

TO BE CONTINUED!
Forever Gangsta 2
Coming Soon

## Submission Guideline

Submit the first three chapters of your completed manuscript to ldpsubmissions@gmail.com, subject line: Your book's title. The manuscript must be in a .doc file and sent as an attachment. Document should be in Times New Roman, double spaced and in size 12 font. Also, provide your synopsis and full contact information. If sending multiple submissions, they must each be in a separate email.

Have a story but no way to send it electronically? You can still submit to LDP/Ca$h Presents. Send in the first three chapters, written or typed, of your completed manuscript to:

**LDP: Submissions Dept**
**Po Box 870494**
**Mesquite, Tx 75187**

*DO NOT send original manuscript. Must be a duplicate.*

Provide your synopsis and a cover letter containing your full contact information.

Thanks for considering LDP and Ca$h Presents.

SOUL OF A MONSTER III

By **Aryanna**

THE COST OF LOYALTY **III**

By **Kweli**

THE SAVAGE LIFE II

By **J-Blunt**

KING OF NEW YORK V

COKE KINGS IV

BORN HEARTLESS II

By **T.J. Edwards**

GORILLAZ IN THE BAY V

**De'Kari**

THE STREETS ARE CALLING II

**Duquie Wilson**

KINGPIN KILLAZ IV

STREET KINGS III

PAID IN BLOOD III

CARTEL KILLAZ III

**Hood Rich**

SINS OF A HUSTLA II

**ASAD**

TRIGGADALE III

**Elijah R. Freeman**

KINGZ OF THE GAME V

**Playa Ray**

SLAUGHTER GANG IV

RUTHLESS HEART II

**By Willie Slaughter**

THE HEART OF A SAVAGE II

**By Jibril Williams**

FUK SHYT II

**By Blakk Diamond**

THE DOPEMAN'S BODYGAURD II

**By Tranay Adams**

TRAP GOD II

**By Troublesome**

YAYO II

A SHOOTER'S AMBITION II

**By S. Allen**

GHOST MOB

**Stilloan Robinson**

KINGPIN DREAMS

**By Paper Boi Rari**

CREAM

**By Yolanda Moore**

SON OF A DOPE FIEND II

**By Renta**

FOREVER GANGSTA II

**By Adrian Dulan**

LOYALTY AIN'T PROMISED

**By Keith Williams**

THE PRICE YOU PAY FOR LOVE

**By Destiny Skai**

THE LIFE OF A HOOD STAR

**By Rashia Wilson**

## Available Now

RESTRAINING ORDER **I & II**

By **CA$H & Coffee**

LOVE KNOWS NO BOUNDARIES **I II & III**

By **Coffee**

RAISED AS A GOON I, II, III & IV

BRED BY THE SLUMS I, II, III

BLAST FOR ME I & II

ROTTEN TO THE CORE I II III

A BRONX TALE I, II, III

DUFFEL BAG CARTEL I II III

HEARTLESS GOON

A SAVAGE DOPEBOY

HEARTLESS GOON I II

By **Ghost**

LAY IT DOWN **I & II**

LAST OF A DYING BREED

BLOOD STAINS OF A SHOTTA I & II

By **Jamaica**

LOYAL TO THE GAME

LOYAL TO THE GAME II

LOYAL TO THE GAME III

LIFE OF SIN I, II III

By **TJ & Jelissa**

BLOODY COMMAS I & II

SKI MASK CARTEL I II & III

KING OF NEW YORK I II,III IV

RISE TO POWER I II III

COKE KINGS I II III

BORN HEARTLESS

By **T.J. Edwards**

IF LOVING HIM IS WRONG…I & II

LOVE ME EVEN WHEN IT HURTS I II III

By **Jelissa**

WHEN THE STREETS CLAP BACK I & II III

By **Jibril Williams**

A DISTINGUISHED THUG STOLE MY HEART I II & III

LOVE SHOULDN'T HURT I II III IV

RENEGADE BOYS I II III IV

By **Meesha**

A GANGSTER'S CODE I &, II III

A GANGSTER'S SYN I II III

THE SAVAGE LIFE

**By J-Blunt**

PUSH IT TO THE LIMIT

By **Bre' Hayes**

BLOOD OF A BOSS **I, II, III, IV, V**

SHADOWS OF THE GAME

By **Askari**

THE STREETS BLEED MURDER **I, II & III**

THE HEART OF A GANGSTA I II& III

By **Jerry Jackson**

CUM FOR ME

CUM FOR ME 2

CUM FOR ME 3

CUM FOR ME 4

CUM FOR ME 5

An **LDP Erotica Collaboration**

BRIDE OF A HUSTLA **I II & II**

THE FETTI GIRLS **I, II& III**

CORRUPTED BY A GANGSTA I, II III, IV

BLINDED BY HIS LOVE

By **Destiny Skai**

WHEN A GOOD GIRL GOES BAD

By **Adrienne**

THE COST OF LOYALTY I II

**By Kweli**

A GANGSTER'S REVENGE **I II III & IV**

THE BOSS MAN'S DAUGHTERS

THE BOSS MAN'S DAUGHTERS II

THE BOSSMAN'S DAUGHTERS III

THE BOSSMAN'S DAUGHTERS IV

THE BOSS MAN'S DAUGHTERS **V**

A SAVAGE LOVE **I & II**

BAE BELONGS TO ME I II

A HUSTLER'S DECEIT I, II, III

WHAT BAD BITCHES DO I, II, III

SOUL OF A MONSTER I II

KILL ZONE

By **Aryanna**

A KINGPIN'S AMBITON

A KINGPIN'S AMBITION **II**

I MURDER FOR THE DOUGH

By **Ambitious**

TRUE SAVAGE

TRUE SAVAGE II

TRUE SAVAGE **III**

TRUE SAVAGE **IV**

TRUE SAVAGE **V**

TRUE SAVAGE **VI**

By **Chris Green**

A DOPEBOY'S PRAYER

By **Eddie "Wolf" Lee**

THE KING CARTEL **I, II & III**

By **Frank Gresham**

THESE NIGGAS AIN'T LOYAL **I, II & III**

By **Nikki Tee**

GANGSTA SHYT **I II &III**

By **CATO**

THE ULTIMATE BETRAYAL

By **Phoenix**

BOSS'N UP **I , II & III**

By **Royal Nicole**

I LOVE YOU TO DEATH

**By Destiny J**

I RIDE FOR MY HITTA

I STILL RIDE FOR MY HITTA

By **Misty Holt**

LOVE & CHASIN' PAPER

By **Qay Crockett**

TO DIE IN VAIN

SINS OF A HUSTLA

By **ASAD**

BROOKLYN HUSTLAZ

By **Boogsy Morina**

BROOKLYN ON LOCK I & II

By **Sonovia**

GANGSTA CITY

By **Teddy Duke**

A DRUG KING AND HIS DIAMOND I & II III

A DOPEMAN'S RICHES

HER MAN, MINE'S TOO I, II

CASH MONEY HO'S

**By Nicole Goosby**

TRAPHOUSE KING **I II & III**

KINGPIN KILLAZ I II III

STREET KINGS I II

PAID IN BLOOD **I II**

CARTEL KILLAZ I II

By **Hood Rich**

LIPSTICK KILLAH **I, II, III**

CRIME OF PASSION I & II

By **Mimi**

STEADY MOBBN' **I, II, III**

By **Marcellus Allen**

WHO SHOT YA **I, II, III**

SON OF A DOPE FIEND

**Renta**

GORILLAZ IN THE BAY **I II III IV**

**DE'KARI**

TRIGGADALE I II

**Elijah R. Freeman**

GOD BLESS THE TRAPPERS I, II, III

THESE SCANDALOUS STREETS I, II, III

FEAR MY GANGSTA I, II, III

THESE STREETS DON'T LOVE NOBODY I, II

BURY ME A G I, II, III, IV, V

A GANGSTA'S EMPIRE I, II, III, IV

THE DOPEMAN'S BODYGAURD

**Tranay Adams**

THE STREETS ARE CALLING

**Duquie Wilson**

MARRIED TO A BOSS… I II III

**By Destiny Skai & Chris Green**

KINGZ OF THE GAME I  II III IV

**Playa Ray**

SLAUGHTER GANG I II III

RUTHLESS HEART

**By Willie Slaughter**

THE HEART OF A SAVAGE

**By Jibril Williams**

FUK SHYT

**By Blakk Diamond**

DON'T F#CK WITH MY HEART I II

**By Linnea**

**ADDICTED TO THE DRAMA I II III**

**By Jamila**

YAYO

A SHOOTER'S AMBITION

**By S. Allen**

TRAP GOD

**By Troublesome**

FOREVER GANGSTA

**By Adrian Dulan**

**BOOKS BY LDP'S CEO, CA$H**

TRUST IN NO MAN

TRUST IN NO MAN 2

TRUST IN NO MAN 3

BONDED BY BLOOD

SHORTY GOT A THUG

THUGS CRY

THUGS CRY 2

THUGS CRY 3

TRUST NO BITCH

TRUST NO BITCH 2

TRUST NO BITCH 3

TIL MY CASKET DROPS

RESTRAINING ORDER

RESTRAINING ORDER 2

IN LOVE WITH A CONVICT

**Coming Soon**

BONDED BY BLOOD 2

BOW DOWN TO MY GANGSTA

CPSIA information can be obtained
at www.ICGtesting.com
Printed in the USA
LVHW051059170321
681672LV00022B/1539